COLD
AND
PURE
AND
VERY
DEAD

BOOKS BY JOANNE DOBSON

The Raven and the Nightingale
The Northbury Papers
Quieter than Sleep

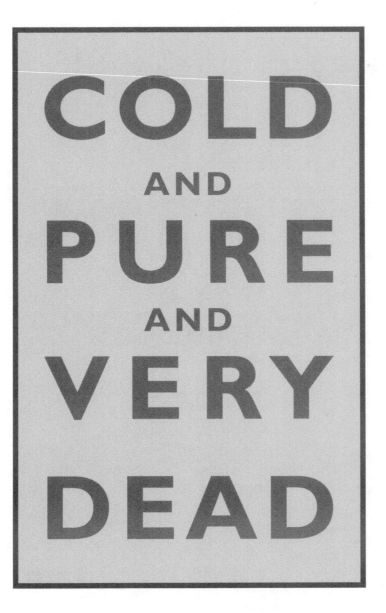

COLD
AND
PURE
AND
VERY
DEAD

JOANNE DOBSON

A Karen Pelletier Mystery

Doubleday

New York   London   Toronto   Sydney   Auckland

PUBLISHED BY DOUBLEDAY
a division of Random House, Inc.
1540 Broadway, New York, New York 10036

DOUBLEDAY and the portrayal of an anchor with a dolphin
are trademarks of Doubleday, a division of Random House, Inc.

Book design by Paul Randall Mize

Library of Congress Cataloging-in-Publication Data

Dobson, Joanne, 1942–
Cold and pure and very dead / by Joanne Dobson.
p.   cm.
1. Women college teachers—Fiction. 2. English teachers—Fiction.
3. Massachusetts—Fiction. I. Title
PS3554.O19   C65   2000
813'.54—dc21
00-043144

1   3   5   7   9   10   8   6   4   2

For my children
Lisa, David, Rebecca

Acknowledgments

Any reader of Grace Metalious's *Peyton Place* will recognize the debts that Mildred Deakin's *Oblivion Falls* owes to the *real* 1950s blockbuster novel. Scholars of American literature can trace the origins of the critical question, "but is it any *good*?" to Jane Tompkins's groundbreaking study *Sensational Designs: The Cultural Work of American Fiction, 1790–1860*.

I wish to thank Miles Cahn and the workers of Coach Dairy Goat Farm in Gallatin, New York for the delightful and informative tour of a truly world-class operation, nothing like Milly Finch's small local goat farm.

As usual, I am grateful to my agent Deborah Schneider and editor Kate Miciak for the fine professional presentation of the Karen Pelletier novels. My good friend Sandy Zagarell has read so many versions of this novel that she qualifies as the world's foremost scholarly expert in the works of Mildred Deakin. My family, as always, is an unending source of support and inspiration. To Dave—thanks again and again.

Our American professors like their literature clear and cold and pure and very dead.

—Sinclair Lewis, "The American Fear of Literature"

COLD

AND

PURE

AND

VERY

DEAD

I

"So, Professor Pelletier, what do *you* think is the best novel of the twentieth century?"

At the request of the Enfield College Public Affairs Office, I was giving an interview to *The New York Times* about the Northbury Center, a research library for the study of American women writers soon to be established at the college. If Dr. Edith Hart's last will and testament survived family lawsuits, I would someday be director of the center.

Martin Katz, the *Times* arts reporter, was young and jittery. His dark hair was cut close to his head, his sallow skin pulled tight over flat cheekbones. Although he was slight, and at least two inches shorter than his rigidly disciplined posture suggested he wanted to be, the black polo shirt hugged a buffed torso. "Novel in English, I mean," he continued, as if he were, of course, intimately familiar with literary work in Urdu and Singhalese. As I considered my response, the journalist flipped a page of his long, skinny notebook and recorded the query. Then he glanced up at me impatiently. Interviewing an Enfield College Assistant Professor about a scholarly research center was not the ambitious Marty Katz's idea of a cutting-edge assignment. He'd put in his dutiful half hour in my green vinyl office armchair, gotten the tedious academic facts, was concluding the interview with a throwaway question.

Afternoon sunlight spilled through my office windows and across the plush-covered cushions of the window seat, forming a luminous rectangle. The patch of sun crept across floorboards in the direction of Marty's black-leather running shoes. When it touched his toes, the reporter yanked his feet back toward the safety of the chair and tapped his pen on the page of his notebook. He clearly wanted a response, and he wanted it fast, so he could point his rented car toward the Interstate and escape back to Manhattan without additional risk of contamination by the un-sullied New England air.

"Best novel of the century?" What a question. I supposed I should give a thoughtful answer: Toni Morrison's *Beloved* was the obvious choice. Then, because I'd recently read it, Jake Fenton's prizewinning *Endurance* came fleetingly to mind, but . . . no. Of course not. No matter how well-written it was—and it was masterfully written—*Endurance* was just the kind of testosterone-driven adventure story that always got defined as "great literature." Anyhow, this reporter's attitude irritated me, and I wanted to give a provocative response. "Oh . . . I'd say . . . *Oblivion Falls* by Mildred Deakin." I'd only finished reading the 1950s page-turner that morning—at 2:17 A.M.—and its haunted characters and steamy sex scenes were fresh in my mind. All *too* fresh. I was beginning to suspect that my friends were right: I definitely needed a man in my life.

"*Oblivion Falls!*" Behind the reporter's gold-rimmed oval lenses, green eyes popped open from their previous half-mast boredom. "What's that?"

"You don't know *Oblivion Falls*, Mr. Katz? I'm surprised. It was a bit of a cultural phenomenon in the fifties—a blockbuster erotic novel, very controversial."

He flipped another skinny page and began scribbling. This was hot stuff compared to my droning on and on about libraries, archives, and state-of-the-art information-retrieval systems. "Really? I was an English major at Brown, but I never heard of it. How good can it be?"

"What do you mean by *good*? *Good* is a relative term. And

good for *what?* College English programs are snobbish about popular fiction, so of course you wouldn't have studied it at Brown. But *Oblivion Falls* was immensely popular when it was published in 1957, partly because of the graphic nature of the sex scenes, certainly, but also because it was a damn good story about the hypocrisies of life in a smug New England college town. And it was a *roman à clef*—a very thinly disguised account of an actual scandal."

"Smutty, huh?" The keen journalistic nose was quivering on the scent of a torrid story: ENFIELD ENGLISH PROFESSOR ENDORSES LITERARY TRASH!

I shrugged. "The arbiters of morality certainly seemed to think so at the time. Sermons were preached against the novel. It was banned in libraries all across the nation."

BANNED, Marty scribbled in his notebook, then underlined what he had written. I could see his swift hand swoop in the double loops of the capital *B,* then skim abruptly across the page in the emphatic line of the underscoring. He had the hook for his story.

"And why shouldn't a book like *Oblivion Falls* be on the Best Books list?" I didn't really think Mildred Deakin's scandalous bestseller was a "great novel"—whatever *that* means—but I felt like tweaking Marty Katz's smug preconceptions about literature. "It certainly helped pave the way for a far more honest treatment of erotic experience in literature. And—that's a stupid question you just asked me anyhow. The *best* novel! Who's qualified to decide?"

"Well," Marty said, frowning, "the professionals, of course. Editors, scholars—"

I held up a hand to forestall the predictable response. "Nonsense. The whole literary rating thing is a joke. All those lists of 'the hundred best books of the century'? Tell me, what makes one novel incrementally superior to another? You might as well try to list the hundred best *ball games* of the century, or the hundred best *meals!* Or the hundred best—"

I shut my mouth just in time. I'll say this for Marty Katz: He could write fast. I suffered a professorial qualm as I saw my outburst recorded for publication. Did I really want to go on record as endorsing the literary qualities of an erotic blockbuster? After all, in two years I come up for tenure in the Enfield English Department. But—what the hell? My literary politics are no secret at Enfield. They hired me because they wanted a specialist in popular literature, and they'll tenure me for the same reason. Still, ten minutes later, as I stood in the massive front doorway of Dickinson Hall and watched the journalist's insubstantial figure with its bulging backpack disappear across the rose-scented summer quad in the direction of the college parking lot, I consoled myself with the probability that his editor would most likely find my response silly, and Marty's hot story would be doused.

This year, the traditional Enfield College English Department end-of-semester party was an evening affair. As I entered Miles Jewell's backyard, the fragrance of new roses infused the early-June twilight with an intoxicating bouquet. My professorial colleagues clustered in groups of four or five among the American Beauties, buzzing with the newest high-minded literary theories from Paris and the latest lowdown on college politics. It had been a hellish day for me, what with the *Times* interview—about which I was experiencing increasing pangs of regret—the near-fatal drug overdose of one of my freshman advisees, and a phone call from a father irate about his daughter's final grade. I wished I were almost anywhere tonight but here, at a department gathering in the midst of this incestuous little college community.

I took two steps down into the rose garden and poured myself a glass of sauvignon blanc from the array of bottles on Miles's patio table. Before I could bring myself to take another step—toward the nearest group of colleagues and their debate about the integrity (or lack thereof) of cross-ethnic literary hybridization—

Miles, my department chairman, came up beside me with a stranger in tow. Male, I noted instantly—very. Fortyish, medium tall, medium burly. "Karen," Miles said, "I'd like you to meet Jake Fenton."

Jake Fenton! The Jake Fenton? The *novelist?* I was astonished. During the interview that afternoon I'd considered mentioning his novel *Endurance* to Marty Katz as a candidate for best of the century. But, then, I'd had to be a smart mouth and nominate the outrageous *Oblivion Falls.* Now here was *Endurance*'s author in person.

"Jake, this is Karen Pelletier," Miles continued, "one of the English Department's junior faculty. I'm certain this gentleman needs no introduction to you, Karen. As you may have heard, we've been fortunate enough at this late date to entice Mr. Fenton to the college to serve as Distinguished Visiting Writer for the coming school year."

No, I hadn't known; I'm not that far inside the corridors of power. I smiled at the writer. He rated a rather extravagant smile.

Jake Fenton took my hand in both of his. "This *is* a pleasure," he said.

When I got home that night, my mother's voice awaited me on the answering machine. *"Karen? Karen? Well . . . I guess you're not there. Connie—she's not there."* My sister muttered in the background. *"Karen? Connie says to leave you a message. She says to ask you to come for Fourth of July. You and Amanda. She says to tell you we'll have a picnic in the backyard— what, dear? Oh, Karen . . . Connie says if you're too busy to come, it's okay. We know how important you are."*

I sighed and kicked off my party sandals. Connie's passive-aggressive jab drew blood, just as she intended it to.

The little house on the back road was lonely that night. My daughter Amanda, home from Georgetown for the summer, had

taken off for Lowell to spend the weekend with her cousin Courtney. My mother lived in Lowell, too, with Connie, her husband,
Ed, and their four kids—of whom Courtney was the oldest. I, on
the other hand, avoided Lowell as if there were a plague notice
tacked to the city gate. Amanda says I have "unresolved family is-
sues." She's right. I don't belong in Lowell anymore.

I listened to the answering machine rewind my mother's voice
into silence. Even now, if I'm not expecting it, the sound of her
wavering voice comes as a shock. I unbuttoned the red cotton sun-
dress I'd worn to Miles's party. The machine beeped, ready to receive future messages from Lowell. I sighed, and thought back to
the party from which I'd just returned. Sometimes I don't think I
quite belong in Enfield either, as my reluctance to partake of the
high academic discourse buzzing around in Miles's garden re-
minded me. I don't know where I *do* belong. Maybe somewhere
in a world peopled entirely with characters out of books. But—I
have to admit it—I'd been intrigued by Jake Fenton.

Jake was famous. He wrote the type of rugged lone-man-
against-the-wilderness novel that somehow managed to beat the
odds and win both wild popular success and sober critical ac-
claim. But I hadn't realized the writer was such an attractive man,
better-looking even than the black-and-white photographs of the
flannel-shirted he-man splashed across hundreds of thousands of
book jackets.

Tonight the writer had worn khaki pants and a navy polo shirt
that fit him well. Dark of hair and eye, he sported the bronzed tan
of a devoted sportsman rather than the golden hue of the casual
beach lounger. He'd clasped my hand between his for at least three
seconds longer than absolutely necessary. My heart had pounded
out a totally retrograde tattoo. I'm a literary critic; I should have
been contemplating Jake Fenton's narrative world view. Instead I
was gaping at his biceps.

Bolting doors, checking window locks, I wandered through
my house, securing it for the night. Then, in the bedroom, I

switched on the bedside lamp, and pulled the red dress over my head. In the oval pier-glass mirror I glimpsed a slender, dark-haired woman in lacy white bra and bikini panties—a woman who would be forty in six months, but who, in the forgiving dimness of the single lamp, didn't look a day over thirty-nine. I stood there for a minute—maybe a minute and a half—studying my mirrored image, and recalling—half-unwillingly—Jake Fenton's speculative gaze.

"Jake's just this week relocated to Enfield," Miles had continued, tipping a bottle of merlot inquiringly in the writer's direction. Jake nodded. As he sipped the red wine, and Miles continued the flow of social banalities, my new colleague regarded me with a faint smile. His eyes were a stormy gray, with deep lines etched at the corners.

"And," Miles concluded, "perhaps Karen wouldn't mind showing you around town one day?" It was phrased as a question but was, in fact, an order from the boss.

"Perhaps she wouldn't," Jake agreed, and drowned a crooked smile in his merlot.

Perhaps I wouldn't mind at all. I'd just opened my mouth to concur, when Miles suddenly commandeered the novelist's arm in a no-nonsense "follow-me" grip. "That's Harriet Person over there, Fenton. *She's* a power in the Department; let me introduce you." Halfway across the yard, Jake Fenton had looked back at me and winked.

That night at bedtime my face got the full restorative treatment: lemon-scented micro-moisture cleanser, exfollient clarifying lotion, advanced night-repair cream, multi-action moisturizer. When I finished cleansing and repairing, the eyes staring back at me from the bathroom mirror were still shadowed. With exhaustion? I wondered. With anxiety? With loneliness? I opened the medicine cabinet again and took down the extra-emollient cucumber-based eye cream.

This is just the kind of man you've learned the hard way not to trust, I'd scolded myself, as Miles had led Jake away. Then I'd watched Jake's broad shoulders for a helpless minute, until Harriet wrested him from the chairman and frog-marched him toward a wicker garden bench positioned cozily beneath Miles's arbor of climbing roses.

It took an eternity to get to sleep; my brain simply wouldn't click off. My mother's message haunted me. I knew I couldn't go to Lowell for the Fourth—I'd already made plans to spend that weekend on Cape Cod with my friend Jill Greenberg at her parents' cottage in Wellfleet. Single-mother Jill and her baby Eloise were counting on me. Anyhow, I simply didn't want to do holiday-time with my family. I'd gone to Connie's for Easter—and suffered through a dinner fraught with unspoken resentments. Connie and her family *loved* Amanda—who, against my express wishes, had sought them out after years of estrangement—but I was a problem. No one else in the family had ever attempted any education higher than a few community-college vocational courses, and here I was an *English professor,* of all things—with a Ph.D. "We're all gonna have to watch every word that comes outta our mouths," my brother-in-law, Ed, said. I tried to explain that it didn't make any difference, that my work was no reflection on my family, that I simply loved books and loved to teach—and that, anyhow, they *talked fine.* But every word out of *my* mouth sounded academic and patronizing—even to me.

And, as for Jake Fenton . . .

The party had dragged on. With three colleagues, I'd engaged in a tedious debate about implementation of the revised curriculum requirements, then I joined a gossip session with a couple of faculty wives. We'd snagged Jake Fenton from Stallmouth College, I learned. Before that he'd been a visiting writer at Princeton. And before that . . . The man's credentials were impeccable. I'd left for home without further contact with Jake. No way was I about to augment the enthralled cluster of women around the famous man—Patsy Walker, Latisha Mohammed, Sally Chenille.

Although I'd picked up on Jake's signals, and was . . . well, attracted, the writer seemed to be just a little too easy with the opposite sex for his own good—or mine. Then, halfway home, I'd remembered that Amanda was gone for the weekend, and I almost turned around and went back to the party.

At about first light, the birds began their maddening diurnal clamor, and I gave up the effort to get to sleep. Two pages of the latest issue of *American Literary History* must have knocked me out, however, because I awoke at ten A.M. with the lamp still burning and a cramp in the hand clutching the scholarly magazine.

Oblivion Falls

August lay over the earth, hot and heavy, like a desperate lover.
*Sara Todd reclined on the granite ledge jutting perilously over
Oblivion Falls, a cataract that plummeted a full fifty feet into a
maelstrom of churning water, a cataract long reported in local legend to lure young people to a watery grave. As indeed, it may well
have done. Within the span of Sara's own short memory, no less
than three of her schoolmates had been taken by its dark waters,
taken by the yearning for the fathomless known only to the very
young, taken by the lure of the dangerous depths. Sixteen was a
dangerous age, Sara knew. Sixteen was aimless and driven. Sixteen
was beauty without knowledge. Sixteen was the age at which
Sara's mother had given birth to Sara, confining herself forever to
the narrow rooms of Satan Mills, New Hampshire, and the narrow
life of those who labor for others and never for themselves, confining herself to the drunken embraces of a husband who despised her
almost as much as he despised himself. This will not happen to me,
Sara vowed, clutching to her chest the book of Christina Rossetti's
poems she'd been reading in her aerie. Yet she studied her indis-
tinct, wavering image in a reflective pool caught in a basin of rock
at the edge of the precipitous cliff. A nymph, a water sprite, a love-
liness she had only to reach out and grasp. Instinctively, without an
instant's thought, she stretched a slim white hand over the puddled
image to the very brink of the precipice, farther, farther . . . Then
she heard a footstep in the brush behind her.*

2

Good for you, Karen!" Greg Samoorian pulled out the chair opposite me at Bread & Roses Bakery and Cafe a week after my interview with Marty Katz, and plunked himself down. Banana-nut muffins were the Monday-morning special at the cafe just across Field Street from campus, and the air was redolent with banana and nutmeg. I'd just finished my muffin and started on a second coffee.

I lowered the international news section of the *Times*. During the teaching-free summer months I read the newspaper in one long, slow, uninterrupted stretch before I start my research or writing, but Greg's a pal, and for him I'd tear myself away from war and famine anytime.

"Hi, Greg." Something was up: the voltage generated by Greg's devilish grin might have lit the entire town of Enfield. "So, what have I done now?"

"What have you *done?*" He smacked his forehead with the heel of his hand. Greg was stocky, dark, and bearded. Today, like me, he was in summer dress-down mode—cotton T-shirt, denim shorts. He was freshly barbered for a change, and the impact of his hand against his brow did not disarrange the habitually unruly curls. "You mean you really don't know? Well, sweetheart, let me be the first to tell you—you've just been quoted in *The New York Times*! I thought you were sitting there, hunched over the paper, gloating about it."

"Quoted in the *Times?*" I folded the first section of the paper in neat quarters and ceased breathing. Greg fished around in my stack of newsprint and retrieved the still untouched arts section. He flipped pages, found what he was looking for, slid the newspaper across the table. Over Marty Katz's byline, the two-column headline queried: IS BESTSELLER BEST NOVEL OF CENTURY? The subhead continued: *Professor Nominates Banned Book for Great-Books List.*

I sucked in a deep breath, then glanced hastily around the sparsely populated cafe. Good thing it was summer vacation. Two work-study Economics students hunkered bleary-eyed over scones and coffee, and Michael Mastrangello from the Political Science faculty was lost in the sports section of the *Boston Herald*. No literary types, thank God. It wouldn't do for the Enfield English Department to observe me going into psychotic meltdown.

"Read it," Greg commanded, and went in search of sustenance. Reluctantly, I turned my attention to the narrow columns.

Is a literary potboiler such as Mildred Deakin's 1957 bestseller *Oblivion Falls* as worthy of accolades as James Joyce's masterpiece "Ulysses"? This is a question raised by Professor Karen Pelletier of the English Department at Enfield College, one of the nation's most highly regarded four-year liberal-arts schools. Ms. Pelletier challenged a reporter's assumptions about what constitutes valid literary achievement.

"A best-selling novel," Professor Pelletier asserts, "often reflects social, political, and economic complexities of cultural matrices in ways at least as intriguing and enlightening as the most carefully wrought literary work of art. All too often in this century the tools of high aesthetic mastery have been available solely to the elite—and to men. When a juicy woman's novel such as *Oblivion Falls* catches the fancy of a mass readership . . ."

Greg returned with a muffin and a white ceramic mug brimming with cappuccino. I glanced up at him and groaned. "Did I really say 'juicy'?"

"You said it, girlie. And in the pages of *The New York Times*."

"The little twerp caught me at a weak moment. Oh, God. I'll never get tenure now!"

"Keep reading. I think you come across fine."

"Ummn." I began to read out loud.

> "According to this accomplished scholar of women's literature, political and theoretical developments of the final decades of the twentieth century have served to problematize the notion of an irreconcilable split between popular culture and what used to be known as 'high culture.' Therefore it would be equally valid to claim great achievement for a popular success such as *Oblivion Falls*, a lusty potboiler of a novel which took on the freighted issues of sex and class, as for any of the more strictly literary works recognized by the many cusp-of-the-millennium 'Great Books' lists that have proliferated of late."

I raised my head again. "I did not say 'cusp of the millennium.' "

"Good."

"Nor did I say 'lusty potboiler of a novel.' "

"I didn't think so."

I sipped coffee, then set the cup precisely in the center of my empty muffin plate. "Well, he *did* call me an 'accomplished scholar.' And at least I put my eccentric nomination for 'great book' into some respectable theoretical framework. Maybe I don't look like a *complete* fool." I spread the newspaper on the table and began to smooth it back into its original folds.

A hand swooped down from above and plucked the paper from my grasp. It was a large hand, brown, and masculine, with wide, flat fingernails clipped extremely short.

"Mildred Deakin," said deep, vaguely familiar, tones, "well, what d'ya know?"

I glanced up. *Jake Fenton:* The name slipped easily into my consciousness, as if it had never slipped out in the first place. Even with the five o'clock shadow—five A.M., that is, as if he couldn't be bothered to shave first thing in the morning—Jake was eye candy. After I'd met him at Miles's party, I'd reread *Endurance*. As I'd recalled, it was everything the cover blurbs had promised: *stripped-down . . . masculine . . . urgent.* The claim of *universal,* however, gave me a bit of a problem; I, myself—personally, that is—had never eaten bear, bloody and steaming, raw from the fresh-killed carcass. Jake Fenton's universals were different from mine.

The novelist squeezed my arm and smiled at me. Then he slipped into the seat beside me, tapping his forefinger against the portrait of Mildred Deakin I'd failed to notice in my self-absorbed perusal of the Katz article. "This is a face I never expected to see in the pages of the *Times,*" he mused. I, too, studied the black-and-white photo. In the 1950s when this picture was taken, Mildred Deakin had been a fragile beauty. The dark hair was short and sleek. Enormous eyes dominated the small oval face with its charmingly pointed nose and sensitive, dark-lipsticked mouth.

I glanced at Jake, bemused by his avid attention to the fifties image. "You couldn't possibly have *known* Mildred Deakin," I said. "You're far too young."

"No—of course I didn't." He dropped the paper abruptly, as if, really, he'd had only a passing interest in the article, and turned to Greg. "Don't believe we've met. I'm Jake Fenton." The writer gripped Greg's hand in that firm "see—no weapons" clasp that constitutes male greeting. "And, Karen, good to see you again. I've been meaning to call about that tour of the town. Wish I could stay, but right now I've got a . . . an obligation." The words trailed off as he smiled apologetically, rose and moved toward the counter. When he had secured his coffee-to-go, winked at me for the second time in our short acquaintance, and exited the small cafe, a certain kinetic energy went out with him, as if all the particles of oxygen circulating in the room had for a brief second been stilled.

Greg watched me watch Jake leave. When I turned back to my friend, he maintained the assessing gaze.

"What?"

"Careful with that guy, Karen." He hefted the ceramic mug, eyes serious over the rim.

I bridled. "Don't be stupid, Greg; I have no interest in Jake Fenton." I gave him my most forbidding look, the obsidian glint between lashes. "And, besides, even if I did, it's none of your business."

Greg laughed then, and wisely let it drop.

I closed the *Times* arts section and slid the paper into my bookbag. Greg downed the last of his cappuccino. "Aren't you going to finish that article?" he asked. "Your fifteen minutes of fame."

"I'll read it later." My fingertips were black with printer's ink. I wiped them on a paper napkin, then stuffed it in my empty cup. "Right now I can't take any more notoriety." I nodded at Sophia Warzek, who'd just delivered a pan of fresh muffins from the kitchen. The enticing scent of ripe banana wafted anew across the light-filled room. Sophia paused at the counter and smiled at me. She's my protégée and former student—and my daughter Amanda's best friend. I reached across the marble tabletop and broke off a small chunk of Greg's muffin. "Tell me, what other stupid things did I say in *The New York Times* for all the world to read?"

"Nothing. Really. The reporter just goes on to quote from the novel and recount a bit about Mildred Deakin's life. Did she really vanish without a trace?"

I swallowed the muffin bite. "Yeah, she did. It was very strange. *Oblivion Falls* made Deakin an overnight sensation, and it didn't hurt that she was young and attractive, as you can tell by that photo—only twenty-five when the novel was published. For a couple of years pretty Milly was everywhere, giving talks at women's clubs and public libraries, frequenting literary soirees and nightclubs. Living pretty high, from what I've heard. Her picture showed up in *Time* magazine, in the society columns of major newspapers, in scandal sheets. Then, abruptly, she dropped out of sight, and no one's seen or heard anything from her since, I think, 1959. Not her family; not her friends; not her publisher. At the time of her disappearance, the New York City police investigated Mildred Deakin as a missing person, but they never did find her."

"What do you think happened? Was she abducted? Or murdered? Or did she simply have a breakdown and wander off?"

"I don't know anything about Mildred Deakin's mental state, Greg. As a matter of fact, I don't know much about fifties literature, at all—the 1950s, that is. I only mentioned *Oblivion Falls* to the *Times* reporter because I'd just finished reading it. I picked the book up a couple of months ago at a conference; some feminist press had just reprinted it." I glommed another chunk of Greg's muffin.

"Was it any good?" He curved an arm around his plate, guarding what was left of his breakfast from further predations.

People kept asking me that question. I didn't know the answer. "I needed some light summer reading, and it was a great read—downright steamy in places, and the class tensions were just as hot as the sex. The book kept me up half the night."

"Steamy, huh?" He waggled his dark eyebrows. "According to Jill, you need some of that."

"Greg!" What on earth was my friend Jill saying about me?

"But, like I said, Karen, watch out for that Fenton guy. There's something about him. . . . He looks like he could be bad news."

"Back off, Greg." I raised both hands, palms out. Is there no private life in this town?

"Okay, okay! Well, anyhow, Karen—looks like you're into another literary mystery here."

George Gilman from the History Department passed by in his usual disorganized rush. Loaded down with a briefcase and a large coffee, our short, pudgy, bespectacled colleague wagged fingers at us around the paper coffee cup. I wagged back. George pushed the door open with his shoulder and vanished through it.

"You mean Mildred Deakin? Pu-leez," I responded, and snagged the last morsel of Greg's muffin. "Really, I have no interest in what happened to Mildred Deakin—where she went, or why." I licked crumbs off my fingertips. Then I thought about it for a minute. "Wouldn't it be terrific, though, if the Northbury Center could acquire Deakin's papers? I wonder where they are? *Oblivion Falls* was hot stuff, and the correspondence about it must be fascinating. Not too many erotic novels circulating in the fifties."

"*Peyton Place, Forever Amber, Naked Came the Stranger.*" Greg tallied them on his fingers.

"How do you know this stuff?" Greg is an anthropologist, not an English professor, but the breadth of his literary knowledge is mind boggling.

He gave me a good-natured leer. "Sweetheart, when it comes to smut—"

"Give me a break, Greg! You're the most smut-free guy I know! So . . ." I waved the subject away. Mildred Deakin wasn't in my period of literary specialization, the American nineteenth century. With any luck this short newspaper article on a Monday morning would be overlooked by my friends and colleagues in the academic world, and I wouldn't hear any more about it. "I'm on vacation; I don't want to talk about literature. How are the babies? And Irena, of course."

"Everyone's great." Greg's brown eyes gleamed with paternal pride. "Did I tell you Sally says *Da-Da* now? It's the cutest thing! Irena says she's just babbling . . . you know, *ga ga ga* . . . but I swear . . ." And he was off on his favorite topic, Jane and Sally, the twin daughters who had turned this cynical postmodernist scholar into a squidgy ball of marshmallow fluff.

I had no luck at all, as it turned out. Some producer on the *Oprah* show read the *Times* article, and located a reprint copy of *Oblivion Falls*. By mid-August, Mildred Deakin's years-out-of-print novel had made it into Oprah's Book Club, then onto *The New York Times* Best-seller List, into the Amazon.com top ten, and onto the paperback racks of Starbucks' coffee houses across the nation. Usherwood Imprints, the feminist small-press publishing house that had dutifully reprinted the book earlier that year, rushed to print and distribute the multitude of copies necessary to meet the clamor for this "lost woman's masterpiece." And I—Professor Karen Pelletier of the Enfield College English Department—for a few brief unwilling days, became the world's reigning expert in the work of the "lost" Mildred Deakin.

When she heard the footstep, Sara jumped up from the ledge and let her full cotton skirt fall over her knees and shapely calves. Quickly she pulled back her heavy hair and clasped it again in its wide barrette. She had taken to wearing the skirt instead of her one pair of shorts after Percy Simpson at the lumberyard had corralled her in the back room last week when she'd gone to pick up some nails for her father. "Nice ass," Percy had said, grabbing her buttocks. She'd twisted from his grasp and thrown coins on the counter as she passed through the store. As she stalked away up the hill Percy had made a comment to the men on the sidewalk bench. Sara had heard the men laugh. She knew her father would be furious when she got home. Not about Percy. Not about the men. She wouldn't tell him about that. She had learned early that the only safety lay in silence. Her father would be furious because she had come home without his seventeen cents in change.

The second footstep sent Sara looking for another egress through the tangled brush, but with no luck. Only one path led to this remote aerie overlooking the river, and only lovers knew it. Lovers and the occasional dreamy schoolgirl. Sara stood, her back pressed against a slender birch, waiting for the intruder to appear.

3

The Labor Day party was at the home of Greg and Irena Samoorian. A multi-level contemporary on a couple of semi-wooded acres, it was my favorite house in Enfield for kicking back and relaxing. Smoke poured from a restaurant-size gas grill where chicken and ribs sizzled, kids squealed and splashed in the pool, friends and colleagues clustered wherever they could find a puddle of shade on this hot early-September afternoon.

With a baby back rib for a pointer and barbeque sauce instead of chalk smeared on his chin, Professor George Gilman was treating me to an extemporaneous lecture on his favorite topic, the history of the book in America. "A number of social and economic factors caused the publication of popular fiction to escalate rapidly during the postwar years, and led in the 1950s to the rise of the blockbuster bestselling novel. . . ."

I'd asked George about *Oblivion Falls,* because he was the only person I knew who had the expertise to speak knowledgeably about the background for the novel's original popularity. All the sudden hoopla about the book had intrigued me. Throughout the long humid final week of August, every time my phone rang I'd had to field yet another request from the media for information about Mildred Deakin and her sensational novel. Inquiring minds from Regis and Kathy Lee to the cultural reporters for NPR were suddenly agog to know the story of the novel's composition and salacious details of Deakin's life and loves.

Fortunately, since I knew virtually nothing about her, I remembered Sean Small. "Professor Small," I'd told someone from the *Charlie Rose* show, "is a professor at Skidmore College who delivered a paper on Deakin at the last MLA. The MLA? That's the Modern Language Association convention. The major annual conference for scholars of language and literature. That's where I learned just about everything I know about Deakin, from Professor Small's paper. You might as well go directly to him. Yes, Skidmore. Hello? Hello?" I gave Sean Small's name to the next three interviewers who called. After that, the culture vultures left me alone with my ignorance. But now George was giving me an impromptu quick-and-dirty graduate seminar on twentieth-century popular fiction.

"The sudden freeing-up of paper for peacetime purposes after World War Two," he continued, waggling the baby back rib, "as well as increased leisure time for women, who had been nudged none-too-gently back into the domestic sphere from their wartime factory jobs; the rise of the paperback book and the Book-of-the-Month Club; postwar prosperity; and a hunger on the part of the public for a return to normalcy—all these extraliterary factors contributed to sharply increased production and distribution in the popular-print market."

"In other words," I said, glugging down the last of my pale ale, "a lot more books were published."

"That's what I just said," George replied.

George and I had perched on a cast-iron park bench in a small grove toward the back of the yard. George Gilman was one of my favorite colleagues, an historian whose prodigious knowledge, strong intellectual passions, and total absence of intellectual pretense all endeared him to me—but he did tend to get carried away. With a sauce-covered finger, George resettled his half-glasses on the bridge of his nose, smearing his cheek in the process. I resisted an impulse to reach out and daub sauce on the other cheek for balance.

"In the case of *Oblivion Falls* in particular," he said, "a younger generation of writers and readers had come to adulthood, a generation without the wartime responsibilities and deprivations that had focused the energies of their older brothers and sisters on the great public interests of the international community. For this new cohort, the concerns of private life and personal freedom had a heady allure, and Deakin's populist sympathies and graphic sexual honesty appealed to a wider public than she could possibly have reached in any earlier decade of the twentieth century, a far-wider public certainly than the critically acclaimed Beat poets and novelists of the same era. That *Oblivion Falls* should, in our own era of widespread prosperity and narcissism, once again find a popular audience is not surprising. . . ."

He paused to tear a tender chunk of pink meat from the rib with which he was gesturing. There went the other cheek.

"Enough, George. Enough." I laughed. "When I asked for some background on the popularity of *Oblivion Falls,* I didn't mean to turn party time into work time for you."

"Work? Heck—this is *fun,*" enthused my little colleague, sucking the final shreds of meat from the rib, then wiping his fingers on his jeans. I offered him a napkin, but he waved it off. "If God didn't mean us to wipe our hands on our jeans, Karen, he wouldn't have made denim. You want another beer?" I nodded, and George set off on a booze run.

From my vantage point on the bench, I had a good view of the swirling activity in the pool. Kids cannonballed into the water, teenagers deployed gigantic splash-guns, parents dandled babies. "Wheeee." Jill Greenberg hoisted the flame-haired Eloise above her head, then zoomed her down. *Spp-lash!* The baby shrieked with delight. Jill laughed her bubbling laugh and hoisted Eloise into the air again. In a green-and-white-polka-dot bikini, nine months after Eloise's birth, my young friend was as slim and radiant as ever.

"She's so beautiful." George had returned with two sweating

beer bottles, and was watching Jill over my shoulder. He handed me a bottle and sighed. "But . . . she'd never look at me."

Jill was a stunner, mid-twenties, red-haired, stylish with a big-city edge. George was none of those things. In his early forties, he looked something like a garden gnome, small of stature, thin of hair, pale of skin, and decidedly lacking in fashion sense. This afternoon, in spite of the August heat, he wore a short-sleeved white dress shirt and jeans, the stiff, heavy kind more likely to be found on the sales racks at Agway than at any mall. George was right. Jill would never look at him more than the once it took to put a name to the face, and assign the face to the fatal category of Nice Guys to Pal Around With.

She was at the party with Kenny Halvorsen, her constant companion, six-foot-two of hunky soccer coach. When Jill passed Eloise off to the teen-aged daughter of a colleague, Kenny scooped Jill up, hoisted her over his head, dive-bombed her into the pool. *Spp-lash!*

George sighed again. "She is just so *lovely.*" He was on his third beer and beginning to loosen up. I was on my second, and already a little too loose.

"Have you ever been married, George?" I usually don't ask questions like that, because I usually don't want to hear the answers.

He shook his head. "The book . . ." George was the author of a massive and acclaimed study of twentieth-century developments in the history of the book. ". . . took ten years to research and write. When I was working on it, I was obsessed. It was all I could think about. I would have made a lousy husband. And then, it just seemed too late. But . . . you know what I miss the most about not being married? It's the children. I'd love to have children." His tone was wistful.

"It's *not* too late," I said, always the optimist. "You might find someone yet, and—there's always adoption."

"I've thought about that; I was adopted myself, you know."
He glugged down beer.

"Really?"

"Yeah. But it's almost impossible for a single man to get a child. The usual fears . . ."

Then Jill carted Eloise over and thrust eighteen pounds of wet, squirming baby in my arms, and the conversation took a different turn.

You know who you should talk to about *Oblivion Falls?*" Greg poured a tot of brandy into my coffee. The party was over, and I'd stayed behind to help him and Irena clean up. Now Irena was in the babies' room changing a diaper, while Greg and I sat on the deck under a lavish night sky.

"Who?" I didn't really care. It was so relaxing here with the stars and the almost tropical darkness, that I just wanted to float through the night in a brandy haze. I didn't ever want to use my intellect again.

"That new guy in your department. What's his name? The big hire you made last spring? The Cadaver Chair?"

I laughed so loud, Irena came to the window to find out what was funny.

"*Palaver* Chair, you idiot," I said, smacking Greg with a plastic Thomas the Tank Engine place mat. "And his name is Ralph Brooke. Ralph *Emerson* Brooke. But why ask him?"

"Doesn't he do the fifties? I remember talking to him about the Beat Generation at the reception the English Department had for him."

"Not only does he *do* the Beats, I think he *knew* them all. Maybe he even *slept* with them all, given the degree of intimacy he implied during his interview: *As Jack said to me in 'Frisco. Jack? Why, Kerouac, of course.* From what Brooke says, he was a real hipster in the fifties. Hung out with Ginsberg and Ferlinghetti.

Anyhow, he wouldn't know anything about Deakin. Ralph's the old-style sexist type of academic who'd die rather than look at a popular woman's novel like *Oblivion Falls.*" Brooke's hiring still rankled with me. The uproar in the Enfield College English Department the previous spring over the endowed Paul O. Palaver Chair of Literary Studies had torn the department into opposing factions that might well never reunite, the passions had run so hot. By a single vote, the senior male members of the department had voted in a scholar who was anathema to the rest of us: conservative, white, male, and—as far as I was concerned—perilously close to being embalmed. The *Cadaver* Chair, indeed! The academy has no mandatory retirement age, but even I, as open-minded as I am about most things, thought the age of seventy-four was a bit late for taking on what should be a demanding new job. "What Professor Brooke did in his misspent youth is of no concern to me. It's his misspent maturity I'm concerned about. Particularly the fact that he's going to be misspending it in my department."

Greg sipped his brandy pensively. "I'm amazed the department's feminist mafia let a canonist like Brooke get through."

A *canonist?* Well, if that's not already a word, it should be. "We did our damnedest, Greg. But Brooke is Miles's last stand. They go *waaay* back—Princeton for grad school, then teaching together for a couple of years early in their careers—at Stallmouth College, I think. After that Miles came here and Ralphie went off ... somewhere ... maybe on the road with Kerouac, for all I know. But he ended up at the University of Chicago for decades. Now he's here."

"So sweet," Greg said. "Boys together, now together again." He gave me a big smooshy smile.

"Greg, I think you're looped." I pushed my doctored coffee away. I still had to drive tonight.

"Just a leeetle tiny bit," he replied contentedly, "and it feels so damned good."

4

Speak of the devil, I muttered to myself first thing the next morning as I glanced out the front window from my booth at the Blue Dolphin diner. Professor Ralph Brooke, Enfield College's new P. O. Palaver Chair of Literary Studies, plodded up the front steps and into the eatery's narrow aisle. Following the waitress to a booth in the far back corner, he passed by without seeming to recognize me. Over scrambled eggs and home fries, I had a prime rear view—heavy, stooped shoulders, yards of seersucker, and a fringe of curly iron-gray hair encircling a freckled head. He ordered coffee, then hid behind the outspread pages of the *Times.*

Five minutes later Miles Jewell entered the diner, his thick white hair and summer tan set off nicely by a navy-blue polo shirt. He peered through his steel-rimmed glasses, located his buddy, and veered toward him. At the sight of his old friend, Ralph Brooke folded the paper and rose ponderously. In the most secluded corner of the diner, the two senior scholars pounded each other on the back and chortled together like a pair of happy thieves.

That first Tuesday of September promised to be summery— hot and muggy—but when I entered Dickinson Hall at 8:47 A.M. it was clear the fall semester had begun in earnest. Students hustled through the halls, young women greeting each other with squeals, male students with manly back thumps. In the English

Department office, Monica Cassale, our secretary, was enthroned at her desk, deep in a copy of *Oblivion Falls*—I recognized the cover with its flaming orange and red roses. Fielding queries about course offerings and professors' office hours, Monica scarcely glanced up from her book. The English Department secretary was so efficient that if Miles ever sat back in his big, soft, leather chair in the inner office one day and died, Monica could simply close his door and run the department all by herself. At least for a while. At least until the smell got too bad.

I nodded in the general direction of the desk, and the secretary nodded back without taking her eyes off the novel. I was sorting through the junk from my pigeonhole mailbox, when our chairman himself entered the office. I greeted him with the ritual back-to-school question, "Did you have a productive summer, Miles?"

But it seemed he hadn't. "Karen, every damn second of my time was eaten up by petty administrative details—curriculum planning, scheduling, hiring. I got no research done. This is absolutely—indubitably, without any doubt whatsoever—the final year I will serve as department chair."

"Umm," I responded, with an enigmatic smile. I'd believe that when I saw it. Miles had chaired the English Department for the entire twentieth century. It would take nuclear fission to dislodge him from the seat of power. Especially now that he had his boyhood pal, Ralph Emerson Brooke, in that driver's seat with him.

I, myself, had had quite a productive summer, I thought, as I retrieved the only salvageable piece of mail—a note from a former student—and carried it to my desk. And, I gloated, I was now on pretenure sabbatical leave. With no teaching scheduled for the entire fall semester, I planned to spend lovely leisurely days doing research for my biography of the nineteenth-century novelist Serena Northbury. I squared my shoulders in the desk chair, pulled up a yellow lined pad and a blue rolling-tip pen, and inscribed: *To Do This Semester!!!!* Number One: BEGIN BOOK.

By 9:16 I'd become so paralyzed by the thought of Number

One that my pen hovered over the half-page-long list of other ob-
ligations for two and three-quarters minutes without settling on
Number Two. A light breeze nudged a whiff of late-rose fragrance
through my open window, and an evanescent memory of Miles's
rose garden wafted through my mind. *Where was Jake Fenton?* I
wondered idly. Aside from our encounter in the café, I hadn't
heard from the novelist, and, surprisingly in this small town, I
hadn't seen him around. He was probably doing research for his
latest literary adventure, I thought, most likely somewhere in
deepest, darkest, most primitive Montana. Then I brought my er-
rant mind up short: *My God! Why was I thinking about Jake? I
had a book to write!*

When the phone rang, I all too willingly dropped the pen.
Given my experiences of the past couple of weeks, I half-expected
yet another request for an interview about *Oblivion Falls*. In no
way was I prepared for the grim inflections that awaited me on the
other end of the line.

"Doctor." Only one person in the world called me *Doctor* in
that particular way, as if it were my given name.

"Lieutenant Piotrowski?" The lieutenant was with the Massachusetts State Police Bureau of Criminal Investigation. I hadn't
heard from the big cop since the completion of the homicide investigation that had brought him to the quiet Enfield campus last
fall. At that time, my matchmaking friends Earlene Johnson and
Jill Greenberg had gleefully predicted some amorous move on the
part of Charlie Piotrowski, but if he was, indeed, interested, he
had never followed through. It was just as well I hadn't heard
from him, I'd told myself. After I'd broken up with Tony, my long-
lost, long-time love three years earlier, I'd vowed never, ever again,
to get involved with another police officer. Living with a cop
makes for a difficult life. Okay—living with a cop is hell.

And by the somber tone of his voice, Piotrowski didn't seem
to be calling about Chinese and a flick.

"I understand, Doctor," the lieutenant said without social preamble, "that you are acquainted with a New York City journalist by the name of . . . ah . . . Martin Katz."

"Yes?" *Martin Katz?* What possible connection could this New England–based homicide detective have with the *New York Times* reporter? "Yes, Lieutenant, I've met Mr. Katz."

"Well, Doctor . . ." Piotrowski sighed: he's a big man; he has large-capacity lungs; it was a long, slow sigh. "I just this minute got an official inquiry about you from the New York State Police Bureau of Criminal Investigation. It seems, Dr. Pelletier, that Mr. Katz has been murdered—and in circumstances that link him quite directly to you. I'll probably get in deep shit for telling you this, but I wanted to prepare you: Doctor, you're in for a visit from a couple of New York State Police homicide cops."

When the brush parted and Cookie appeared, Sara sighed with relief. It was only Cookie; she was safe. Her friend was sweaty and scratched, dressed in the dungarees and camp shirt Mrs. Wilson, Cookie's mother, despised as unladylike. Sara herself had outgrown the one pair of blue jeans Cookie had passed down to her, and to buy another she was saving the money she earned running errands for Professor and Mrs. Wilson and serving at their parties. She envied her friend the easy way she dressed, her clothes always right for whatever they were doing, from school dances to crashing through the underbrush.

"Joe Rizzo was looking for you," Cookie said. "I didn't tell him you were up here."

"Thanks." Sara smiled at her friend.

"But—I don't understand why you never want to see him, Sar. He's such a hunk. Handsome like a movie star is handsome." Cookie sighed, leaned back against a big oak and slid down until her thin bottom rested on the ledge. Sara, more decorous, as her garb demanded, sat carefully next to her.

The two girls were a contrast in types. Sara was tall and willowy with hair like honey, a creamy complexion, and a body whose fullness belied her youth. Cookie sprang from a less extravagant branch of girlhood, her thin face and her acornlike breasts the despair of her young life. Cookie's real name was Carole, but as an only child of doting parents she bore her pet name still.

"I don't want to see him because . . ." Sara struggled for an expression that would not offend the innocence of her more protected friend. "Because I don't . . . I don't want to . . . to end up living my mother's life. I want to get out of Satan Mills. Someday I want to go to college . . . if I can. There must be a way."

"To live your mother's life? But, Sara, I don't understand. Your mother is old. She's . . ."

"She's fat. She's ugly. She's piss poor. That's all right. You can say it."

Cookie screwed up her face in apology, then blurted, "But I really don't see how going on a date or two with Joe Rizzo would—"

"I know you don't," Sara replied. "Listen, Cookie, I'm tired of this place. Let's go back to your house and play some records."

As they pushed their way through the thorny blackberry bushes, a silent figure slid from behind a pine tree and followed them.

5

Professor Pelletier, you must wonder what we're doing here, so far from our jurisdiction," said the tall, thin New York lieutenant, oh-so-politely concerned with my peace of mind. And rightly so. Piotrowski's call had rendered me confused and apprehensive about what these out-of-state cops wanted from me.

This homicide team was a walking advertisement for Empire State diversity. The senior investigator, a blond woman in her late thirties with pale skin, pink-tinged ears, and virtually transparent eyebrows, stood so ramrod straight she looked uncomfortable. Her partner was much more laid back. A young sergeant, he was a medium-height, pudgy man of some mixed lineage, African-Latino-Caucasian, brewed in the ethnic cauldron of the Bronx.

Although Lieutenant Paula Syverson wore a plain gray pants suit over a peach silk shirt, she might as well have been in uniform. Her shoulders were so square, her demeanor so stiff, I half-consciously checked for the state-police shoulder patch. From the moment they entered my office, Sergeant Rudolpho—*call me Rudy*—Williams was the tactical charmer of the pair, elaborately agog at the beautiful Enfield College campus, ostentatiously impressed at talking to—*conversing with,* he corrected himself—a real English professor. *Give me a break!* I thought, as I settled them in my student chairs and retreated strategically behind the desk, welcoming even the most tenuous barrier between me and these minions of the law.

The news of Marty Katz's murder was a shock, but I couldn't imagine what "circumstances" could possibly link his demise to me. Piotrowski had declined to give me any details other than the basics: The journalist was victim of a homicide—somewhere in rural New York State, I assumed, since the staties were handling it rather than city cops—and the investigators wanted to interview me. But why me? My only contact with Mr. Katz had been the *Times* interview, and that was an open book—an open newspaper—for all the world to see.

"I'm a SUNY-Albany grad, myself," the voluble Sergeant Williams continued, "but I never saw anything at all like this on my campus." He gestured around my office at the polished hardwood floors, the green needlepoint area rug, the floor-to-ceiling bookcases, the tall bay window with its plush window seat. "It was all strictly concrete and cinder-blocks. This is impressive."

The lieutenant gave him a pale glance: *Enough. The wheels are greased; let's roll.* "Well, Professor?" she asked. *"Don't* you wonder what a couple of New York State Police officers are doing all the way out here in western Massachusetts?"

I hesitated for less than a second: No way was I going to con this cool intelligence into thinking I was surprised by the news she was getting ready to spring on me; I'd better come clean about Piotrowski's call. "Actually, Lieutenant, I know why you're here."

Syverson's jaw tightened. "You do?" The thin lieutenant leaned toward me, elbows on her knees, hands clasped at her chin. The studied informality did not come naturally to her; she must have taken a course: *Interrogation Strategies 101.* "Tell me all about it, Professor," she said, in a compassionate manner borrowed from the confessional. I could almost hear the implied interrogational cliche: *You'll feel a lot better if you do.*

I laughed incredulously; did she think I was about to confess to murder? "Wait a minute, Lieutenant. Just wait a minute here— I didn't kill him."

Syverson jerked upright. Rudy Williams's hand flew to his belt: *Get out the handcuffs, baby, we've caught us a killer.*

The lieutenant's pale eyes narrowed. "Who?" she asked, in a voice like a razor. "*Who* didn't you kill?"

"Marty Katz, of course," I replied. "I didn't kill him." She should have said *whom*. Whom *didn't you kill?* But this did not seem to be precisely the right moment for a lesson in grammar.

Rudy Williams, alert as a feral cat, seemed ready to spring out of his chair. "Professor, nobody said nothing . . . anything . . . about the shooting death of an individual named Martin Katz."

Lieutenant Syverson threw him a *stuff-it* look.

I repressed a groan. "I seem to be getting off on the wrong foot here."

"Oh, yeah?" Syverson said. "Professor Pelletier, look at this from our point of view. We walk in here cold, giving you no information about the purpose of our visit, and right off you deny committing a homicide we didn't, until this very second, have any reason to suspect you of. And, then, you identify the victim—whose name we never mentioned. That sounds a lot like the *right* foot to me—at least from an investigative point of view. Professor," she ran the tips of her fingers back and forth over the arm of the green vinyl chair, "have you done something you need to tell us about?"

"No, Lieutenant, of course not." I straightened up in my desk chair, and shifted a vase of purple iris I'd bought from the florist on my way in to work that morning. Then I clasped my hands together—tightly. "Look, the only thing I've got to confess is that I received a phone call a couple of hours ago from an acquaintance with the Massachusetts Staties . . . ah, State Police. He told me you were coming—and why."

For a brief moment she had absolutely no lips. "He did, huh? And who, may I ask, was that?"

I told her. Looked like Piotrowski *was* about to get into deep shit. But, then, any good cop knows what he's letting himself in for when he breaks regulations, and Piotrowski is nothing if not a good cop. He could handle it.

"Lieutenant Piotrowski didn't tell me anything specific about the case, other than the name of the victim," I continued, attempting to smooth things over for him, "but he did say that the circumstances of Mr. Katz's death link it directly to me. Could you please tell me why?"

The investigators exchanged a long, silent look—their favorite means of communication, it seemed—then Syverson shrugged. "Professor, do you know a woman named Milly Finch?"

"Milly Finch?" I sped through a tabulation of friends, colleagues, and students, former friends, colleagues, and students, former employers as far back as the truck stop in North Adams where I'd first entered the work world as a single mother with a three-year-old daughter to support. Then I went back even further, to girls I'd known in high school, junior high, elementary school. "No. No, I don't think I've ever run across anyone named Milly Finch. Who is she?"

"She's a goat farmer."

"A *goat farmer?*"

"Yes. Mrs. Finch is an old . . . ah . . . elderly woman from a small town called Nelson Corners, over in Columbia County. Just across the New York State line from Massachusetts. She's kind of a recluse—raises goats and sells the milk. Goes to church once in a while. That's just about all anyone in that area ever thought there was to her life: raising goats and going to church."

"Oh?" Obviously there was more to this story—and to Milly Finch's life. I waited.

"On Friday afternoon, Martin Katz was found shot to death with a thirty-thirty Winchester in Mrs. Finch's driveway."

"Re-e-e-ally?" This was strange, even tragic, but so far I couldn't see any "circumstances" that linked the killing to me. "That's too bad," I said, then added, inanely, "he wrote so well."

"Did he?" the pale lieutenant asked, and exchanged another significant look with her subordinate. "Well, so did she, obviously. Write well, I mean. We haven't released this information to the general public yet, Professor, but a long, long time ago Milly Finch was a famous novelist. She published under the name of Mildred Deakin."

Joe Rizzo leaned against the brick wall of Stubby's Grill. Sara knew he was waiting for her. She had stayed too long at Cookie's house, reluctant to emerge from its order into the chaos of her own family's tenement flat in Satan Mills, the poor side of town. Her mother would be cleaning up the scraps of fried potato and canned beef, if Sara's father and brothers had left any scraps, and her father would bawl at Sara the minute she entered the house to get her lazy butt into that kitchen and wash those dishes, or did she expect her mother to slave her fingers down to the bone for a great, big, lazy lout of a girl like Sara. A lot he cared about her poor mother, Sara thought, lying around and drinking as he would have been ever since he got home from the shoe factory.

Sara knew Joe was waiting for her because he'd been there for five nights running, leaning against that wall, his hard, lean body encased in tight blue jeans and a white undershirt, a pack of Lucky Strike cigarettes stashed in the rolled-up sleeve, his black motorcycle parked slantwise in front of the bar. Joe was what the girls at school called a "rock," or a "hood," the kind of boy who'd left school at sixteen to go to work at Phillips's garage. He was a good mechanic, everyone said so, a hard worker, but every time Sara looked into his face with its hard lean lines and hard black eyes she saw a hard future, a future that she already knew far too well.

Sara Todd understood herself to be an incipient sinner. But it was not the sin of bedding Joe Rizzo that she was likely to commit. It was the sin of refusing to lie in the bed that Satan Mills had made for her, the transgression of insisting on a far more dignified life than the likes of Joe Rizzo would ever offer her, the immorality of choosing to leave the rank into which she had been born.

Lowering her eyes to the cracked sidewalk, she passed Joe, pretending she didn't hear his greeting, without once looking up at him.

6

The New York cops had just finished grilling me about my interview with Marty Katz, and I was watching their green Ford Taurus pull out of the Dickinson Hall lot when Piotrowski materialized at my side on the marble steps. He must have been lurking around the corner of the square brick building waiting for Syverson and Williams to leave. The sight of his plain, broad face with its brown eyes and Slavic cheekbones somehow reassured me that, in spite of the irrational irruption of murderous violence into my life once again, God might still be in His Heaven and all might still be right with the world. Piotrowski had that effect on people; it was one of the things that made him a good homicide cop.

The weather was glorious, sunny, and so clear that from my position on the wide steps, I could glimpse the outline of the distant Berkshires between the Gothic stone of the college library and the sleek concrete modernity of the Wakefield Dining Commons. In the informality of first-day classes, groups of students and teachers sat cross-legged on the grass under the ancient maples of the campus quad. I raised an automatic hand in greeting to Earlene Johnson, the Enfield Dean of Students, who flashed me a knowing smile when she noted my companion, then hurried on by, but I felt extraordinarily detached from campus life. The New York investigators' news had stunned me with its implications, making the cause of Marty Katz's death all too apparent to me. If I hadn't so flippantly tossed off the title of Mildred Deakin's book in response to his question, the reporter would still be alive. Admittedly it was a stupid question he'd asked, but he didn't deserve to *die* for it. I'd asked a great many stupid questions myself over the years—after all, I was a teacher—and no one had yet come after me with a hunting rifle.

The idyllic leaf-green and red-brick scene before me stood in bald contrast to the ugly fact of Marty Katz's murder—and to the sordid world homicide lieutenant Charlie Piotrowski negotiated on a daily basis. The lieutenant's impressive size—six-foot-three, well over two hundred pounds—was not all that distinguished him from the professors and administrators bustling around the campus on academic errands. A general air of attentiveness to the variegated phenomena—human and physical—that surrounded him, of alertness and readiness to respond—set this plain beige man apart from the abstracted scholars around us. He seemed to inhabit space more concretely than did my colleagues, rendering the space he inhabited intensely more concrete. Slit-eyed, Piotrowski watched the unmarked Taurus until it turned onto the campus ring road and disappeared from sight. Then he pivoted and barked at me. "They treat you okay?"

"Yeah," I replied. His brusque tone put me unexpectedly on the defensive. "As okay as possible for a couple of homicide cops who think I killed a *New York Times* reporter in cold blood." I frowned at him. "What are you doing here, Lieutenant?"

He grumbled. "Thought I should get myself out of reach for a while; your friends from New York are gonna be making mad-as-hell phone calls about me tipping you off." Then, before I could thank him for that tip, he eyed me closely, and his manner gentled. "You don't look so good, Doctor—kinda pale and shocky. They didn't hassle you, did they?"

I shrugged.

"They can't really consider you a suspect...." Lieutenant Piotrowski squinted in the noontime sunlight, his face set in professional cop mode, sussing out the situation, checking all the angles.

"No. Not really. At least, I don't think so. But, Jeez, Pio-

trowski . . . I'm in a state of shock. A reporter from the *Times* is
dead, and all because he sought out a writer I told him about, a
novelist nobody had seen—or heard from—in decades. A deliber-
ate *recluse,* the New York detectives said. I may not have killed
Marty Katz, but, you know, it's beginning to look as if I set in motion a chain of events that did."

"Cut yourself a break, Doctor!" His tone was sharp, and a
woman student passing by gave us a quick glance.

"But it's all my fault," I protested. "When the New York lieutenant gave me the facts of the case—that Marty was gunned
down in Mildred Deakin's, ah, Finch's driveway—it became clear
to me that he would never have been there in the first place if I
hadn't told him about her. He was a journalist; he must have
hunted her down to get her story. From what those cops said, it
looks like she probably freaked out when he told her what he was
there for, grabbed her husband's deer-hunting gun, and killed him.
At least, that's what that skinny lieutenant said—that they've got
Mrs., ah, Finch in custody."

"Hmm, well, you might be right that he wouldn't have
looked her up if you hadn't mentioned her, but you couldn't
know—Hey—whoa—Doctor, don't *cry.*" He reached out to pat
my shoulder, then glanced around and abruptly pulled his hand
back. "At least, don't cry here, right in front of your office. Ya
gotta remember that. It's a cardinal rule: Never bawl where they
cut you a paycheck. No telling who's gonna be watching." He
slid a pack of tissues out of his pocket, handed me one, hesitated
for two seconds, then continued. "Listen, why don't we take a
ride and talk about this? I got some, ah, other things I been
thinking about lately—thinking about a lot, as a matter a fact. I'd
like to . . . ah . . . run them by you. You had lunch? No? Okay,
I'm buying."

"I don't *bawl!*" I dabbed at my eyes. Piotrowski was right; I
had to get out of here. The campus was at its busiest this early

September afternoon, students, staff, and faculty energized for the new school year—and all too curious about their long-unseen peers. "Thanks, Lieutenant. I could use something to eat. *And* a shoulder to cry on."

The lieutenant's eyes widened skittishly, and I hastened to clarify. "I mean, I'd like to run this mess, er . . . situation . . . by you. Who better?"

The New York cops had asked me not to talk about the case, and, especially, to keep quiet about Mildred Deakin's connection to it. I'd agreed, but didn't think that meant I couldn't tell Piotrowski. "We got a few leads to follow up," Syverson had said, pursing her bloodless lips, "before that news becomes public knowledge. So, we'd appreciate it if you . . ."

"This *mess*, huh?" Piotrowski furrowed his eyebrows. "Yeah, who better than yours truly at taking care of messes?" His abruptly expressionless tone surprised me.

"Well, you *are* a pro. Maybe you can help me make some sense of Marty Katz's death."

"Wa-i-i-i-t a minute, Doctor." Any softening in his manner suddenly vanished, and the gruff professional was back in full force. "You're not thinking about sticking your nose in this—"

"Just let me get my bag from my office, and we can talk it over in the car."

Before I could start up the steps, the Dickinson Hall front door opened, and Jake Fenton emerged from the dusky interior. The novelist squinted, then smiled when he saw me. Our paths intersected three steps up from where Piotrowski was standing.

"Heyyyy, Karen," he said. "Good to see you." Ignoring my outstretched hand, he squeezed my arm. "How've you been?"

"Good," I replied, returning his smile. "Haven't seen you around in a while."

"I've been away." Jake's eyes flicked sideways, then back. Uneasy? Evasive? Or was the shock of Marty Katz's death overshadowing all my interactions? "But, hey, I'm back, and we never had that date we talked about. You were supposed to show me the town." He winked at me. For a few seconds I forgot my irrational guilt about Marty Katz's death and allowed myself to be swept into the force field of this man's physical magnetism. With a tan so deep he could have passed for a native of some South Seas island, he radiated health and a muscular energy not-so-subtly sexual in nature.

"Let's set it up," I replied. "I'm on leave, so my time's pretty flexible right now." Jake wasn't much taller than me, I noted immediately, maybe an inch or two. Just enough to make things interesting.

The writer glanced curiously at Piotrowski, who, blank-faced, gave me an almost imperceptible shake of the head, and began ambling down the steps—as if he and I had simply been passing the time of day.

"Thursday?" Jake evidently decided Piotrowski was harmless and tipped his head inquiringly at me.

"What time?"

"Three? Then we'll get a drink—maybe some supper."

"Great," I said, then out of the corner of my eye noted the lieutenant idling before a bulletin board studded with multicolored posters. "Right now, I've got to run."

"Okay. Thursday. Three. I'll pick you up at your office. Bye, Karen." He waggled his fingers at me, then headed down the steps.

I waggled back, then hastened into the building to get my bag.

Walking across campus, on our way to his Jeep in the visitor's parking lot, Piotrowski was silent, responding only briefly to my attempts at conversation. Over burgers at the Blue Dolphin, he listened silently to my recitation of the New York cops' tale of willful death. At his parting caution—"Like I said,

Doctor—you butt out of this"—I realized he hadn't said a word about whatever it was he had on his mind and wanted to run by me. I was so caught up in the mystery of Marty Katz's death, seemingly at the hands of the newly resurrected Mildred Deakin, that I didn't bother to ask him about it.

7

At 3:14 A.M. the morning after the visit from the police officers, Amanda pulled into the driveway. She and Sophia had
been out hunting down one last hot blast of summer, or, in other
words, they'd spent the night engaged in what passed for clubbing
on a Tuesday in western Massachusetts. Tomorrow my daughter
was scheduled to take off for her senior year at Georgetown.
When she opened the back door, quietly so as not to wake me, I
was hunkered at the kitchen table in semidarkness with a cup of
microwaved milk. "Mom?" Amanda queried, as she let the door
slam behind her, "what're you doing up at this hour?" She pulled
out a chair and joined me at the round oak table.

After months of allowing her reddish-brown hair to grow almost to her shoulders, Amanda was back to a short crop. The se-
vere cut became her, highlighting her dark-lashed hazel eyes and
the clean, elegant lines of her cheek and jaw. At twenty-one, despite the lateness of the hour, she radiated energy. She also radiated the stale odor of cigarette smoke. "Yuck," I said, giving a
pseudoconsumptive cough, then waving my hand in front of my
face. "How can you breathe in those places?"

"It ain't easy," she replied. "But the music was great. I had a
good time. Thanks for asking."

"I'm glad," I replied, and reached out to squeeze her hand.
Now that she had a reliable car, I didn't have to worry quite as
much about my daughter when she went traipsing all over the

back hills in the middle of the night in search of tunes. This summer, thanks to a timely combined raise and merit award from the college, I had purchased a five-year-old Subaru station wagon, and Amanda had graduated to my gray 1988 Volkswagen Jetta. It was the end of the American Century, and things seemed to be looking up for the Pelletier family.

"So?" Amanda reached out and switched on the hanging lamp over the table. As usual she was dressed in jeans and one of her variegated wardrobe of Georgetown sweatshirts—cobalt-blue, this time. Also as usual, I thought she was stunningly beautiful.

"So . . . what?" I replied, squinting in the sudden light.

"What are you doing up so late?" she continued. "And sitting in the dark, too."

"Insomnia," I muttered into my milk.

"Again? Mom, what's going on with you?"

Murder. Loneliness. Lust. I shrugged. In the blackened window, a sepulchral woman's shoulders bobbed up and down in their shroudlike oversized T-shirt. "Just stressed, I guess."

"Stressed? But, Mom, everything's going so well." The shoulders bobbed again, but before I could respond, Amanda blurted, "It's the law-enforcement thing, isn't it?"

Kids always think they're the center of the universe. Amanda, who'd been set on med school when she'd entered Georgetown three years ago, was now toying—against my express wishes, I might add—with the idea of following her beloved Tony Gorman into police work. My ex-boyfriend is a high-level official with a New York State Police Drug Enforcement Agency based in Manhattan. He's also a mesmerizing raconteur, and, when we lived together, Amanda had consumed his wild tales of undercover derring-do with each and every dinner—when Tony had managed to make it home for dinner, that is. Which wasn't often. The stories had rooted in fertile soil—thus the course in criminology for which Amanda was registered during the fall semester.

"Well, honey, now that you mention it, I'll add that to the list." And I did: *Murder. Loneliness. Lust. Extreme Maternal Anxiety.* "But the truth is, your career plans hadn't crossed my mind tonight. Something else has come up. Remember Lieutenant Piotrowski? I spent most of the afternoon with him."

She grinned. "He finally asked you out?"

"No." I brushed her frivolous comment away with an impatient hand.

"Another *homicide?*" Her voice scaled up three notes.

"Looks like it." I removed the mug of cold, scummy milk to the far side of the table.

"At the *school?*" Up two more notes.

"No. Thank God." Amanda, of course, knew all about the rediscovery of *Oblivion Falls,* so I told her about Marty Katz seeking out the reclusive Mildred Deakin, and about his subsequent violent death. "So, this has nothing to do with Enfield College," I concluded, "except that I gave the interview, and I'm employed by the college."

"Cripes, Mom. You're the one who should be signed up for a course in criminal investigation, not me." Amanda bent down to unlace her Doc Martens.

"I seem to be taking an independent study."

"What are you gonna do about it." Her heavy boots clunked against the floor as she kicked them off. Suddenly my bare feet felt cold against the slick linoleum.

"*Do* about it? According to Lieutenant Piotrowski, I'm going to *butt out* of the case and let the pros handle it."

"Really? I'm surprised. This homicide obviously has causative factors rooted in the literary world, and you're a literary investigator." She was already talking like a police detective. "No cop knows the literary world the way you do."

"You're right," I said, sighing. Sometimes my daughter's unyielding faith in me feels like a burden. "If I don't look into it, there's a lot the cops might miss. Also, to tell the truth, I feel responsible. I initiated the chain of events that led to the reporter's death. I have an obligation at least to look into Mildred Deakin's background. She was a writer, after all."

"Good for you, Mom!" My daughter jumped up from the table and hugged me. Then she held me out at arm's length and studied my insomniac face. "Somehow I don't think that's all that's eating you. And if it's not the thought of me maybe going into law-enforcement that's keeping you awake, what is it? The folks in Lowell?"

"No!"

"Jeez, Mom. You don't have to bite my head off! It wasn't so bad having your family here for that picnic, was it?"

My mother had been silent most of the rainy August day we'd finally gotten the family together. Connie had turned her nose up at the enchiladas and nachos I'd slaved over, saying, "I don't eat Mexican." Her husband, Ed, had gone around tapping the walls of my rooms for soundness. Finally he said, "You must make pretty good money at that college of yours. Why do you live in such a cheap house?"

"Amanda, I'm *not* thinking about the family. You're the one who keeps harping on them."

"I'm just trying to make sure that you won't be all alone—"

"Amanda—cease and desist!" What had I been thinking: *unyielding faith!*

"All right." She held up her hands, palms out. "Chill, okay. Just—chill." She yanked open the refrigerator door. "And speaking of *chill,* is there any of that chili left from the other night?" She rummaged around. "Oh—cool," she said, retrieving the blue pottery bowl from the bottom shelf. "All that beer sloshing around in my empty stomach—"

"All that *beer!*" I shrieked. "Amanda, you haven't been drinking and driving . . ."

. . .

Massive rock ledges blurred past on the Massachusetts Turnpike as I crossed the Connecticut River Bridge, keeping to the slow lane. Since they've raised the speed limit on the Pike to sixty-five, traffic has speeded up accordingly. I was doing a steady seventy, but, then, I've always been an overly cautious driver. Tractor trailers whipped past me, effortlessly accelerating up the endless hills that constitute the westbound lane at this point. SUVs going eighty-five or ninety left me eating their dust.

I was headed for New York State, for the small town of Nelson Corners in Columbia County, where, according to the New York investigators, Mildred Deakin Finch had spent the forty most recent of her sixty-seven years. What did I intend to do there? I really didn't know. Drive by the scene of the crime, maybe. Buy the local paper. Drink coffee in the local luncheonette. Loiter in the local grocery store. Keep my eyes and ears open. Try to get the scuttlebutt on Mrs. Milly Deakin Finch. Try to find some clue as to why she would panic at the unexpected intrusion into her country life of a big-city news reporter. Across the blur of highway and horizon, I projected an image of the novelist—the only picture I knew—black and white, young and beautiful, poised for her book-jacket photo, cigarette held gracefully in a long, thin hand. Then I added forty years to that image: black and white, mature and beautiful, cigarette held gracefully in a long, thin hand. Then I added goats.

When I arrived in Nelson Corners, having left the Pike at the first New York exit and navigated a labyrinth of winding roads, my plans to stake out local establishments promptly evaporated. There were no local establishments in Nelson Corners. There was no *town*. Along the main road, Route 295, long driveways led back to derelict barns and farmhouses in dire need of fresh paint. I slowed as I came to the intersection of 295 and County Route Three, which on the New York State road map pinpointed the town's name. Sure enough, here was a green rectangular road sign announcing NELSON CORNERS. The intersection offered a white post office, converted from what had once been a small house, a shuttered brick church with a sign that promised ANTIQUE EMPO-RIUM—COMING SOON, and two houses, one a run-down Gothic Revival with peeling yellow paint, and the other a spiffed-up gray Colonial sporting a dried-flower wreath on its plum-colored front door. Beyond that—more long driveways leading back to more derelict barns, and a road sign directing me to CHATHAM 8 MI. What on earth could have brought a Manhattan sophisticate like Mildred Deakin to this forsaken speck on the map? Whatever connections Nelson Corners might possibly have in this age of cyberspace to the larger world of life and literature would not even have been dreamed of in 1959.

I must have missed something, I thought. Turning the Subaru in a narrow lane, I headed back. As I slowed again at the Nelson Corners intersection, a heavy woman in orange stretch pants and a sleeveless beige shell stepped out of the post office with a broom and began sweeping the small porch. *Good. Someone I can ask for directions.* I pulled into the three-car parking lot and rolled my window down. The woman stopped sweeping, but remained where she was. I stuck my head out of the car window. "Could you tell me . . ." Then I hesitated. Did I really want to begin my acquaintance with this hamlet by asking directions to a house where a sensational murder had just taken place? The locals would think I was nothing but a sensation-hungry ghoul. There must be more subtle ways I could get the information I needed. The sweeper waited for me to complete my question, dark eyes neutral in a round, ruddy face. "Can you tell me . . . uh . . . where I could get a good cup of coffee?"

She leaned her broom against the porch railing and ambled down the steps, over to the car. "Coffee, huh? Well, turn around and head back for Chatham." She eyed me speculatively. "Don't know how *good* you'll think it is—won't be none of your *ex*-pressos or lat-*tees.* But it's coffee. Best bet's at the Homestead, just off Main Street."

My informant watched me steadily as I turned the car. When I pulled out onto 295, I glanced into the rearview mirror. The dark eyes were fixed on the Subaru. Obviously not much happened on a Wednesday morning in Nelson Corners; the postmistress would know me again if I ever came back to town.

As far as its central business district went, Chatham was a two-block town, one block of Main Street and one block of Church. The Homestead Restaurant was just across the railroad tracks from the intersection of those two streets, adjacent to an elegant old stone train station that had been restored as an elegant new bank. At 12:37 on a September Wednesday the Homestead was doing what my mother would have called a land-office business—the parking lot so jammed you would have thought they were giving the food away for free. As I opened the restaurant door, my appetite was instantly aroused by the heavenly aroma of frying bacon. A tray of sandwiches floated past, carried at shoulder height by a slim young woman in tight black pants and a pink uniform blouse. I tracked her progress toward a section of tables at the rear of the restaurant. HOT TURKEY. HAM AND SWISS. GRILLED CHEESE. Each sandwich was plunked on a thick china platter and anchored with a mound of potato salad or a raft of slab fries; there wasn't a portobello mushroom or a radicchio leaf in sight. I felt as if I had traveled from a far country and arrived unexpectedly at my gastronomic home. Commandeering the remaining counter stool, I grabbed a menu. ALL SANDWICHES SERVED ON HOMEMADE BREAD, announced a banner positioned kitty-corner across the cover. *That's what I want*, I thought, *all sandwiches. Oh, and serve them on HOMEMADE bread.*

The counter waitress—Betty Anne, according to the white letters on her shiny black name tag—was sixty and skinny, with that run-half-off-her-feet look career waitresses get. Her gray hair was tight to her head in prim curls, and her pink open-neck uniform blouse revealed more wrinkled skin than I would have cared to show. With my eye on the mirrored pie rack behind the counter—HOMEMADE! announced the hand-lettered sign—I ordered coffee and a grilled cheese, bacon, and tomato sandwich. Then I turned my attention to my fellow diners; after all, I'd come to town to schmooze the locals. The men crowding the long counter with me didn't look like talkers. Hardworking men, I thought, with hard-looking hands. Farmers, carpenters, plumbers. None of these people were going to give any information about their neighbors to a nosy woman from God-knows-where. My intrusion into the life of this community suddenly seemed presumptuous. The reality of the lives lived in this town by these laboring men and women made me feel silly playing detective—silly and a little frightened. But then Amanda's words came back to me: *You're a literary detective and this is definitely a literary crime.*

I gave myself a pep-talk in a silent hard-boiled snarl: *Someone in this joint's gotta know this Milly Finch broad, and I'm the dick that's gonna make 'em squeal.* Sometimes I think I only know my life through the books I read.

The Homestead's clientele was a mix of locals and exurbanites. At tables toward the rear of the restaurant, young women in pressed Gap khakis and pastel jerseys tended distractedly to preschoolers. I ignored them; they were not old enough or local enough to tell me anything useful about Milly Deakin Finch.

Other diners looked more promising, grizzled dark-clad men and hefty women in double-knit pantsuits who addressed themselves seriously to the business of refueling their bodies. These people looked battered by life—by sun and soil and decades of a declining rural economy. At a corner booth one mature man—in his late fifties, maybe sixty—good-looking with a shock of thick white hair and a tanned weathered face, flirted with the floor waitress. As she delivered his burger and fries, he grabbed her wrist lightly and muttered something that made her laugh. I was too far away to hear the words, but the brief tableau was striking: the bulky, well-muscled man, bone-white hair startling against the dark skin, and the slender, pale young woman silhouetted against the large plate-glass window, united momentarily in laughter.

"So, Betty Anne," I ventured to the waitress as she set the heaping china platter in front of me, "anything exciting ever happen in this town?"

"You kidding?" she replied. "Ya want more coffee?"

"Sure." I nibbled a fry while she poured. "Thought I read about a murder around here somewhere," I said casually, and bit into the sandwich.

"Oh, that." Her lips tightened, turning down at the corners. "That crazy Milly Finch." A scrawny man next to me shifted uneasily on his stool, then cleared his throat. The waitress glanced at him. He touched the brim of his green Caterpillar gimme cap, then jerked his head backward. Betty Anne's dun-colored eyes flicked in the direction of the window booth, where the white-haired man now joked with one of the young mothers. Suddenly the counter waitress got busy, hustling the coffeepot back to its burner, then wiping down the counter at its far end. *Strike One,* I thought. My neighbors on either side, the scrawny man and a young freckled guy in a feed store uniform, were strikes two and three. They weren't even interested in talking about the weather.

I devoted myself to the apple pie—two inches of thick sliced apples in a flaky crust sprinkled with cinnamon and sugar, worth a three-and-a-half-hour round trip any day. When I went to pay my bill, a rack of newspapers by the register caught my attention. The *Chatham Courier* headline read LOCAL WOMAN ARRESTED ON HOMICIDE CHARGE. I grabbed the paper and, standing there with the check and a ten-dollar bill tight in my hand, I read the brief article:

> According to Chatham police spokespersons, Mrs. Mildred Finch of Nelson Corners is being held in custody in the

> shooting death of a New York City man at her home yesterday. The victim is Martin Katz of Manhattan. As this issue went to press, no further details were available.

I glanced at the masthead. The *Courier* was a weekly, dated last Saturday. Not much to be learned there. Gossip was still my best bet. But where to find a good reliable gossip monger?

That's where the body was found, right there in the driveway, by the woodpile, next to the porch," the realtor said. On my way out of Chatham, I'd passed the Country Estates Realty Office, spiffy white and charming behind a picket fence and rows of fresh-faced purple pansies. I'd slammed down my brake pedal, and on the spot invented a software-executive husband, three school-aged kids, and a Frisbee-playing golden retriever, all crammed into a two-bedroom New York City co-op and panting for a spacious, peaceful home in the unspoiled countryside.

I lucked out; Wendy Vandenberg seemed to be the single most talkative person in town—maybe the *only* talkative person in town. But then, Wendy wasn't really local. The realtor had moved to Columbia County from Queens a mere thirty-five years earlier, she said—when property was a steal. And it was the best move she could have made. New Yorkers had been snapping up houses ever since—like they were candy—and prices had skyrocketed. Then she glanced over to where I sat in the passenger seat of her safari-green LandCruiser. "Not that there aren't plenty of bargains left," she hastened to add, in a voice that still held outer-borough intonations, "for smart purchasers willing to put a little honest elbow-grease into a charming, untouched country original." *Untouched country original*, I thought. *Well, okay, but, I've always been partial to indoor plumbing.*

"I'm not certain this is *precisely* the area we wish to invest in," I said, in that superbly informed, all-options-open Manhattan manner that I'd found so grating during the six years I'd lived in the city. "A number of factors will come into play, of course, including tax base, school district, health-care availability. . . ." The realtor nodded; she'd heard it all before. When push came to shove—or when contract came to mortgage—her clients would purchase with their hearts, not their heads. The green slope of a hill, the rugged texture of a wood-shingled roof, the warm slant of morning sun on old brick, an accidental lilac, and they'd be lost hopelessly in a dream of the one perfect life available in the one perfect, unique—gotta-have-it-at-any-cost—country home.

We were pulled over on Granite Quarry Road, on a low hill overlooking the Finch place—one of the few functioning family dairy farms, Wendy informed me crisply, remaining in the Berkshire foothills. When we'd left her office, I'd asked a few wide-eyed, titillated questions about the Nelson Corners homicide, and the realtor—not averse to dishing the dirt—had brought me straight to the scene of the crime. The Finches' sprawling white farmhouse sat back a hundred and fifty feet from the road at the end of an unpaved driveway. To the left of the house stood two well-kept red barns and a tall royal-blue silo, to the right, a smaller barn and a compound of fenced-in sheds. A herd of Holsteins graced the sloping fields, whimsical black and white against verdant hills.

"I still can't believe it." Wendy shook her head, baffled. "No one could ever have predicted that Milly would do such a violent thing. She was so quiet and private-like." I noticed that the realtor was referring to Milly Finch in the past tense, as if she had already been tried, convicted, executed, and buried. "And she didn't even *know* the man—whatshisname . . . ?"

"Marty Katz," I replied without thinking, then hoped the realtor wouldn't wonder how I knew.

"Katz—yeah, that's it. A reporter, someone said he was. But what the heck was he doing all the way up here at Finches' place?

Must of got lost, and was asking for directions. Tsk. Tsk." *What's the world coming to?*

"Must of," I repeated. "Must of got lost. Tsk. Tsk." So the news about Milly's literary fame wasn't out yet. If it had been, Wendy Vandenberg would have told me instantly.

There was a moment's contemplation as we sat, looking over at the peaceful farmyard scene. "Those are Milly's goat pens, those sheds over there," the realtor informed me, breaking the silence. "She sold goat milk to some gourmet-cheese maker down county. Did pretty well, too, at least according to my husband, Fred," the realtor said, pulling her vehicle back on the road and accelerating past the Finches' well-kept acreage. "Fred's a fireman. He knows everything that goes on around here."

"I can imagine."

"Jimmy Finch is in the department, too. One night when the boys were out for a few," she bent her elbow, flexed her thick wrist twice, "Jimmy told Fred quite a story. . . ." She let it trail off, tantalizing me.

"Oh, yeah?" Maybe *this* was what I'd come to Nelson Corners for.

"Yeah. About how he met Milly." She shifted down as we climbed a steep hill between a hayfield on one side of the road and a half-built housing development on the other. "It was maybe thirty-five, forty years ago—late one Saturday afternoon—and Jimmy was driving home from the cattle auction. I think Fred said it was November, cold and getting dark. Two miles out of Chatham, he sees something strange on the side of the road. He pulls the pickup over—Fred says it was a big old blue Ford F-150—Jim's truck, that is, not the thing on the side of the road . . . like it matters what kind of a *truck* it was! Men! Anyhow, Jimmy pulls over, gets out of the truck and finds a suitcase. Nice monogrammed leather piece with a good bronze lock—initials, M.D."

M.D.? I was paying heightened attention now. "Really?"

"Yeah. So Jimmy figures maybe it fell off a car, and he tosses the thing in the cab. He'll take it to the police station next time he's in town. Then he goes along another couple of miles, and there's something else on the side of the road—smaller. So he pulls over—and it's a portable typewriter. You remember the kind? In a case? With a little handle? Kind of like a laptop, only bigger? Anyhow, Jimmy picks the typewriter up, and says to himself, *What the hell is this*? He throws it in the cab, gets back in the pickup, starts up, then jams the brake—there's a body lying in the middle of the road. Well, Jimmy's freaking out—he's just a kid at this point, maybe eighteen, nineteen, and he jumps out of the truck again. There's this beautiful girl lying unconscious in the road. He doesn't know what to do. There's no traffic, so he can't flag someone down and get help, and of course he can't leave her there. So he picks her up and puts her in the cab of the truck with the suitcase and the typewriter and takes her home to Mama. And the rest is history. They get old Doc Daniels in—he wasn't old then, of course—and Betsy Finch nurses the girl back to health, and she's got nowhere to go, so she stays with the Finches. A couple years later Jimmy married her." Wendy paused as she cut a tight right onto a narrow dirt road. Then she glanced over at me, with a wistful smile. "Isn't that the most romantic thing you ever heard in your entire life?"

"Right out of a storybook," I agreed. "But who was she? Where'd she come from?"

"She never told him, he says—not very talkative, our Milly. But the station master—this is back when Chatham was a big railroad town—the station master says she got off an express out of New York—Chatham was the end of the line then—picked up her bags and just started walking. He figured she knew someone in town, was going to their house. But it looks like she had no idea where she was going, just decided to walk—until she dropped." Wendy pulled the LandCruiser into a secluded driveway and suddenly got professional. "Okay, Mrs. Pelletier, here's the home we're showing. Nice four-bedroom Cape, two and a half baths, six acres . . ."

I don't remember a thing about the house. I was so entranced by Milly Finch's story, it was as if I'd been transported to another time. Forty years earlier Mildred Deakin had stepped out of her life of fame and fortune and onto a north-bound train. She'd traveled to the end of the line, then, on a raw November afternoon, she'd gotten off the train and, lugging her suitcase and typewriter, she'd trudged through the darkness until she'd fallen in her tracks.

"ookie, sweetheart," Cookie's mother said. "I was just thinking, for your sixteenth birthday we should do something really nice."

Cookie grimaced. "I don't want one of those awful pink corsages with the roses and bubble-gum."

"No, of course not. We'd never do anything in such poor taste. But I was thinking, how about if you invite two or three of your nice little friends, and we go to Boston for an all-girls pajama party. We could stay at the Copley, have dinner somewhere special, and maybe take in a concert. It would be really special. Would you like that?"

"Oh, wow. That would be terrific, Mom. Thanks!" She jumped up, threw her arms around her mother, and hugged her. Then she pulled away. "I'll just go call Sara—"

Mrs. Wilson took Cookie gently by the arm. "Just a minute, honey. Don't you think it might be kinder not to ask Sara? After all, she's probably never been in a nice hotel, and she might feel very uncomfortable. How about some of your other friends. There's that nice Norton girl. . . ."

Cookie stared at her mother uncomprehendingly. "Not ask Sara? What do you mean? She's my best friend. I'd never go anywhere without Sara!"

8

Jake Fenton was a born storyteller; I sipped my vodka martini, mesmerized—by his words and by his intense gray gaze. It was 11:52 the evening of the day after my visit to Nelson Corners. I'd wanted to share Mildred Deakin Finch's poignant tale with Jake— he'd been so interested when he'd seen the writer's picture in the *Times* a couple of months earlier—but I couldn't seem to get a word in edgewise.

We sat at the battered oak bar at Ernie's Grill in Greenfield. I worked on my martini and listened to Jake spin tales of heroic adventure. Jake was on his third Crown Royal—double, straight up—and heading for the fourth. How he could handle that much booze without slurring so much as a single consonant of his kayaking-the-rapids-of-Tibet story mystified me. My eyes were drawn to the biceps straining the sleeves of his close-fitting black T-shirt. Must have something to do with muscle mass.

From its posters of "college girls" in pasties to the rich fug of beer and cigarettes and the lethal thunk of stiff, whizzing darts, Ernie's Grill was a testosterone-powered, down-and-dirty kind of place. Aside from the bartender in her seam-stretched jeans and midriff-tied white blouse, I was the only woman in the bar. If there was a guy in the place who didn't have lingerie shreds dangling from his eyeballs when he looked at me, he wasn't letting their absence show. The leering contest was less about me—or any woman—than it was about the other guys at the bar, less about my body than about the perceived prowess of their own: competitive *cojones*.

After a few minutes in Jake's presence, I forgot all about Milly Finch. The man knew how to tell a tale. The lead kayak on the Tibetan whitewater expedition had just capsized and vanished beneath the waves, and my companion turned his relation of this fatal incident into a nuanced disquisition on the fragility of the human soul embarked on its perilous journey from zygote to coffin. "The boats battle the rapids," he mused, "but the man inside the boat, his spirit, the muscle of the man, determines the fate of the craft." He paused for a slug of Crown Royal, then continued. "It's ironic, but I've never felt so alive as I did when that kayak went over. For poor Saunders, it was ending; for me, the quest was at its most intense."

"And you couldn't rescue him?" I was horrified.

"Nope. Didn't even try." His gray eyes were murky in the smoky dimness of the bar. "The current was too strong—would've taken us all." Jake slugged back his drink and raised a finger to the bartender. Rescuing Saunders wasn't the point; the point was the profound impact of Saunders's demise on the Alpha male seated next to me. The murk in Jake's eyes, I decided admiringly, was a brave attempt to mask this strong man's pain. Then I thought again—and sighed. The murk in Jake's eyes was most likely pure unadulterated murk.

That afternoon, twenty minutes late for our three o'clock tour of the town, Jake had come striding into my office. "Page proofs," he announced, thunking a thick overnight-express envelope on my desk. "I'm going to have to beg off that tour we were planning and spend the rest of the afternoon going over these." He shuddered in mock horror.

"That's too bad," I said, and meant it. I'd been looking forward to his company.

"So, how about maybe this evening?" Jake asked.

"This evening? A town tour?"

"No tour; I can find my own way around. Always have." He perched on the edge of my desk and flashed me a smile. "How about a late supper and a few drinks? About ten?"

My heart went *dum, dum, dum,* but I hesitated a cautious five seconds: That was a very late date. Was he trying to set me up? There was something about Jake Fenton that made a woman ask herself a question like that. But, hey, what the hell, I'm a big girl now. I could always say no. Or *yes.* I *could* say yes—if I wanted to. It was not an unprovocative thought. "Sure. I'm free this evening."

"Great," he said, fiddling with the pencils in my pencil cup, caressing one gently between his fingers. "Where do I pick you up?" He plucked the pencil from the cup and scribbled directions to my house. Then he winked at me. "See you around ten."

"Sure." To mask my unsophisticated excitement at this serendipitous date with the world-famous novelist, I hefted his UPS envelope from the desk. The thing must have weighed five pounds. "So, Jake, what's the new book called?"

"Birds of Prey," he replied, immediately retrieving the envelope from my hands. "But keep that to yourself. This baby's slated for a huge promotional blitz, and the title's part of the tease. We're not gonna reveal it until the very last second."

"Really?" Most of the writers I read are dead—Shakespeare, Dickinson, T. S. Eliot—and the live ones are lucky to get a cup of cappuccino from their publicists, let alone a *huge promotional blitz.* "What's the novel about?"

"A kid and his sister, lost in the woods."

"Sounds like 'Hansel and Gretel.' " I've always been such a smart-mouth.

"It's *nothing* like 'Hansel and Gretel,' " Jake replied sharply.

. . .

The fourth Crown Royal double was proving to be the proverbial straw for Jake. Having wound up his tale of the recovery of poor Saunders's body and the perilous journey with the funeral litter down the Tibetan mountainside guided by a single lonely but loyal native boy, the adventurer abruptly ceased his tale.

Two hours and counting of Jake Fenton's company was beginning to disabuse me of romantic fantasies I might have entertained about the man. Jake Fenton wasn't about Romance. Jake Fenton was all about Jake Fenton: the Fenton wit, the Fenton charm, the Fenton brilliance, the Fenton sex appeal—the Fenton *cojones*. This masculine self-absorption would ordinarily have put me—a staunch feminist—off my feed, but the difference between garden-variety narcissism and literary genius was epitomized by the difference between the drunken blather of the other guys at Ernie's and the world-class word-spinning of the man beside me. As long as I accepted the evening on Jake's terms, I could enjoy the Fenton take on the blood sport of life—and the ephemeral catch in my breath every time Jake stopped talking and granted me another shot of his sexy little smile.

Eventually Jake's hand found a casual perch on my thigh. The catch in my breath was no longer ephemeral, but this man was a little too slick for me. Just as casually, I removed the hand, replacing it on his own thigh. As if I had pushed a button or switched a lever, Jake ceased talking. Suddenly he concentrated on smashing bar snacks. One by one, tiny goldfish, sesame sticks, pretzels, met their fate, crushed to crumbs between the oak bar top and Jake's broad thumb. Then he buried his gaze in the booze, and kept it there, despite my earnest attempts to resuscitate the conversation.

Great. Just great! I thought. My evening in the presence of literary genius was going downhill a good deal faster than Jake, his native guide, and poor Saunders's corpse. And my heroic escort was looped, obviously in no shape to drive the big brown Range Rover he'd picked me up in. *How in hell am I going to get home?* I wondered.

As Jake brooded into his whiskey, the atmosphere in the bar began to heat up. I hadn't been paying much attention to the two guys next to us. They'd been downing draft Buds for the past hour and a half and reminiscing amiably about high school glory days, but suddenly they struck out over who'd made the winning run in game twelve of senior year. Their voices rose, and I glanced over at them. The redhead with the shoulders unexpectedly hooked a right at the pudgy guy in the "I got shucked at Pete's Oyster House" T-shirt, connected, and knocked him off the bar stool. He crashed into Jake. The impact jolted the writer out of his sulk. Jake caught the guy, staggering as the impact of Pudgy's weight hit the impact of the Crown Royal. Without even pausing to think about it, he shoved him powerfully back into his assailant. Then he socked him in the stomach. The pudgy guy vomited all over the redhead—and over every one else within range. I vaulted off my stool.

"Who do you think you're shoving, asshole?" The pudgy guy, back on his feet, caught at Jake's arm with a barf-spattered hand. Jake met him with a mean elbow, and Pudgy grunted and doubled over. The redhead steadied Pudge, his bosom pal again, and took a wild one-arm swing at Jake.

"Shit." The novelist slurred even that simple integer of Anglo-Saxon verbiage. "I don't have time for this crap." He tossed two twenties on the bar and grabbed my arm. "Let's get out of here." For someone with such a heavy load on, my companion was pretty fast on his feet. He quick-stepped out the door behind me like a man who'd exited many bars in his lifetime and knew the moves.

No one showed any signs of following us out of Ernie's, maybe because they too had gotten a good look at the Fenton biceps. As Jake aimed the car keys in the general direction of the brown Range Rover, I snatched them from his hand. "I'm driving, sport," I announced, hoping Jake wouldn't turn out to be a violent drunk. In my short years with Amanda's father, I'd had more than a lifetime's worth of experience with nasty drunks.

"Good," Jake said, climbed into the shotgun seat, and promptly lapsed into unconsciousness.

took him home with me. What else was I going to do with him? I had no idea where Jake lived. I could have called Enfield College Security to find out, but, perhaps stupidly, didn't want to humiliate the novelist. If I reported it to Security, Jake's bender would be all over campus by third period tomorrow—and my name would be permanently attached to that of a drunken barfly writer. *That* would be a disaster: I wasn't tenured yet.

Jake semirevived as we pulled into the driveway, and followed my instructions like a good boy. He stumbled out of the SUV, through my front door, and onto the couch as if he'd done it a thousand times before and knew the drill. It was almost two A.M. before I'd gotten the booze brushed off my breath and the puke spatters scrubbed off my arms and legs. Then I put myself, clean and relatively sober, to bed. Alone. Behind a locked door.

When I woke up at 9:28 and made my way to the living room, the afghan was folded neatly over the back of the uninhabited couch, Jake and his Range Rover had vanished, and a one-word note in bold capitals on the kitchen table was the only sign that I'd spent the night with Jake Fenton, master of the pen and sword, eloquent interpreter of post-modern masculinity, world-famous novelist. The note read: SORRY.

In an interpretive quandary, I read the word aloud. *Sorry?* What did Jake Fenton mean by *sorry?* Was it a curt, abrupt, pro forma sorry? Was it an abject, humiliated, repentant sorry? Or a wry, philosophical, we're-all-in-the-same-human-condition sorry? Or an I'll-call-you-in-a-day-or-two-and-see-if-you're-still-speaking-to-me sorry? Or *what?* My Ph.D. in literary studies didn't help me one bit in trying to deconstruct the meaning of *sorry*.

9

The short, wiry woman with the cropped gray hair sat erect in her chair, torso rigidly upright, thin shoulders squared under the drab fabric of the prison uniform. Only in her eyes could I detect any resemblance at all to the chic young 1950s writer I'd seen pictured in the *Times*. Those eyes, still intensely dark, glared at me with suspicion. "What do you want from me?"

I didn't know. Absolution, most likely. "I wanted to say I'm sorry—"

"Sorry? *Sorry?* You open your mouth, and my peaceful world is shattered, and you're *sorry?*" It seemed that Mildred Deakin Finch wasn't in the absolution business.

"But, Ms. Deakin, I had no intention—"

"Finch. *Mrs.* Finch."

"Mrs. Finch—"

"You *had no intention*," she mocked me. "You destroyed my life, but you *had no intention*. What are you doing here, anyhow? What do you want?"

"I'm not quite certain." I could hardly tell this bitter woman that the haunting image of her younger self had kept me awake two nights running, floating in hazy black and white just below full consciousness, threatening to sink to the level of dreams. I couldn't tell her that what I *wanted* was for that . . . that girl . . . to tell me *why*. I wanted to know what had sent a novelist at the height of literary celebrity bolting from Manhattan to seek the obscurity of the rural hinterlands. I wanted to know what placed her, decades later, on a Columbia County goat farm with a hunting rifle in her hand. I wanted to know what personal demon it was that had pulled the trigger.

'd spent an afternoon that weekend in the college library researching everything I could find about Mildred Deakin. After my visit to Nelson Corners and the realtor's compelling story about Milly Finch's arrival in that hamlet, I'd become almost obsessed with the writer. But the scholarly world in general didn't seem as interested as I was. Falling in some ambiguous crevasse between the scholarly categories of "literature" and "popular culture," *Oblivion Falls* and its author had attracted precious little academic attention. A computerized MLA bibliography search turned up two essays in books on 1950s popular fiction and one biographical sketch—by Sean Small in his introduction to the reprint edition of the novel. That was all. However, Professor Small's bibliography noted a few potentially useful primary sources—a handful of newspaper articles from the fifties and a file of Deakin's personal papers in the archives of the New York Public Library. If I needed to look up the newspaper articles, I could probably find them on microfiche in the Enfield Library. I tucked the NYPL's Deakin file away in my mind for possible perusal the next time I found myself in Manhattan. Then I read *Oblivion Falls* again, hoping against all odds to find some clue to Mildred Deakin's inexplicable flight from literary fame.

The novel wasn't half bad. It recounted—in sexual detail that was considered explicit at the time—the love life of Sara Todd, an ambitious and talented young woman from Satan Mills, the working class section of Beaumont, a New England college town. This story had no Cinderella ending, however; the girl dies during an illegal abortion. After all, this was the 1950s, and as far as respectable society was concerned, Sara Todd of Satan Mills was a "bad girl," and deserved punishment. Deakin's prose was spare and clear, and the sex scenes were effective—if somewhat more clinical than erotic. But it was *Oblivion Falls*'s subtle analyses of class aspirations, struggles, and prejudices that I found most compelling. Mildred Deakin's fictional Satan Mills was all too familiar to me, reminding me vividly of Lowell, and the hard life and hard people of my own childhood and youth.

For the second time I read the novel's haunting final lines: *As for Sara, she had been a particularly flamboyant specimen of the hardy summer roses that push their way into evanescent bloom in this otherwise unyielding northern soil. When Prentiss thought of her, if he thought of her at all, it was with the vague regret one feels for the passing of such a common flower.*

The tear I wiped from the corner of my eye was not simply for Mildred Deakin's fictional Sara.

I turned back to the Introduction for another look at the author's life. According to Professor Small, Mildred Deakin was the motherless daughter of a Stallmouth College English Professor. Born in 1932, she'd been abandoned to a life of airless intellection in the college town of Stallmouth, New Hampshire, by a mother who'd absconded to Los Angeles with a Hollywood scriptwriter. From her early years, Mildred had spent her days in the family kitchen with Bernice Lapierre, the housekeeper who raised her. Bernice had a daughter, Lorraine, who grew up along with Mildred—"like a sister," Deakin had told a reporter in a rare interview. That "sister" had died as a teenager in some unspecified way. *Ah,* I thought, *an illegal abortion, like Sara in the novel.* Subsequently, Bernice, Mildred's beloved foster mother, had committed suicide, devastating the young writer. As Professor Small put it, *Oblivion Falls* was "Deakin's poignant attempt to redress the wrongs—sexual and emotional—suffered by the unfortunate members of her family of women."

. . .

So, what *was* I doing here, in this Columbia County jail on a mid-September Monday morning? Well might Milly Finch ask. Mildred Deakin's life story was a tragic one, and, having inadvertently brought it to a crisis through my flippant comments to the *Times* reporter, I could not simply walk away. I'd felt compelled to seek the novelist out—but to what end? In the fluorescent light of the prison reception room, Mildred Deakin—Milly—was wan, her small, oval face etched with a multitude of fine lines. Two deeply engraved vertical grooves cut between her arched eyebrows. In the large, institutional-green chamber, she looked as out of place as a deer in a goat pen. Suddenly overwhelmed by pity, I leaned toward her. "Is there anything I can do to help you, Mrs. Finch?" I asked this ghostly shadow of the passionate young woman who had written *Oblivion Falls*. She recoiled, a shudder running through her spare frame. Her eyes went perfectly opaque.

Fueled by a combination of compassion and guilt, I pressed on. "Mrs. Finch, I know you must have had powerful reasons to seek reclusion . . . ah, privacy . . . the way you have. And, I must admit, I do feel somewhat responsible for what happened with Martin Katz. You're absolutely right. I opened my mouth, and a man died in your driveway. I was a catalyst. But a few links were forged in that chain well before my interview with the *Times.* . . ." *Such as whatever traumatic event in your past life caused you to hide among goats for the past forty years,* I thought. *Such as why you felt the need to pick up a gun.* "I want to understand why things happened the way they did, and I want you to help me. I do realize that if I hadn't mentioned *Oblivion Falls* to Martin Katz, he would never have written about it in the *Times.* And, if he hadn't written about it, there wouldn't have been any hoopla in the media about the book. And if there hadn't been all that hoopla in the media, he would never have sought you out in Nelson Corners. And if he hadn't sought you out, you never would have . . ." I paused, struggling for some delicate way of saying it.

She completed my trailed-off statement. "Never would have shot him down in cold blood. Go on, that's what you were going to say, wasn't it?"

I nodded. I hadn't intended to phrase it quite so bluntly.

"Five minutes," announced the hefty blonde in the guard's uniform waiting by the door. Milly did not acknowledge her. Instead she stared to my left, avoiding my gaze, her dark eyes still hedged, the parallel lines between her brows deepening. I had a sudden realization that Milly Finch at this stage of her chosen life was far more comfortable consorting with goats than with human beings.

"Hah! I get it." Her head swiveled; abruptly she focused on me. "You're writing a biography, aren't you?"

"No!" I responded, emphatically. Then, perhaps fatally for my purposes. "Well, I am doing a biography, but not about you—"

"Oh, yes you are!" Her eyes narrowed, and her gaze attempted to bore into my soul. "A tell-all book about Mildred Deakin and her scandalous novel and her scandalous life. That's what you're doing here, isn't it? Just like that reporter, you're digging around in the dirt for whatever tidbits you can scratch up. Well, no thank you. It's my dirt, and I don't want any books written about it. You writer types are all alike—jackals! It doesn't matter whether you're reporters or academics, you make me sick." Her voice had sunk to a barely audible hiss. This time *she* leaned forward in her chair, and *I* shuddered, thankful, perhaps with good reason, for the hefty guard at the door.

"Well, Professor Jackal," Milly Finch went on, tapping a forefinger on the table, "put this in your book, why don't you? And get it right, because I'm not going to talk to you again. I did not shoot that reporter. I never saw him or heard of him until I came out of the goat barn that Friday evening and found him lying dead in the dirt with his head in a puddle of blood—ruining an otherwise perfectly beautiful sunset."

I nodded wordlessly. According to the *Chatham Courier*'s follow-up story in this week's issue, even though her fingerprints had appeared clearly in several places on the murder weapon, Milly Finch had pled not guilty. She'd been arrested, and was being held on suspicion of homicide, but had not yet been formally charged.

"You *need to understand*, do you?" she said. "Well, understand this. Somebody else shot Mr. Martin Katz, shot that reporter dead with my husband's thirty-thirty. That's all I know about his death, and that's all I'm saying about it. Go write your *biography*," she spit out the word as if it left a foul taste in her mouth, "about someone else, someone who's done something evil enough to deserve being dragged through the literary mud. Now, get out. I don't want you here."

She rose abruptly from the straight wooden chair and beckoned imperiously to the guard, who moved forward at once.

Would you like a canapé?"

Cookie's mother had taught Sara how to hold the heavy silver tray, how to arrange the caviar on toast, how to pronounce the word canapé. Mrs. Wilson had even had the black dress and little white apron "made up" especially for Sara, and bought her the flat black shoes. Professor Wilson was the Chairman of the English Department at the college, and the Wilsons did a great deal of entertaining. Mrs. Wilson had told Sara that she felt it was her duty as a good wife to support and further her husband's career. Sara enjoyed working in the Wilson's bright, well-equipped kitchen, and appreciated the opportunity to listen to the literate conversation at the parties.

When she didn't get an immediate response from the guest, Sara repeated her question: "Would you like a canapé?"

"I'd like a great deal more than a canapé," said the tall, slender man with the curly dark hair and the dancing eyes as he smiled down at her. Sara knew this was Professor Andrew Prentiss, because Cookie had pointed him out to her several times in town. Cookie had a mad crush on Professor Prentiss. Once last spring when she and Sara were having a Coke in Jacobs Pharmacy after school, the young professor had come in and ordered an egg-salad sandwich. He had passed Cookie where she sat at the soda fountain without noticing her, even though he had been at her home several times for dinner. She had burst into sobs and Sara had hustled her out of the store. After that the two girls had vowed off older men forever. Now here was Professor Prentiss, with his deep-set gray eyes, heavy brows, and triangular smile, gazing at Sara as if he would like to eat her up. Sara thought he looked like a handsome young Satan. She felt a breathless catch somewhere in the region of her heart. "And what is your name, pretty girl?" he asked.

Off in the corner of the room, Cookie sat in a green plush wing chair. She was hiding in the corner because she hated the dress her mother had made her wear, an embroidered blue chiffon with a high neck, gathered skirt, and bow that tied in the back. A "perfect frock for the sweet jeune fille" *the woman at the shop had called it. A perfect frock for a baby, Cookie thought.*

"Sara," said Sara, in response to the question from Professor Prentiss, feeling unaccountably as if with the mere utterance of the word she were giving up something far more precious than a simple name.

Mrs. Wilson stopped in the middle of a conversation with Edwina Price and stared hard at Sara and Andrew Prentiss. Then she excused herself and stepped sharply up to the girl. "Sara," she said, "keep those canapés circulating."

10

Harriet Person motioned to me from her position at the head of the long, pale-ash English Department conference table and jerked her head at the chrome-framed chair next to her. I slid it out and sat down. "So," Harriet said, sotto voce, "I understand you've got a hot thing going with our hunky Visiting Writer." Her eyes were steely slits.

"What?" I practically shrieked it. Ned Hilton looked up curiously from the large, trapezoidal paper clip he was compulsively unbending and rebending. Joe Gagliardi stared across the table, avid for any hint of scandal. Ralph Brooke, oblivious to anyone but himself, fixed Craig Markoff, our new, extremely young Shakespearean, with his intense gaze. Ralph's gray eyes were magnified behind black-rimmed, thick-lensed glasses, and the effect was uncanny.

"Then there was the time," Ralph intoned, "when Papa and I were marlin fishing off the Keys—*Papa?* Why, Hemingway, of course. We all called him *Papa.*" Craig nodded and stroked his gold nostril ring nervously. Being in the presence of someone who'd actually fished with Ernest Hemingway most likely had convinced young Craig that he'd been sucked into some eerie academic time warp.

The first English Department meeting of the fall semester was about to get under way. Still stunned by my encounter with Mildred Deakin Finch the day before, I'd seriously considered not attending. But, even though I was on research leave and wasn't obligated to go to meetings, I knew that, as an untenured faculty member, I was well advised to show my shining visage at every department gathering. So the morning after my visit to the Columbia County jail and the disquieting talk with Milly Finch, I strolled into the English Department lounge at eleven A.M., attired in khaki shorts and a sleeveless olive T-shirt—and shivered. Although summer still prevailed on the Enfield campus this third week in September, the lounge, with its ice-blue walls, ice-gray carpeting, and ice-green draperies, felt as wintery as always—an appropriate metaphor, I thought, for the chilly relations between department members.

"Shh." At my outburst, Harriet's hand sliced the air. I shushed. Ned went back to his murderous-looking length of wire. Shut out of the good dirt, Joe pouted, the gold stud that pierced his lower lip momentarily vanishing in the folds of skin. Ralph droned on and on. Craig glanced wildly around for someone to take pity and rescue him. Harriet leaned over and hissed in my ear. "Come into the hall, Karen, so we can talk without your little secret getting out."

"*What* little secret?" I hissed back at her. "There *is* no little secret!" But I pushed my chair back obediently and followed my senior colleague. The door sighed shut behind us.

Standing there with Harriet in the empty hallway, I noted, irrelevantly, that she seemed somehow different today—younger, maybe. Then it struck me: The trademark streak of white in her otherwise dark hair had vanished.

"Monica says she saw Fenton's Range Rover in your driveway the other morning—before six A.M.," Harriet informed me in clipped tones. Monica—our department secretary. "She recognized the New York plates. Said Jake's car was tucked up to your front door 'real cozylike.' "

A wave of anger threatened to choke me. "What the hell was Monica doing, spying on my house in the middle of the night?" I thrust my hands in my pockets so my colleague couldn't see that they'd curled into furious balled-up fists. *And what the hell business is it of yours?*

"She had some sort of sunrise ritual up Greenfield way—one of her coven things." Monica is a witch. Literally. And proud of it. *And* she's nosy as hell. "Karen." Harriet leaned toward me, her expression unreadable. I shivered again. "Jake Fenton may be hot, but he could mean trouble for you. Even if what you had with him was only a one-night stand, you'd better watch your back."

"It wasn't a one-night stand," I protested—then didn't like the way that sounded.

Harriet continued as if she hadn't heard me. "I tell you this for your own good. As junior faculty, you are not best advised to become sexually involved with even a temporary member of the department. Your tenure decision comes up in a year or two. Think of the position such a . . . a questionable professional history would put you in when your senior colleagues vote on—"

Ordinarily I would have stormed away from such an intrusion into my privacy, but I had a misbegotten notion that if only I could clarify what had actually happened, I could staunch this gossip before it bled me to death. "Harriet, there's no involvement! Nothing happened!"

This time she heard me. "But he was there? At your house? At six A.M.?" She frowned. "And *nothing happened?*"

"It's not what you think. He was just dr—"

Miles Jewell pushed open the door at the top of the stairs. He was followed by Jake Fenton and three other stragglers. From the sudden fire that flashed in Harriet's eyes when Jake came into view, I realized why she and I were having this conversation. And I knew instantly why the white streak in Harriet's hair had vanished.

Jake nodded at us. I hadn't seen or heard from the writer since I'd put him to bed, bombed, on my couch during the wee hours Friday morning. I clamped my mouth shut on the word *drunk*. With an eyebrow-puckering frown at Harriet, who was smirking at Jake, I followed the entourage into the English Department lounge.

Twenty colleagues were already gathered around the long table in the center of the room. My eyes scanned the group: Ralph Emerson Brooke, current occupant of the Palaver Chair of Literary Studies; Kenneth Beatty, Shakespeare; Ned Hilton, seventeenth century; Latisha Mohammed, African-American; Sally Chenille, coappointment with Comp Lit; Nicole Gottesman, queer theory; Edmund Friendly, the Puritans; Anne McQuade, Shakespeare; Joe Gagliardi, postmodernism; Stanford Franks, postcolonialism; Bob Banks, post-Shakespeare; Deborah Minter, eighteenth century; Michael Dunkerling, animality; the newcomer Craig Markoff, neo-Shakespeare; and on and on. The usual crew.

Jake Fenton pulled out the chair next to Ralph Brooke. He sat, stroked his sexy three-day beard contemplatively, then leaned over, and whispered something in the older man's ear. Ralph turned to him, whipped off his clunky glasses, and stared. Jake smiled a snarky smile, whispered again. Ralph choked and went bone pale. Odd. But before I could observe the two further, Miles called the meeting to order. Under the influence of the chairman's mind-numbing tones, I sank into a deep funk, furious at Jake for putting me in such an awkward position vis-à-vis the college community, furious at the college community for the titillated gossip that was bound to fly around campus like wild fire.

I don't remember a thing that transpired during that meeting. I know I signed the attendance sheet, voted on measures brought up for voting, dutifully watched my colleagues' mouths open and shut in eloquent debate, but my mind had vacated the room and was back in the corridor with Harriet Person. All the biting things I should have said goose-stepped into my mind like a platoon of storm troopers. I felt my face grow hot and my jaw set into a truculent jut. *A person can't even have a Goddamned private life around this place without her Goddamned colleagues playing Big Brother. Goddamned full professors, nothing but a Goddamned bunch of Goddamned fucking fascist thugs. . . .* I wanted nothing more than to jump out of my seat and launch into a diatribe against this intrusion into my personal freedom. Thank God for Robert's Rules of Order, or I might have scuttled my hard-won career right there and then.

Twenty minutes after the department meeting ended, Jake Fenton sauntered into my office. Behind him, Monica lurked in the hallway, four-square and solid in chinos and a red cotton sweater with a pattern of gray diamonds. She caught my eye and grinned. Before I could muster up a scowl—or stick my tongue out at her, I was in such an evil mood—Jake pushed my office door shut, and stood there with his hand on the knob. I thought, apropos of nothing, that perhaps Jake Fenton always kept his hand on the doorknob. That must make it a hell of a lot easier to get away.

"Is it always like that?" The crooked just-between-us grin illuminated his bronzed face; the gray eyes crinkled.

I didn't feel like being charmed. My big night with this literary legend, and its aftermath of gossip, had left a bitter taste in my mouth. "Is *what* always like *what?*"

"That strange meeting we just endured. The turf battles. The impenetrable sesquipedalian language. Those obscure resentments underlying each debate like massive, ancient icebergs."

I shrugged. I had no memory of anything other than my own sullen funk. And what was so strange about all that, anyhow? That's just the way things are in an English Department. Jake had taught elsewhere; he should know that.

Jake relinquished the doorknob, walked across the office, and sank into my green armchair. "I'm really here about what happened the other night, Karen." His lips tightened. "As you can see,

I have a bit of a problem with alcohol. How much of an ass did I make of myself?"

"That depends on what you mean by 'ass.' You got drunk; you got involved in a fistfight with strangers; you passed out in the car." I shrugged again. "I've seen worse."

He cringed. "Did I . . . ? You know . . . ? I mean, face it, Karen, you're a very attractive woman. And I . . . Well, I hope I didn't . . ."

"You tried."

Jake grimaced. "I hope I didn't . . . make myself obnoxious to you. I'd really like to spend more time with you, Karen—lots more. That is, if you . . ."

I gave him an enigmatic smile. *In your dreams, big boy.*

The narcissist in him chose to interpret the smile positively. "I'll give you a call someday soon, Karen. We'll set a date." He rose from the chair and headed for the door. Then, his hand on the knob again, Jake turned back. "I didn't *say* anything, did I?"

"*Say* anything? You *said* a lot."

An anxious expression crossed his rugged features. "About . . . anyone in particular?"

"You talked about a number of people. There was some native guide—"

"No." He shook his head impatiently. "Not *that* kind of talk. Did I say anything about . . . well . . . anyone . . . ?" Then he seemed to register what I'd told him, and his face relaxed again. "Never mind, Karen. I don't know what comes over me sometimes." He pointed his index finger at me as if it were a gun, then cocked his thumb. "Hey, listen, Karen, I'll call you." He flashed me his hot-guy grin, turned the knob, and strode down the hall.

"Don't bother," I replied, but he didn't hear me.

J ake Fenton?" George Gilman queried, when he ran into me outside the library. My little colleague's arms were loaded with books. I was on my way to Earlene's office to pick her up for a late lunch.

"Don't *you* start," I warned. "It's nothing but unfounded gossip."

"I hope so, Karen, because I know things. . . ."

"I don't care." I wanted to snap at him, but his wrinkled gnome's face was so full of concern that I modulated my tone. "It's all a misunderstanding, George. There's nothing going on."

"You're sure?" We were standing on the bottom library step, and he set his stack of books on one of the stone pillars.

"Yes." I did snap at him this time. "And, besides, even if we were screwing our brains out, it wouldn't be anyone's business but our own."

"I know. I know." He raised his hands defensively. "It's just that . . ." He paused. It was a long pause, as pauses go, and I was about to break into his frowning abstraction when he continued abruptly. "It's just that with the work I'm doing on this new book, I hear a bit about what goes on with contemporary writers."

Something wasn't being said, but I nodded anyhow. George's new book would provide the first major overview of *fin-de*-twentieth-*siècle* American book history.

"I'm doing a chapter on institutional cross-influence—you know, the effect of university writing programs, writer's retreats, conferences—on the shape of literary fiction. I've seen how nasty Fenton can be. At a conference at Iowa, he was having an affair with . . . well . . . with a writer whose name you would know, whose fiction has been characterized as defining the female literary voice for the past three decades. He got soused at a party, announced to the gathering that she was a 'tight-assed little cunt,' and jammed an ice cube down her cleavage."

"Jeesh! And I thought academics were bad."

"Oh, we are." George was silent as Ralph Brooke passed us on the steps. Ralph inclined his head ponderously. We nodded in response. My companion watched the Palaver occupant until the older man was well past us. Then he said, speculatively, "I didn't realize anyone still sold seersucker suits."

I laughed. "Maybe he special-orders them."

"But where do they get the fabric? I thought the world's entire seersucker population had died out—oh, say, about 1968." Then, without missing a beat, he dropped the facetious tone. "Do you know Brooke at all, Karen?"

"He's new in my department, but I can't say I know him. Why?"

"He's such a pompous son of a bitch. He got hold of me at lunch the other day and blathered on about his salad days as a hipster in the Village with Kerouac, Ginsberg, and Delmore Schwartz. I can't believe you guys hired him. He puts himself forward as a big expert on the Beats, but what he doesn't know about the fifties . . ." He let it trail off. "Have you read any of his work?"

"Oh yes," I replied, "during the hiring process." I laughed, distracted from my own problems. "To me the most impressive thing about it is the name he publishes under: *Ralph W. Emerson Brooke.* Can you beat that name for scholarly credibility?"

"Rumor has it . . ." George drew closer. His mood seemed to have lightened. ". . . that Brooke's name had no W. in it until he published his first book. Then suddenly, magically, old Ralphie was named after the Sage of Concord: *Ralph Waldo Emerson Brooke.*"

I gave him a quizzical glance. "George, what's going on? It's not like you to be so bitchy about a colleague."

He looked a little shamefaced. "It's just that, well, Brooke's been lobbying to get the contract for the Library of America edition of the Beat Generation writers, and I had my eye on that little project for myself." The campus carillon chimed twice, and George hastily scooped up his books. "Gotta run, Karen. Office hours. But remember what I told you. Be careful. Jake Fenton may be a terrific writer, but sometimes I don't think he's much of a human being."

Earlene hangs out in Emerson Hall, the administration building, and after I left the library I cut through the classroom wing on my way to her office. It was warm in the building, and professors' voices droned out from open classroom doors. Terms such as *epistemological contingencies, cultural relativism,* and *transnational immigration patterns* faded in and out as I traversed the hallway. Harriet Person's pedantic tones snagged my attention as I approached her classroom: . . . *due to the objectification of women,* Harriet pronounced. I slowed down. My colleague was teaching Women's Studies 101, the Intro to Women's Studies course. Next fall when she went on sabbatical I was slated to serve as her replacement, and I needed some pointers. The prospect of teaching WS 101 intimidated me. How to deal adequately with all the complicated, contradictory, and confusing ramifications of gender—biological, sociological, cultural, economic, political—in one twelve-week course without resorting to reductive sloganizing eluded me. Harriet's confident voice continued, and I took mental notes: *the persistent trivialization of female literary endeavors stems from a deep-seated misogyny. A fear of female sexual power* . . . I passed out of earshot, but not until the words *vagina dentata* crossed my ears—the dread male image of the all-devouring female, the toothed vagina that castrates and devours. I sighed as I turned the corner. I couldn't quite imagine myself uttering the words *toothed vagina* in front of nineteen young women and the inevitable lone male Women's Studies major.

I climbed a flight of steps and entered Earlene's outer office. The work-study student at the desk slid what looked like a copy of *Oblivion Falls* underneath a thick manila folder and informed me that Dean Johnson had said I should go right in. "Karen," Earlene queried before I was halfway through the door, "what's this I hear about you and that Jake Fenton? Did you really . . . ?"

When I got home, there was a message from Jill on my answering machine. *Jake Fenton? Call me!*

I poured myself a large glass of California merlot and took it to the green chaise in the backyard. I drank it very slowly, and stared at the leaves on the cherry tree above me. By the time I'd finished the wine, I thought I could discern a separate outline for each and every leaf. Soon the days would be too short to catch that particular transparent quality of late afternoon light. I drained the last drop of wine from the glass and rose to go inside. I walked slowly. There was a long evening ahead, and I had nothing planned.

*T*he morning after the Wilsons' party Sara and Cookie were supposed to meet at the granite ledge to picnic on party leftovers. When, well after the sun had reached its apex, Cookie did not appear, hunger drove Sara home. A lunch of bread and fried bologna satisfied her appetite, but did nothing to assuage her unease about why her friend had missed their rendezvous. Perhaps Cookie was ill, or was suffering from the agonizing cramps that always accompanied her monthlies. Sara counted on her fingers, but couldn't make it out to be Cookie's time of month.

After helping her mother hang wash on the line, Sara combed her hair and changed from the cotton skirt into her shorts. The day had become blisteringly hot, the town torpid with heat the way only a New England town, accustomed to its chilly climes, can swelter. A sturdy climbing rose provided the single floral decoration for their four-flat wooden building, and Sara gathered a few pink blooms from high on the bush where the depredations of children had not destroyed the late August flowering. She arranged the blooms nicely in a nosegay, thinking that, when she reached the Wilsons' house, she would add a paper doily left over from the party decor.

Cookie, who usually bounced down the porch steps at Sara's appearance, did not answer the bell. After what seemed to be a long two or three minutes, Mrs. Wilson opened the door wearing a cotton-print dress and house shoes. Her long face was set in a disapproving frown. "Sara," she said, "Sara, my child. I am very sorry to have to communicate this message to you, but Professor Wilson and I have decided that in Carole's best interests, it would be better for her if she . . . ah . . . socialized with young people of her own . . . her own like . . . from now on. I'm certain, Sara, that you will understand. After all, neither of you is a child any longer. Good-bye, Sara."

And she closed the door in Sara's face.

11

The muffin of the morning at Bread & Roses was fresh blueberry. I ordered two—one for now, one for later—and black coffee. When Sophia Warzek pushed backward through the double kitchen door transporting a tray of chocolate croissants, I changed my order immediately: one muffin and one croissant. "What else do you have back there?" I teased her. "Whatever it is, don't bring it out until after I'm gone."

She smiled wanly, and slid the tray into the display case. Then she frowned and touched me lightly on the hand. "Karen, look, there's something I need to talk to you about—get your advice." She glanced furtively around. The palest of blondes, she tended to flush without the slightest provocation, and now her cheeks turned a rosy pink. "But I can't do it here. Can I call you?"

"Better yet, let's have lunch. I miss you, kid!" I punched her on the shoulder. When Amanda was home from school, I always bought groceries for three; Sophia practically became a member of the family.

She made a big pretense of rubbing her arm. "Hey, Professor, that's abuse!"

"Yeah, right. Take it to the Faculty Behavioral Standards Committee. See what they think constitutes abuse."

The laugh didn't reach her blue eyes. "I don't get off work until three, Karen. That's kind of late for lunch."

"How about dinner?" I was suddenly worried about my young friend; I hadn't seen her look so . . . so haunted . . . since her father had been incarcerated two years earlier. "Not tonight. I've got a . . . a thing over in New York this afternoon. How about tomorrow? At Mai Thai? Around six?"

"Sure, Karen. Thanks. See you there." She headed back to the kitchen.

"My treat," I called after her. The only downside of her father's absence was that Sophia was now sole breadwinner for herself and her hapless mother.

As I turned from the register, a poster on the Bread & Roses community bulletin board caught my eye. Or, rather, it was the photo of Jake Fenton on the poster that caught my eye—that familiar flannel-shirted hero-of-the-wilderness photograph that graced all his book jackets. READING & BOOK SIGNING, THURSDAY, SEPTEMBER 16, 7 P.M., SMITH'S BOOKSHOP, FIELD STREET, ENFIELD, JAKE FENTON, AWARD-WINNING AUTHOR OF *ENDURANCE, SURVIVAL, WILDERNESS, PREDATOR, DEADFALL, HUNTER.* Hmm. Tomorrow? Sophia and I could go after dinner. Maybe. Jake might be a lousy date, but I'd bet he could put on quite a show.

Juggling my goodies—muffin, coffee, croissant bag, newspaper—I surveyed the cafe. This drizzly mid-week morning the small room was packed with students, faculty, and townspeople. Behind me, I heard a woman grouch to her companion, "I hate it when the students come back; you can't ever get a seat in here. And it's so noisy." Her accent was somewhere between Boston and Britain.

"Well, it *is* right across from campus. Maybe we should try going somewhere else."

"Yeah, but—the scones . . ."

In front of me on line, a tall, athletic female student in a buzz cut said to her friend, "Really, Tiff, you should get some help. It won't be hard to find someone to talk to around here. You can't throw a *stick* in this town without hitting a therapist."

"Yeah. Yeah. I know." Tiff tightened the scrunchie that held back her sleek dark ponytail. "But . . . listen . . . I tell you what . . . instead of a therapist, I'm thinking of consulting a psychic. . . ."

Her friend shrieked, "A *psychic!* Are you bonkers?"

The place *was* noisy. I frowned. *With the students back,* I thought, *I can't hear myself think.* Then I recalled the conversation behind me, and snorted. Was I turning into a curmudgeon? *Patience,* I admonished myself, *patience.* But I was wearing new shoes, and I'd been standing on line forever. I glanced around for distraction. Since my last visit, Bread & Roses had changed its art display. Large, brownish-pink oil paintings covered the white-stuccoed cafe walls—indeterminate close-ups of what appeared to be either human anatomical parts or root vegetables. They distracted me, but not in the way I'd hoped.

"Karen." From a table in the corner, George Gilman beckoned me over. "I'm just off to class. You can have my table." He gathered up teaching notes, slid them in a folder, and stuck the folder in a battered leather briefcase that looked as if it had gone through grad school with him.

"Thanks." I set my breakfast on the round marble tabletop, and followed it with the rolled-up copy of the *Times* I'd carried clutched under my arm.

George peered at me over his half-glasses and tapped the newspaper. "There's a story in here that I guarantee you—*you,* in particular, I mean—will find riveting."

I smiled at him quizzically: *What?*

He shook his head. "The stuff life does to people! You couldn't possibly make it up."

Wha-a-a-t?

He hesitated, always inclined to gab. Then he unrolled my paper and pointed. "Read this."

I took a bite of the muffin, and glanced at the front page. George's stubby finger indicated a one-column, bottom right, headline: MURDER SUSPECT IDENTIFIED AS MISSING NOVELIST.

I inhaled muffin crumbs, choked. George slapped me on the

back, force-fed me water. When I'd wiped the tears from my eyes,
I read the article.

> HUDSON, N.Y.—Mildred Finch of
> Nelson Corners, charged with homicide
> by New York State Police, has been iden-
> tified as the best-selling novelist Mildred
> Deakin, who vanished from the public eye
> in 1959. Ms. Deakin-Finch's indictment
> on one count of homicide in the first de-
> gree comes following the shooting death
> of Martin R. Katz, a reporter for this
> newspaper, on her Nelson Corners' farm
> September 3. Ms. Deakin, 69, a popular
> novelist in the 1950s, was the subject of
> an article by Mr. Katz published here last
> spring. Over four decades ago she precip-
> itously left the literary world and van-
> ished, keeping her whereabouts unknown
> to even her closest family and friends. The
> search for the beautiful young novelist
> was highly publicized in the media at the
> time of her disappearance. According to
> the lead investigator, Lt. Paula Syverson
> of the Claverack barracks of the New York
> State Police, Ms. Deakin, using the name
> Milly Finch, has resided in the small
> Columbia County community of Nelson
> Corners for many years. No motive for the
> shooting has been revealed.

"Oh, my God! I thought the police were keeping her identity
secret. Poor, poor Milly."

"You *know* her?" Before I could respond, George glanced at
his watch and grimaced. "Sorry, Karen. Gotta run." He rose from
his chair, then paused. "But, you know, the funny thing is that I
think I *talked* to the victim once."

"You did?"

"Yeah. I'd forgotten his name, but he was a *Times* arts reporter, right? Martin Katz . . . yeah that sounds right. He called
me this summer—"

"He did?" I was astonished.

"Yeah. He was researching some article and wanted an expert

opinion on 1950s book culture. I told him that I thought the conservative fifties were the cradle of both the counterculture and the postmodern. He liked that . . . *the cradle of the postmodern.*" George grinned, amused by his facility at condensing complex cultural phenomena into five-second sound bites. Then he glanced at his watch again. "Yikes, my disciples await."

"See ya, George." My little colleague bustled off in his usual Mad-Hatter flurry.

The article continued with details of the homicide and a summary of the writer's career. In spite of the *Times*'s deliberately understated presentation, Mildred Deakin's reappearance made a sensational story. "Fame is a bee," Emily Dickinson once wrote, and it looked as if the reclusive novelist was about to get stung again.

thought you didn't want Milly Finch's true identity revealed, Lieutenant," I said to Paula Syverson over the phone. After finishing the article, I'd headed to my office through a downpour, the first real rain of the season.

"That's right, Professor Pelletier, as long as it served our purpose that the public didn't know who she was. But now . . ." The lieutenant let it trail off. Mildred Deakin Finch had been indicted on a murder charge, and, as far as Syverson was concerned, the case was closed. "I'm curious, Professor . . . tell me, what business is all this of yours?" Before I could reply, she went on. "I don't mean that to sound hostile. I really want to know."

"I saw her, you know . . . Milly Finch . . . the other day. At the jail. She told me the same thing she told you, that she didn't shoot Marty Katz. And—you know what?—I think I believe her." I tapped on my desk with the eraser end of a number-two pencil.

"Hmm." It was a noncommittal utterance.

"I assume," I went on, "that, as part of your investigation, you've considered motivation—why Mildred Deakin would want Marty Katz dead. Am I right?"

"Milly Finch—not Mildred Deakin. Well, *that's* a no-brainer. Obviously Mrs. Finch is pathologically reclusive. Everything about the way she's lived her life confirms that. So, when the victim showed up, she knew he was gonna snatch her out of her cozy . . . ah . . . retirement, she panicked, and—*bam,* he's a goner. She's not talking, of course, but that's the way it musta happened. It's too bad, really; she seems like a nice lady."

I paused for two seconds, then burst out: "You know, Lieutenant, as far as I'm concerned, that theory just doesn't wash. This country has had all sorts of famous literary recluses—Emily Dickinson, Henry Roth, J. D. Salinger—but none of them ever ensured their privacy by committing murder. It's simply not a strong enough motivation. There's got to be something else going on here." This time I tapped my pencil on the phone's mouthpiece for emphasis.

I heard her sigh. "Professor, I know this is a real sad situation—pathetic, really, that poor old lady—but you can't let pity blind you to the—"

"Lieutenant Syverson, listen, I've had some experience investigating literary crimes. So, I want to ask you—what if we started looking into Deakin's literary past? See if maybe we can't uncover some long-buried motivation for this killing. Some reason someone other than she herself wanted to keep Mildred Deakin's identity secret?"

"We?" There was a long pause; I heard papers rustle. "Your friend? That Massachusetts investigator—what's his name? Piotrowski, that's it. He *said* you might start messing around in this. But, I don't know—"

"Lieutenant, ask yourself one question: Who else would want to keep Marty Katz from dragging Mildred Deakin back into the limelight? Who would benefit from Mildred Deakin's continued disappearance?"

"That's two questions. And her name is Milly Finch. *You* tell me. Who *would* benefit?"

"That's what we need to find out. Did she have heirs? Would someone profit from the recent boom in sales of *Oblivion Falls?*"

"Professor—"

"Or did she have enemies? After all, the book was a *roman à clef*—"

"A *rommana clay*—what's that?"

"A *roman à clef* is a novel whose story is a thinly disguised version of actual people and actual happenings—in this case, the death of Lorraine Lapierre, a young woman in Deakin's home town. What if someone is afraid that after all these years his involvement in that ancient scandal will become known? What if—?"

"Professor . . . I'm just not sure you should—"

"Or did she have a professional rival? Marty Katz must have been poking around, asking questions about her. Did he reignite long-extinct animosities?"

"Professor—"

"How much do you know about American literature, Lieutenant?"

She actually laughed. "Probably just as much as you know about criminal investigation, Ms. Pelletier. Now listen, in my own mind I'm a hundred percent that we got the right perp here. But Piotrowski did say you've got good instincts, and you've been real useful to him in the past. And I'm never averse . . . Is that the right word? *Averse?*"

I nodded—as if she could see me over the phone. How the hell did *I* know what word she wanted?

"I'm never *averse* to a little expert consultation—especially if it's free. What do you have in mind?"

I swiveled in my desk chair. The heavy autumnal rain continued, and two umbrellas passed directly outside my window. One was large and black, the other a frivolous yellow with a tweety-bird on it, staring directly at me. I wished I had either one of them; I was still damp from crossing Field Street earlier, and was going to get soaked again when I headed for the parking lot.

"I want to talk to anyone I can find who was associated with Deakin's life and career," I told Syverson. "The 1950s were a long time ago, but many of those people would still be alive. She must have had an agent, an editor, some family. Or, listen—maybe it's *not* a profit motive. Maybe there *is* some secret . . ." I paused to think about that; it was a curiously satisfying—even poetic— thought. "Some *deep, dark* secret." I could hear a muffled snort on the other end of the line and erupted, defensively, "Well, what *else* would have caused her to flee the way she did?"

"I dunno, Professor." The police officer was suddenly all seriousness.

"I could talk to the townspeople in Stallmouth, New Hampshire, where she grew up and to people she knew in Manhattan at the height of her fame. If there was any particular . . ." I tried to think of a synonym for *secret* but couldn't come up with anything satisfactory. ". . . ah, incident, someone should know. And later today I'm getting together with a Deakin scholar who lives somewhere over in your neck of the woods. I thought he might know the names of some people I could contact. Did you interview Sean Small, Lieutenant? He's a professor at Skidmore in Saratoga."

"You kidding? Why would we interview a scholar? I'm telling you, Professor, we have solid forensic evidence that puts Finch on the scene—her fingerprints on the gun, her footprints in the mud. And we have motivation." I sensed a creeping impatience, and wasn't surprised. This detective didn't know me from Adam, and so far she'd been quite forebearing. So far—but maybe not for much longer. "And besides, for your information, Professor, Saratoga is not in this 'neck of the woods.' It's way the hell north of here."

"Oh."

"Now, Professor, I don't know why you want to take this on. That's a hell of a lot of work you just laid out there. But, hey, no skin off my teeth. If you want to ask a few questions around among the literary types, that's harmless enough. Nothing else,

you might get a good scholarly article out of it." She seemed to
think this was funny, and in the background I could hear Rudy
Williams chortle. "And as long as you keep within the bounds of
the law, I won't . . . can't . . . do anything to stop you. Just, you
know, get in touch if something comes up—which it's not gonna,
you know; you're wasting your time here. Oh, and by the way,
your lieutenant—" She said the last words in a tone of amused in-
dulgence that irked me.

"He's not *my* lieutenant!"

"No? I coulda sworn . . . Well, whatever. Piotrowski says
you've been known to take an unnecessary risk or two, so . . .
now listen up, Professor Pelletier: no hotdogging. You hear me?
Just in case you're right—which you're not. I don't need another
homicide on my plate."

Sean Small was a plump young man. What was left of his red
hair was curly, pulled back at his nape in a ponytail. He wore
a yellow knit shirt with three faux-wood buttons at the neck, the
requisite academic khaki shorts, and complicated sandals that
strapped around his ankles. His voice burbled over his words like
a spring freshet over stones. He was so excited that Mildred
Deakin was still alive, he could hardly sit still in his chair.

I'd called the Deakin scholar immediately after I'd returned
home from visiting Milly Finch in jail, and we'd set up a Wednesday date for coffee at the Homestead Restaurant in Chatham. Re-
specting her desire for anonymity—and Syverson's injunction to
keep quiet about it—I hadn't told him then about Mildred
Deakin's reappearance. Today Small had shown up at the Homestead clutching a clipping of that morning's *Times* article, absolutely agog over the news. My account of the jail visit blew him
away.

"You *saw* her? You actually *talked* to her? What did she say?
How did she seem? What does she look like now?"

"She said nothing. She seems miserable. She looks like hell." I hated to burst his bubble, but there was no romanticizing the situation. "She's in jail, Professor Small, charged with homicide. How do you think she feels?"

He plowed on, oblivious to the very real and present—nonliterary—nature of the tragedy. "Call me Sean. 'Professor Small' always makes me think someone's talking to my mother. You, know, Karen, I've started collecting material for a Deakin biography. Now I'll be able to talk to her in person, get her own story in her own words."

I recalled what the novelist had called me: *Professor Jackal.* And I wasn't even *her* biographer. "Don't count on it, Sean."

He paid no attention to me, he was so deeply into the myth of the beautiful, lost, tragic writer. "A firsthand account of literary history! You know what this is like, Karen? It's just as if Charlotte Brontë had come back to life again. Or Virginia Woolf, or—"

"Sean . . ."

"—or Sylvia Plath. It's much more like Sylvia Plath, don't you think? Did Deakin know Plath? Hmm. I'll have to ask her." He scribbled on a yellow lined pad.

"Sean . . ."

He put down the pen, picked up his fork, and broke off a piece of flaky apple pie. "How did you get in to see her, anyhow? Did you just show up at the jail—"

I glanced around the restaurant cautiously. Not very many people out on this rainy Wednesday—a few pie-eaters and coffee-drinkers at the counter, and, in a booth by the window, the good-looking white-haired man who'd been flirting with the waitress during my last visit to the Homestead. I'd chosen Chatham as a meeting place because it was just about halfway between Saratoga and Enfield. But perhaps meeting here had not been such a good idea; it was, after all, Milly Finch's home turf.

"Sean, please keep your voice down. People around here know Milly Finch; Nelson Corners is practically next door."

"Re-e-e-ally." His head swiveled, as if he were looking for someone to interview about Mildred Deakin right then and there.

"Listen, Sean," I said. I'd told him on the phone that I was researching a book on sensational fifties literature. Well, maybe someday I would. Only it would be the *1850s*. "My study focuses on identity construction in novels that violate social codes of personal disclosure. My thesis is that the female subject position in fifties popular fiction transitions hegemonic domestic gender constructions intertextually, prefiguring feminist resistance narratives, particularly in the realm of female sexuality." I paused, hard put to come up with any further jargon. He nodded; it all made sense to him. "Now, what I thought you might be able to help me with . . . In your research have you uncovered anything that would explain Deakin's decision to vanish like that? Just walk out of her life the way she did?"

Sean's plump pink lips turned slowly upward in a smug pink smile. "We-e-e-ll, maybe I have. . . ."

"What?" I beckoned to the waitress for a refill on the coffee.

"Now that would be telling, wouldn't it." He gave me a sidelong look from his amber eyes: the scholar as irresistible tease. Then he rearranged his face in a more serious expression: the scholar as man of the world. He granted me a level look. "But, seriously, Karen, you can't really expect me to disclose to you a piece of extraordinary biographical information that will solve a forty-year-old literary mystery and make my biography the final word on this significant novelist?" He ran the tines of his fork over the remaining crumbs of pie crust.

This smug young man knew something, and I could sense that, against his professional best interests, he was bursting to tell. I sat back in my chair. "No, of course not. How foolish of me to ask." The waitress—it was Betty Anne again—arrived with the coffeepot. My companion was still scraping the empty pie plate. "Sean, can I get you another piece of pie? Maybe you'd like to try the lemon meringue?"

No sooner had Betty Anne brought the slab of pie than Sean leaned over the table toward me as close as he could get without smushing the airy white meringue. His voice was hushed, almost sacramental. "What the hell, Karen. With Deakin's reappearance, this isn't going to stay secret very long, anyhow. You might as well know. She had a baby, Karen. Just before she disappeared, Mildred Deakin gave birth to a baby boy out of wedlock, and then she gave him up for adoption."

Joe Rizzo was waiting at the granite ledge. Sara gasped when she saw him. She had been looking for a place where her stunned tears would draw no attention, and the granite ledge had long been her private sanctuary.

"Why are you afraid of me, Sara?" Joe asked, frowning. "I won't hurt you."

"Joe, I . . . I'm not afraid of you. It's just that I . . . I came here to be alone."

He took her hand and drew her down to a seat against the rock. "You always want to be alone, Sara. And you never talk to me. That's why I had to follow you, find out where you hide yourself. But you're always here with that . . . that little girl . . . that Cookie. Where is your little shadow today?"

Joe's voice was kind, and Sara, in the extremity of her pain, found herself telling him about the encounter with Cookie's mother.

"Her own like," Joe mimicked, scathingly. "You should of expected it, Sara. People like that only want one thing from people like us—the sweat of our bodies. You shouldn't have nothing to do with a girl like that milk-toast Cookie Wilson."

"But we're friends," Sara wailed. "We like to read the same books and talk about the same things and listen to the same music."

Joe placed a consoling arm around Sara's shoulders. "Do you like this?" he asked, and pressed his lips to hers.

After a long moment, she pushed him away. "No," she said, "I don't. And don't you ever try to do that again, Joe Rizzo."

12

Sometimes when I'm in the car on my way home from work," Sophia told me over the puffed vegetable chips at Mai Thai, "I just want to keep on going, just get on the Interstate and press that pedal to the floor and *go*. Get *out* of here. *Never* come back. Then I pull into our driveway and get out of the car and open the door and see my mother hunkered in front of her soaps, and I know she'd never make it without me. It wouldn't be a matter of . . . self-actualization . . . for her, it would be a question of whether or not she'd have food to put in her mouth—she's that helpless. When my father . . . took care of things, I had no idea what kind of shape she was really in. She could make lunches, do the laundry, clean. She had the . . . the semblance of normality. But now that he's . . . away . . ." She meant, in prison. "Forget it. As far as having anything to do with the outside world—she'd starve to death first."

I reached over and took her hand. "That's rough, Sophia."

"I feel so trapped." Her blue eyes were misty with incipient tears. "And I don't think I can stand another day in this town. It's just a big pity party. I'm *that poor, poor girl, that scholarship girl, that girl with the agoraphobic mother, that girl whose father . . .* well, you know. They're very nice to me at Bread & Roses, but, face it, it's basically a minimum wage job, and that's a trap. I earn just enough to maintain the status quo—pay the rent and buy groceries, and—oh yes—keep the television working. I fiddle with my poems on the weekend, but lately even that . . . And, I'm sick of muffins! I can do more for the world . . . *than* . . . *bake* . . . *muffins.*" With each of her final words she smacked the table hard with the flat of her hand. Then she looked down into her lap and whispered, "But that's all life seems to hold in store for me."

"Sweetie," I said, "it's not that bad." Amanda had hinted that things weren't going well for her friend, but I'd had no idea that Sophia was this deeply depressed. After her father's arrest, she'd attended classes part-time, and had finished her B.A. over a year ago. Since then she hadn't made any career moves. I'd been sur-prised at that. Even staying in Enfield to care for her mother, Sophia could have found a job with a better future than baking at Bread & Roses offered her. But every time I'd broached the sub-ject—how about teaching school? how about a job at the col-lege?—she'd shied away. Now I thought I understood why; she was desperate to get away from Enfield.

Just then the waitress brought our meals, shrimp for me and Pad Thai for Sophia. Whenever I took her out to eat, Sophia or-dered the cheapest thing on the menu. "That looks yummy," I said, and forked up a clump of her rice noodles. "Can I trade you some shrimp for an oodle of these?" Against her protest, I laid three jumbo shrimp on her plate. She burst out sobbing; evidently I'd just joined the pity party.

I waited out her tears, then asked, "Did I ever tell you about . . . about when Amanda was a baby?" I knew I hadn't; I didn't talk to anyone about that grim period of my life. But maybe it would help Sophia to hear the Great Karen Pelletier Saga. Maybe it would even help *me* to tell it. So, as we ate, I recounted the tale of my star-crossed youth—the high-school pregnancy, the re-nounced college scholarship, the abusive marriage. "And then, when I had to get Amanda out of that house, I asked my father if I could come home. He freaked out. Not only did he refuse to take us in, he forbade my mother and sisters to help us. Sophia, I had a high-school diploma, nothing else—no contacts, no references, no work experience. I made it on my own—with a little help from a few kind people and a few farsighted educational programs. Oh, yeah, sweetie, I was a scholarship girl like you—all the way through. I know how pity feels. But I also knew what kind of life I wanted for myself and my daughter: books, music, ideas—*choices*. I could have stayed there in North Adams, waitressing for the rest of my life and bemoaning my miserable lot, but I'd be *damned* if I was going to be *cheated like that.*" I slammed my fist on the table three times, then grinned shamefacedly at my companion: *The anger never really goes away, does it?* "And, now, I'm here at Enfield and Amanda's at Georgetown. We did it. So can you."

"Amanda is *so* lucky." She was looking at me reverently, as if I were the second coming of Mother Teresa.

"That's *not* the point, sweetie. The point is that you *can* get out of the box. *You,* Sophia Elisabeta Warzek, can get out of the box. Now we just have to figure out *how.*" I pushed my plate away, signaled to the waitress, then asked Sophia. "Tell me, in an ideal world, what would you want to do now?"

"Maybe grad school—an M.F.A. in poetry. Maybe a publishing job in Manhattan. But I can't, Karen—I can't leave my mother."

I hesitated before I ventured my next thought. "There are programs for people like her. Assisted-living types of arrangements."

She flinched.

"Think about it," I said gently, and turned to the waitress. "Coconut ice cream, please. Anything for you, Sophia? No? Make that *two* coconut ice creams."

After dinner, we hustled over to Smith's Bookshop for Jake Fenton's reading and book signing. The streets were slick with rain, and the bookstore lights spilled onto the sidewalk like luminous yellow paint. Sophia and I shared a large red umbrella, tipped against the wind-slanted rain. Blindly entering the narrow doorway, I collided with a tall, slender figure, snapped the umbrella shut, and smiled apologetically at a man with gold-rimmed glasses and a gray ponytail. "Sorry." I leaned the closed umbrella against the wall in the tiled entrance to drip with the others.

"My fault, entirely," he replied, bowing slightly, in the continental manner. With a gallant flourish of the arm, he stepped back and ushered Sophia and me through the door. We detoured around a double stack of *Oblivion Falls* paperbacks by the front counter and into the main section of the store.

The event was a sellout, drawing the full range of Jake's audience, from the intelligentsia to the rugged, out-doorsy, shit-in-the-woods crowd. Book signings usually feature bulk cookies and jug wine, but tonight Smith's Bookshop had gone all out. For this momentous event, Whit Meyers had laid out *meat:* roast beef, corned beef, and liverwurst sandwiches cut in bulky quarters, accompanied by thick, ridged, hand-cut potato chips, and a blood-red bordeaux. If cigars and brandy hadn't been so prohibitively expensive, we would have been puffing and sipping ourselves into a fine masculine fug.

The bookstore chairs, grouped in a small semicircle in front of the lectern, were already occupied when Sophia and I arrived, and people were beginning to jam the narrow aisles between the floor-to-ceiling bookshelves. Interspersed among the guys in the plaid flannel shirts, were a few students and a number of my colleagues: Miles Jewell, leonine as usual, with his tweeds and mop of shaggy white hair; Sally Chenille and Joe Gagliardi, the downtown twins, with their multiple tattoos and piercings; George Gilman in old khakis and a baggy brown sweater, gazing yearningly across the room to where Jill sat with Kenny; Greg, who'd managed to tear himself away from his babies for the evening. Ralph Brooke, in a black beret and navy-blue raincoat with epaulets, leaned against the counter, as far away as he could get from the main event and still see what was going on through his thick-lensed glasses. Even Avery Mitchell, our president, he of the elegant bones and smooth lines, slipped in at the last minute.

As Sophia and I found a nook, in the New Age and Spirituality section, that offered a partial view of the author, Harriet Person sidled up to me and muttered in my ear. "Karen, I'm distressed to see that you haven't taken my advice to stay away from Jake Fenton. You'd be much better off if you did." I gave her a straight look—*bitch!*—then turned my attention pointedly to the main event. She sidled away again.

Jake, clad tonight in the universal male book-signing costume, sweater and jeans in monochromatic black, was off in a corner, engaged in an intense, low-voiced discussion with the man I'd crashed into in the doorway. The newcomer was an intriguing guy; round, gold-rimmed glasses lent a scholarly air to a slender face featuring high cheekbones, a strong jaw, and a strong straight nose. And then there was that iron-gray ponytail.

The two men didn't quite *glare* at each other, but if the brute unflinchingness of their eye contact was any measure, they were not the best of pals. Even in such an ultracivilized setting as this college-town bookstore, there was something primal about this scene. A confrontation between two males in the heat of life, I mused—but then, I've always been a bit fanciful as far as a certain type of manly man is concerned. When Whit stepped up to the lectern to introduce the author, the conversation between the two men terminated with what looked like a muttered imprecation from Monsieur Ponytail. The latter stalked down the book-laden aisle, his facial muscles revealing a struggle to contain anger, brushed past me, and slammed out of the store just as Jake began to read.

And thus we walked in the woods' "—Jake wound up the selection from *Endurance*—" 'and it would not be wrong to say that thence forward the woods walked in us, its brute knowledge stalking through our veins with every spasm of our too-young-wounded hearts.' "

The applause was enthusiastic. In the question-and-answer period that followed the reading, Sally Chenille was the first to raise her hand. A nationally known, even notorious, theorist of literature and sexuality, Sally fancied herself a celebrity, even though her brief flurry of talk-show appearances had died down. She had chosen the slim black tunic she wore over ebony tights to enhance her media-friendly, skeletal frame. Her gaunt features were embellished as usual with an application of woundlike makeup. Leaning against a tall shelf, she gestured languidly with her plastic wine glass. "Mr. Fenton," she asked, "would you postulate that the semiotic field of masculine entextualization is inseminated with a fetishized phallic signification?"

"Excuse me?" Jake gripped the black metal lectern with both hands and leaned forward with an exaggerated attentiveness, as if anxious not to miss one iota of her meaning.

Sally ran a beringed hand over her bruise-colored brush cut. "Let me put it in layman's terms, Mr. Fenton. Since the mechanisms of masculine sexual desire exert themselves through assumedly preideological bodily drives, and given the common linguistic etiology of the words *pen* and *penis* from the Latin *penna,* or feather, does it not therefore stand to reason that penile engorgement and the act of taking up the pen to write derive from a common physiological impulse—"

Jake glanced around at his admirers with a *would-you-believe-this?* expression. "Lady," he queried, playing to the gallery, "are you asking me if I write with my balls?"

Sally, oblivious to nuances and titillated by this plain speaking, flashed a vermillion-lipsticked smile. "Well, I wouldn't put it quite so *bald*ly." She paused to grin at what she obviously considered a clever pun. "But, yes, in essence, that's what I'm asking."

Jake pulled his earlobe. "That's what I *thought* you were asking." He looked out over her head at the gathered audience. "Next question, please?"

Guffaws from the audience clued Sally in to the fact that she'd been had. Her self-satisfied expression evaporated; her face went blank. Until just this very moment, I would not have been able to imagine a situation in which I could feel sympathy for someone as obtuse as Sally Chenille.

"Questions?" Jake asked again. After his response to Sally, he had no immediate takers.

Then Miles, with as macho a swagger as possible for a man of sedentary lifestyle fast leaving seventy in his dust, rose from his chair. "Jake, my friend, your own work excepted, don't you find that the past two or three decades have seen the waning of *virility* in American literature . . . ?"

I couldn't bring myself to listen to Jake Fenton's reply.

W ell, if it isn't that pretty girl, Sara." Andrew Prentiss spoke to Sara from his top-down red MG, which was pulled up at the stoplight in the center of town.

Walking down Main Street on her way from having applied for an after-school job at Jacobs Pharmacy, Sara felt young and pretty and free. With the money she'd earned from working at the Wilson's party the week before, Sara had finally purchased the dungarees she'd been yearning for all summer. It gave her particular satisfaction to spend her earnings on the blue jeans, because she knew how much Mrs. Wilson disapproved of her own daughter's preference for such attire. And it gave her even more satisfaction to be dressed like all the other girls in town on this early September Saturday afternoon, the last before the beginning of Sara's senior year in high school.

"Hello, Professor Prentiss," Sara replied, flattered that the professor had remembered her.

"Where are you off to, pretty girl?"

"I'm just on my way home."

"Let me give you a—" Then he noticed Mrs. Wilson walking toward Sara on the sidewalk. She was pushing a wire shopping basket on wheels and a bunch of celery poked out from one of the brown paper bags in the cart.

He lowered his voice. "—a ride . . . sometime." The light turned green. "Good-bye, Sara." He took off with a squeal of tires.

Mrs. Wilson passed Sara by with a chilly nod, as if the girl had never spent all those long summer hours in her kitchen, sipping juice and nibbling the big molasses fruit bars Cookie's mother knew her daughter's best friend loved.

13

found the letter in my mailbox Friday afternoon, along with a memo from the College President about plans for a new state-of-the-information-arts library, a memo from the Academic Dean urging faculty to hold the line on grade inflation, a memo from the Security Office about parking regulations, a memo from the Department Chair about hiring plans. I'd scooped them all up and taken them to the coffee shop to read over a cup of hot tea.

It had just stopped raining, and a chill gray damp pervaded the air. My light denim jacket did nothing to keep me warm. I navigated the narrow paths that crossed the quad, carefully skirting the puddles.

When lit by autumn sunshine, the campus seems sparkling, magical, a place somehow outside of time and power and money and all the other imperatives that drive the modern world. In gloomy weather like this Enfield College looks more like a fortress or a nineteenth-century asylum, a blocky square of straight-edged buildings imprisoning a forlorn patch of green. We were a week and a half into the semester, and the lighthearted mood of the first days was beginning to dissipate. Students walked in earnest couples, rather than boisterous clumps, or else they walked alone. Two greeted me abstractedly. A clump of prospective students and their eager parents passed, guided by an earnest young man who walked backward as he intoned statistics on the percentage of Enfield graduates who entered law school.

In the coffee shop a tall, broad kid in an Enfield sweat suit munched on mid-afternoon pizza. Four girls hunched over class notes, preparing for a late-afternoon quiz. The scent of stale coffee permeated the air. I took my cup of English Breakfast tea to a table by the window and began sorting through the mail. The small cheap envelope with the pinched handwriting had no return address. I drew my breath in sharply; it was postmarked *Hudson, NY.* I ripped the envelope open, jostling my cup in the process. Milky tea sloshed across the table.

September 14

Dear Ms. Pelletier,
There is nothing to do in this place from sunrise to sunset except think, and I have been thinking about your biography of me.

"I am *not* writing your biography," I protested. Aloud, it would seem; a student at the next table, a light-skinned African American girl with short, bleached hair, glanced up from her notes. "Of course you're not," she agreed with a straight face. "I'm only nineteen years old; I haven't done anything worth writing about yet." I laughed and went back to my reading.

That my early life could provide the material for a dozen scurrilous books, I have no doubt. I understand what it is you want to know, but those things have nothing to do with who I am or how I have lived. They have nothing to do with my real life, the life on the farm, the depth and texture of it. No biographer can track the development of a soul in a state of quietude, and what could a woman's soul want more than quietude? To grow her food in peace, to harvest the wild berry in the field, to know the tart intensity on the tongue, the sweet stains on the fingers, the glory of each bright jar on the shelf, of each new-risen loaf of bread. All this is real—not simply words. Will you

*get any of it in your book? Will anyone read it if you do? The
warmth of the goat's flank on a winter morning? The hiss of the
steaming milk in the pail? The rest of it, the early days, the false-
ness, all those men, all that hollow laughter, all that gin, the
thick taste of it all in the mornings. The pain. That makes for
good reading, perhaps, but not good living. The past four
decades, while for me dense with life, will be of no interest to
the world. No beautiful people. No illicit sex. Just a woman living her days as most women live their days, in repetitious cycles
of quiet tasks. I justify my living—and my having lived—by doing something useful. Can you say the same for yourself? Leave
me alone.*

Mildred Finch

*P.S. That gun stood in the kitchen by the door for over thirty
years, and I moved it every time I cleaned. Of course it had my
fingerprints on it.*

I sat at the table, tea forgotten, stunned by the novelist's powerful plea. Or, perhaps I should no longer refer to Mildred Deakin
Finch as a *novelist*, but as a *farm woman*, or *goat farmer*: the identity she had chosen for herself. As a literary scholar, I'd made the
unthinking assumption that literature defines a writer's self: that
the fact of writing, of having written, takes primacy over all else.
Mildred Finch was telling me otherwise. *The warmth of the goat's
flank. The wild berry in the field:* For her, the life itself—the *lived*
life, without the words about it—had become everything.

"Got something interesting there?" I looked up. George
Gilman stood by my table with a mug of coffee. "Let me guess: A
former student wants a letter of recommendation, right? Or a university press wants you to read and evaluate a six-hundred-page
erudite manuscript for pennies a page? Or a government agency
wants you to review a grant proposal for free?" He grinned, but

his banter seemed forced, as if he had something more serious on his mind.

"None of the above, George." I smiled at him. He looked . . . nice. In a blue tweed jacket and neatly pressed gray flannels, he'd taken more care than usual with his appearance. "Can you sit for a minute? I have something I'd like to show you."

"Sure." He sat, carefully centering the creases in his pant legs over his knees.

"George, you're the one who put me on to the article about Mildred Deakin in yesterday's paper. Maybe you'd like to see this letter; it's from her."

"From Mildred Deakin?"

"Mildred Finch, really," I amended, recalling her insistence on that identity.

He read the letter quickly, then, without commenting, read it again. When he'd finished, he sat in silence for ten seconds. Then he frowned. "I didn't know you were writing a Deakin biography, Karen. Maybe you ought to rethink it." He said it soberly, as if there were more than one level of significance to the statement.

"I'm *not* writing her biography. That's just an idea she's gotten in her head. I'm still working on research for the Northbury book. At least, I am when I get any time for it," I said wryly. "But isn't this an amazing letter?" I picked up my cup and sipped tea.

"I like the way she thinks," George said, deliberately. "The focus on the sensory life, on . . . quietude. What a lovely word: *quietude*. A retreat from the noise of the world. She doesn't use the word *spiritual* here, but that's what she's talking about—the spiritual life. The immanence of spirit in the natural world."

I glanced over at him, surprised by these musings from a hard-headed academic careerist. Then I took in the blue-striped dress shirt, the snazzy tie with its whimsical pattern of children's drawings. "You look nice, George. Very spiffy. I haven't talked to you in a while. What are you up to these days?"

I wasn't certain whether I imagined it or not, but I thought his gaze became evasive. He shrugged. "Teaching, grading, thesis supervision, committee work, research. Same old same old. But right now, I've got to run. I've got an . . . an appointment." He rose from his chair, straightened his shoulders, adjusted his tie. "Seriously, Karen, Mildred . . . er . . . Finch wants the literary world to leave her alone, and it might be a good idea for you to back off."

By the time I'd finished reading Milly's letter for the third time, what remained of my tea was lukewarm. I rose to get a fresh cup. As I tipped boiling water from the stainless-steel urn, I heard a snatch of conversation behind me: ". . . all the evidence I need to make the case . . ." Then Jake Fenton's bass tones faded out. Casually, I turned with my refilled mug and scanned the room. Jake was sitting with Ralph Brooke in a partially sequestered nook. That I heard anything at all must have been a trick of the large room's acoustics, for the body language of the two—leaning sharply toward each other—suggested the intention of strict confidence. Ralph's back was to me. All I could see was the curly iron-gray fringe of his hair and the old-man hunch of his shoulders. Jake faced me, sporting a complicated smile, part gloating, part something not quite so healthy even as a gloat. When he glanced up and saw me watching him, all expression vanished instantly from his handsome features.

I tipped milk into my steaming tea and carried the cup back to the table. As I drank, I forgot about Jake, engrossed as I was in pondering Milly Finch's letter. Maybe there was something I could do, after all, to help the elderly novelist out.

Lieutenant Paula Syverson greeted me in her office at the Claverack barracks of the State Police wearing a russet suit with a knee-length skirt and mid-heel brown loafers. "Professor Pelletier, you're a long ways from home. What brings you the hell over here to New York State?" The police officer's ramrod straight posture imposed all the stiff formality of a dress uniform on her ordinary business attire. The only human touch was a pair of reading glasses pushed hastily to the top of her head, releasing one tendril of fine, pale hair onto her temple. In my navy cords, off-white jersey, and denim jacket, I felt at a decided sartorial disadvantage.

In spite of George's injunction against meddling in Milly Finch's business, I'd called the lieutenant as soon as I'd gotten back to my office from the coffee shop. Syverson had not been thrilled about my request to meet with her. Obviously she'd assumed that by now the professor would have tired of playing sleuth. But, polite as always, she told me she'd be in her office until six, and if I could get there by then, she'd see me. Otherwise it would have to wait until Monday morning.

The drive through the mountains would have been beautiful if I'd been able to pay attention—rising mist and an occasional fringe of crimson on the trees. I drove very fast, saw very little, and got to the police station at a quarter to six.

Now, settled in a molded plastic chair across from Lieutenant Syverson, who had barricaded herself behind her metal Corcraft desk, I considered the best way to approach her. Two framed portraits of little girls in blond pigtails graced the desktop. "Cute kids," I said. It surprised me that Syverson was a mother. I found it difficult to imagine this stiff woman in the throes of childbirth—or of any process that led to childbirth.

"Thanks," she replied—stiffly. And waited. A buckled briefcase on the floor by her chair spoke of her readiness to depart for the weekend.

"I won't take up much of your time, Lieutenant," I said. "I'm sure you want to get out of here as soon as possible. Since we spoke on Wednesday, I've learned two things, and I thought I should tell you about them in person."

She nodded, still waiting. She wasn't about to make this easy for me.

"Did you know that Mildred Deakin Finch had a child out of wedlock just before she fled Manhattan for Nelson Corners?"

A noncommittal *umm*. Her thin face couldn't have been any less expressive if it had been cast in plaster. "And what is your source for that information, Ms. Pelletier?"

"Sean Small—you know, the Skidmore professor I told you about. He located a previously unknown archive of Deakin papers at the library of some small woman's college Deakin had attended in New Hampshire. Evidently it was stuff someone had hastily bundled up from Deakin's desk after her disappearance and donated to the school without looking at it. Professor Small was the first scholar to request the papers, and in them he found both the birth certificate and the adoption papers. The adoption was arranged by some big Manhattan agency, and the papers don't list the adoptive parents' names.

"Now, Lieutenant, here's what I'm thinking. If Sean Small—who is not the swiftest of men, let me tell you—could stumble across those papers, Marty Katz—who was pretty *damn* swift—could easily have located them. That's another reason why I think we have to keep looking for a killer. Maybe Marty was murdered because someone didn't want this adoption revealed. Maybe the adopted child himself—"

"Or, maybe Mildred Finch, herself—" Syverson interjected. She rearranged the framed photographs so they sat at a precise ninety-degree angle to each other. Then she sat back, folded her hands, and gave me a level look. "Professor, I'll be straight with you—I did *not* know about this child until just now when you told me. But as far as I can see, that doesn't let Mrs. Finch off the hook at all. It simply gives her one more reason to panic and kill the reporter who threatened to expose her—and her sins—to the world. Nowadays an illegitimate . . . er . . . a child born out of wedlock would be no big deal, but forty years ago . . . ? And, if you ask me, this woman is living in the past."

"No, she's not," I protested, pulling Milly Finch's letter from my jacket pocket. "The past means nothing to her. Read this."

Syverson flashed me a long-suffering look, plucked the letter from my hand, retrieved her reading glasses from the crown of her head, and read. Then she shifted her glasses back to their perch on her hair, met my eyes—and waited.

"The gun," I said. "She moved the gun when she cleaned. *That's* how it got her fingerprints on it."

"So she's told us. Over and over again."

"Oh."

Syverson sighed and leaned toward me, her hands clasped. "Look, Professor, I know you mean well, but there's nothing here . . ." She waved the letter at me. ". . . that provides any new leads." She lifted a file folder from her desk, checked out a set of handwritten notes. "I tell you what: See these notes?" She turned them toward me. *"Agent. Editor. Family. Townspeople,"* she read. "I got them all down here from our last conversation. Now I'll add *child* to that list: *child—given up for adoption.* Okay? And how about *lover?* If there was a child, there was probably a lover. Right? That's how these things work." She entered *lover* on the list, then returned it to the folder. "Okay? Now, listen—I'm tired. It's been a long day. I want to go home and take a bubble bath, then have dinner with my husband and kids. And I don't want to think about Mrs. Mildred Finch again until Monday morning. What about you, Professor? Isn't there someplace you'd rather be than here?"

"Lover," I mused.

I hadn't thought about that.

ara sat at a table in the Stallmouth Public Library with a book of poems. The long summer afternoons she had always spent at Cookie's house reading, talking, and listening to music, now dragged heavily. She could not read at home, for her three brothers were constantly in and out of the house, yelling and arguing, and the radio blared with her mother's programs, so she had taken to spending her days at the library. Books were to her a home and family more real than the flesh and blood people to whom she had been born.

      Our birth is but a sleep and a forgetting: [*she read*]
      The Soul that rises with us, our life's Star,
        Hath elsewhere had its setting,
        And cometh from afar—

"It's that pretty girl again." Sara looked up from the poem just as Professor Prentiss perched on the chair across from her, looking as if he meant to stay just a moment.

"Hello," she whispered, casting a quick glance at Miss Patterson, the gray-haired librarian.

"Hello, beautiful," he whispered back, with a grin that did strange things to Sara's heart. Then he said, "Why, I do believe you're blushing. It's very becoming." He glanced down at her book. "And reading Wordsworth, too. My. My.

      'A violet by a mossy stone
        Half-hidden from the eye!
      —Fair as a star when only one
        Is shining in the sky.'

That's what you make me think of, Sara."

Sara was *blushing. She was embarrassed to feel how warm her face had become.*

"*I would love to have a chance to get to know you better, pretty girl,*" *Professor Prentiss said,* "*but we can't talk here—Miss Patterson, you know.*" *He pulled an old-maid face that caused Sara to giggle.* "*I have a few errands to run, then I'm going over to Lafayette Park—by the statue of the great man himself. Do you think you can join me there in, oh, say, forty minutes?*"

Sara's eyes widened. Almost without volition, she nodded. He rose, dipped his head at her formally, and stopped politely to chat with Miss Patterson before he left the library.

14

Autumn was more advanced in New Hampshire than in Massachusetts: along mountainous I 91, maples, oaks, and birches blazed scarlet and gold against a backdrop of giddy sunshine and sober evergreens. I pulled the Subaru up in front of the Stallmouth College campus, across from the elegant Stallmouth Inn. The austere college buildings, cut stone with granite pillars, stood back from the street behind a meticulously tended lawn. Students sat cross-legged on the grass or wandered across the main street of town, oblivious to traffic. A gray-haired runner laughingly dodged a young skateboarder. The runner looked familiar: wildly curly shoulder-length hair, broad shoulders, extremely fit physique, long muscular legs, all set off to perfection by a threadbare blue Princeton T and black cotton-knit running shorts. I've seen that guy somewhere, I thought briefly, but couldn't put a name to him. I frowned at him for a second, then turned my attention back to the purpose at hand.

I'd been to Stallmouth before, for an academic conference on Civil War writers, but this time I was in Mildred Deakin's town to take a walk on the town side of the town/gown divide. This was the side instinctively familiar to me, the working-class side of the tracks where Bernice and Lorraine Lapierre, Mildred Deakin's foster mother and sister, had lived. *Oblivion Falls* had been based on the scandal of Lorraine's pregnancy and death, or at least I assumed it had, but now it seemed that Mildred Deakin had been involved in an illicit sexual affair of her own. Her lover could have been from anywhere, I supposed, Stallmouth or Manhattan—or any nook or cranny in between. But small towns have longer memories than major metropolitan areas, and it would be useful to ask a few questions of the people who had known her back then. And in New England towns, working-class people tended to stay put. If the roots of Marty Katz's murder did go back as far as the birth of Mildred Deakin's child—or even to the death of Lorraine Lapierre—I might be able to dig them up here.

Sophia Warzek was with me. At dinner Thursday night, I'd told her Mildred Deakin's story—to distract her from her own woes. Sophia had been fascinated, and she knew the New England small-town turf even better than I did. Besides, I wanted the company. The downside of my semester's research leave was that I was spending far too much time alone—except, that is, when I was hanging out with suspected murderers and homicide cops.

Across from the wide campus common, on the sidewalk in front of the white brick Stallmouth Inn with its wide old-fashioned porches, a reggae band played Bob Marley tunes. The band was composed of one African American girl and four white wannabee–African American girls, all in scruffy dreds, multiple earrings, midriff-baring halters, and ragged pants. I looked over at Sophia. "How many of those Jamaican lassies do you suppose hail from Scarsdale?"

"All but the one from Beverley Hills." She crinkled her face up into a mock-sour expression, and I laughed. Getting away from Enfield seemed to be good for her.

"So, my dear Watson," I asked, "what do we do now?"

"Just cruise," she answered. "We'll know the neighborhood we want when we see it." I drove slowly up and down the residential streets until, after four or five blocks, dignified white Victorian and Greek Revival homes belonging to college administrators and tenured professors gave way to small frame houses, asphalt-shingled in tones of pale green and blue. These modest places with their fifteen-by-twenty lawns were most likely the homes of college custodians, groundskeepers, secretaries—and assistant professors. On a farther street, where the houses met the sidewalks without even the pretense of a yard (cafeteria workers), a neighborhood coffee shop caught my eye. GRACIE'S. I glanced at my companion again and raised my eyebrows questioningly. She nodded. I pulled over to the curb and parked. Perhaps the clientele of a coffee shop in Stallmouth, New Hampshire, would be more forthcoming than their peers in upstate New York. Besides, a two-and-a-half-hour drive on a crisp autumn Sunday morning had left us both with appetites.

The luncheonette smelled of bacon, onion, and potatoes. It was long and narrow, featuring on one side a counter with a dozen or so red vinyl-topped stools, and, on the other, six small tables covered in a red plastic that almost, but not quite, matched the stools. A stout elderly woman with sparse white hair tugged back tightly in a bun sat alone at the back table nursing a coffee and reading the Boston *Herald*. Other than her, we were the only customers. We sat at the counter, and I smiled at the waitress: just another happy tourist a little out of my element.

"Coffee?" She slapped menus in front of us.

"Sure."

She filled two brown mugs at a stainless-steel urn behind the counter and slid a hinged-top metal cream pitcher and a glass sugar shaker in our direction. It had been years since a restaurant had offered me sugar in any form other than a paper packet.

The waitress was small and wiry, the muscles in her thin arms ropy, her frizzy hair the monochromatic black that comes only with a color job done at home. "What can I get you?" she asked.

History, I thought. *Local history. The past and all its sorrows.* But I ordered a three-egg western omelet instead, and Sophia asked for a short stack with bacon. No chocolate croissants on this side of town.

"Are you Gracie?" I asked when the waitress delivered the omelet.

"Nah. I'm Anna Mae. Gracie's gone. Died in '83. Gallstones."
I had a feeling I wasn't the first customer to ask this question, or
the first to get the story that followed. "Gallbladder so full of
stones, it split like a rotten plum, Doc Samuels said. I was here
when it happened. She was frying burgers at the grill just like always, and then she squeals like a sow with her throat slit, goes
down like a ton of bricks, hits her head on the grill, and passes,
right there in front of where you two are sitting now." With the
pancake turner, she pointed to the worn brown tiles. Since Anna
Mae seemed to expect it, Sophia and I leaned over the counter and
respectfully noted the precise spot of Gracie's expiration. I nodded
gravely, not daring to glance at Sophia, and the waitress, perceiv-
ing that she had an enthralled audience, continued. "I dropped the
coffeepot right in Billy Doyle's lap—there at table three." The
pancake turner came into play again as she pointed to an empty
table. "Old Billy never darkened our door again. According to his
wife, he never could . . . well, you know . . ." The turner jerked itself into a forty-five degree angle with the pink Formica counter-
top.

"Tsk," I said. Sophia cleared her throat.

Anna Mae went on with her tale. "By the time I got to Gracie,
she was gone, poor thing. And her only forty-seven. That family
never had no luck."

"That's too bad," I commiserated.

"Nope—no luck at all. Gracie's old man got croaked in Ko-
rea, back when she was about eight months gone with Lolita. She
was just a kid—seventeen or so—but she never got hitched again.
Never saw the sense in it, she said. Lived with her sister and *her*
kid, and they were doing okay—had a sweet little place over by
the trailer park. Then Lorraine—the sister's kid, ya see—gets
knocked up." Anna Mae scratched her nose, then pushed frizzy
hair back from her forehead. "This is all before Roe vee Wade, ya
understand—the most important law ever passed in this country,
to *my* way of thinking—and Lorraine . . . well . . . checks out."

Something wasn't being said. "Then Bernice—that's the sister—can't stand it. A coupla years later she hangs herself in some professor's office at the college. You girls want some more coffee?"

"Uh-uh. We're fine."

Anna Mae went on. "Nobody ever knew why she did it that way, ya know? At the college, I mean. Why not kill herself at home where she could be comfortable? Ya know?"

"Tsk," I said again. This story was beginning to sound eerily familiar.

"Yeah. Like I said, them Lapierres never had no luck."

"Lapierre!" I exclaimed. "I thought so!"

"You *knew* them?" The little waitress stared at me as she replaced the pancake turner on its hook by the grill.

"Yes! I mean, *no.*" I glanced helplessly at my companion.

Sophia came to the rescue, crossing her arms on the pink Formica, and leaning forward in the universal posture of feminine confidences. Her softspoken tones caused the waitress to lean in toward her. "We don't really *know* them. It's just that . . . well, you know, that writer who wrote that book about this town . . . that bestseller? The book that was on Oprah's Book Club? Now what's that author's name?" She looked over at me, all youthful perplexity.

"You must mean Mildred Deakin," Anna Mae said.

Sophia snapped her fingers. "That's it—Mildred Deakin!"

The waitress shook her head disapprovingly, and so did Sophia. Without missing a beat, I followed. "Tsk. Tsk."

"It's just," Sophia continued, "that we were reading about Mildred Deakin—my mother and me." She gestured in my direction.

Her *mother!* I was scarcely old enough to be twenty-one-year-old Amanda's mother, let alone *hers.* Sophia must be at least twenty-four by now. I would have had to be pregnant at fifteen!

". . . And the book we read said Mildred Deakin had some connection with the Lapierre family."

"Some connection! I should say." The waitress exploded indignantly. "Bernice practically raised that kid—Milly. Then for her to go betray Lorraine like she did, baring her shame to the world before the girl was half-cold in her grave. . . . No wonder Bernice did away with herself. Couldn't stand the disgrace of it."

"Oh," I interjected, "you mean Bernice Lapierre didn't commit suicide until after *Oblivion Falls* was published?" Why didn't I have a notebook to write all this down?

"Well, yeah. Of course. It wasn't so bad when everyone thought Lorraine had just . . . well . . . but after that damn book come out, there was no way Bernice could hold her head up in this town." The waitress narrowed her eyes at us. "How come you girls are so interested?"

Sophia's eyes widened innocently in direct opposition to the narrowing of Anna Mae's. A blue-eyed, naive, small-town girl. "Well, it's just, like, well, you know, so *fascinating.* You know? Just like something in the *National Enquirer.*"

You're hanging around Amanda too much," I told Sophia when we had left Gracie's and were walking down the sidewalk toward the car. "She's teaching you some of her fresh tricks. *'It's just like, well, you know, the* National Enquirer,' " I mocked her.

Sophia laughed, the first real laugh I'd heard from her in weeks. "Amanda's good for me. I'd be much too well-behaved if it wasn't for her."

"Hey, girlies. Slow down." A voice from behind stopped us in our tracks.

The old woman from the luncheonette hobbled up behind us, the one who'd been reading the *Herald* at the back table, seemingly oblivious to our presence. "You two are real interested in the Lapierres, ain't you?" In the strong sunlight of the Stallmouth sidewalk, I could catch glimpses of bare pink scalp through the tightly pulled-back strands of her white hair.

"Well, yes," I faltered. "Because we read that novel—"

"*Oblivion Falls.* Yeah, I know. Everybody's talking about it again. Tell ya what, girlie. My feet hurt. That your car? I'll make you a deal. You give me a ride home, and I'll show you where Lolita lives."

"Lolita?"

"Yeah, Lolita, Gracie's daughter. The last of the Lapierres."

The minuscule front yard of Lolita Lapierre's double-wide mobile home was ablaze with old-fashioned blooms: climbing roses, black-eyed Susans, salvia, larkspur, bee balm, cone flowers. At the far side of the trailer, sunflowers dwarfed the silver-painted propane tank. We'd dropped off our white-haired guide at the first unit in the Edgemont Trailer Park, and had proceeded according to directions to "the place with all the flowers," pulling the car up in front of this neat, white, green-shuttered home.

"You two aren't Jehovah's Witnesses, are you?" The voice came through the half-open glass-door before we even set foot on the flagstone front walk.

"No, not at all," I replied as I took the six steps from the road to the front door with Sophia trailing behind me.

"Well, I'm not *buying* anything." Lolita had the still-scratchy voice of the one-time smoker. I couldn't see her behind the door; it was summertime-bright in the yard, darker inside the house.

"We're not selling anything, Ms. Lapierre. I'm Karen Pelletier, an English professor from Enfield College, and this is Sophia Warzek, my . . . assistant. We're here to talk to you about your aunt and cousin."

"My aunt and cousin? You mean—Bernice and Lorraine?" The heavy glass door opened abruptly, and the woman who stepped out surprised me. Blonde, petite, well-groomed, she looked like nothing either her name or her smoker's rasp had prepared me for. Or, I realized with a jolt, my preconceptions about "trailer trash." Lolita Lapierre radiated self-discipline: A woman in mid-life, she kept her compact body in shape. Her short hair had been cut and colored by a savvy stylist, and she was dressed in olive-drab shorts and a slate-gray sleeveless T that had most likely come straight from the racks of the Banana Republic I'd noted a half block down from the college. She assessed me with steady grape-green eyes. "An English professor, huh? Then this must be about *Oblivion Falls*. Come in."

We stepped into a small dining area furnished with a yellow fifties enamel-top kitchen table and four matching chairs. The mobile home's living room was likewise modest in scale, but furnished carefully with an eye to space, light, and color: a simple, straight-armed couch in a bright yellow, a red upholstered chair in a retro fifties print, a restored antique wide-slat oak rocker.

"This is *nice*," I said.

"Surprised?" Lolita's sharp reply was defensive.

"Makes my place look like a dump." I laughed. "You could put a sign on my living room wall: FURNISHED WITH COMPLIMENTS OF THE SALVATION ARMY." Not only was this true, but it seemed to be the right thing to say. Our hostess relaxed.

Sophia sat on the red chair, and I took the cushioned rocker. A striped orange cat jumped into my lap and settled down as if he intended to spend a year or two.

"That's Willie. He's a pest," Lolita said. "Chase him off if he bothers you. Can I get you some iced tea?" she asked. "Coke? Apple juice?"

Willie was purring. He gazed at me with amber eyes, then began washing a white paw. I was charmed. "It's fine. He can stay," I replied. "And iced tea would be nice." I set the chair to rocking, and patted the cat's soft head. That was nice, too; it had been a long time since I'd had a pet.

Lolita was all business when she came back with the tall glasses. "So, ladies," she asked, "how can I help you?" She sat on a blue vinyl swivel chair.

I had my story all ready; in a way, Milly Finch had given it to me. "I'm writing a biography of Mildred Deakin." I hated to lie to this woman, but didn't think an announcement that I was engaged in an unauthorized homicide investigation would be the swiftest way to get her talking. "I know your families were close in the . . . the old days, and I wondered if there was anything you could tell me about her or her childhood—any family stories you would be willing to share. . . ."

"Ha!" Lolita's laugh was like a bark. She stared at me incredulously. "You've got to be kidding. Our families were not *close*. My aunt *worked* for the Deakin family. Oh, there was *charity* of course, but nothing resembling intimacy. And, then, because of Milly Deakin's book my cousin's reputation was dragged through the mud and my aunt committed suicide. You really expect me to come up with warm, fuzzy family stories for public consumption?"

"Well, I . . ." I hadn't expected such a sharp reaction and found myself at a loss for words. Then Sophia spoke. She had been studying Lolita carefully, taking the measure of the woman.

"Karen, I think we ought to tell her—"

"Tell me *what?*" In the blue chair, Lolita swiveled to stare at her, then swiveled back to me. "I may live in a trailer park, *Professor* Pelletier . . ." She stressed the "Professor" sarcastically, making me cringe. If I'd had preconceptions about her, she also had them about me. ". . . but I'm no ignoramus. I read the papers. I know things have been happening—that *Oblivion Falls* has become a bestseller again, that Milly Deakin's just been found after all these years, that she's been charged with homicide." She turned to Sophia. "Is *that* what this is all about—that murder?" My companion nodded, then glanced at me with trepidation. I shrugged. Lolita swiveled back to me. "What are you really, Ms. Pelletier—if that's your name? Some kind of cop?"

"No, no," I said. I felt terrible; I'd screwed this up big time, insulting and alienating the one person who might most be able to help Milly Deakin Finch. "I'm who I say I am. It's just that—I'm not really here about a biography."

"Well, whadd'ya know—"

I raised a hand to forestall whatever well-deserved invective was coming. "Listen," I pleaded. "Just listen for a minute." I went on to tell Mildred Deakin's . . . what would she be? a foster niece? foster cousin? . . . about my visit to Milly Finch in jail. "She's old and defeated, Ms. Lapierre, snatched out of a farming life *I* don't understand at all but that *she* loves. I truly do not think she killed anyone. That's why I'm here. It's possible the roots of the reporter's murder lie in Milly's past life, maybe even here in Stallmouth."

Lolita was silent for a moment. When she spoke again it was with the musing tone of one who reassesses a past so distant that its recollected power surprised her. "My mother resented Milly Deakin for a long time, until . . ." Her carefully shaped eyebrows puckered. "But I never thought she was bad. Milly just didn't think about consequences. I remember her quite well, you know."

"Oh. Really?" I shouldn't have been surprised. What had Anna Mae said? That Lolita was born during the Korean War? That would put her in her late forties now, even though she looked younger. Of course she would have known Mildred Deakin.

"Yeah, I was just a little girl and she was like a fairy godmother to me. So pretty and sweet. Once she brought me a bride doll, once a yellow dress. It was dotted Swiss with eyelet, and I had patent leather Mary Janes. It was the only nice thing . . . And then there was—" She broke off abruptly, and her tone altered. "But that has nothing to do with anything. You come here under false pretenses, condescending to me, lying to me. And you expect—"

Reluctantly I plucked the orange cat from my lap and set him on the floor. "You're absolutely right," I said, rising from my chair. "I feel like such a shit. And I don't expect anything. Please accept my apologies, Ms. Lapierre. I'm sorry for having deceived you and offended you." I picked up my iced-tea glass from the end table. "Thank you for the tea. I'll just put this in the kitchen on my way out."

She took the half-finished iced tea from my hand and replaced it on the small table. "On your way out? Where do you think you're going? I have things to tell you."

She had brought him to the ledge to share her sanctuary with him. It was twilight, and the western sky above Oblivion Falls flamed with the hues of all the roses in the universe. Sara stood at the edge of the precipice, her arm extended to direct his gaze to the beauty before them. But his eyes were on her face. "It is the west," he said, with a slight half smile, "and Sara is the sun."

She wanted to say, don't be silly; I'm no Shakespearean heroine, I'm just a small town girl, but when she opened her mouth she found she couldn't speak.

He touched her cheek with a wondering finger, and then her open lips. She felt an unfamiliar thrill run through her body.

"Such beauty," he whispered, gazing down upon her. " 'for where is any author in the world/Teaches such beauty as a woman's eye?' " His own eyes were the stormy gray of rocks flagellated by the furious sea.

Sara felt as if she had been translated from some mundane earthly existence to a new and far more passionately magical life. "Kiss me," she pleaded, aghast at her own daring.

"Are you certain, pretty girl?" The smile had grown more wise, more tender.

"Oh, yes," she said. There was nothing at that moment that she wanted more than to feel his masterful lips upon her own.

As he kissed her, his long white hand slid from her waist and cupped her peachlike breast. She gasped and pulled away.

15

When Sophia and I left the mobile home community, we pulled up to the stop sign at the end of Edgemont Drive. I signaled to turn left and was waiting for a break in the traffic when someone knocked on the driver's-side window. "You girls goin' back to town?" the stout white-haired woman asked.

"Sure. Hop in." Cadging rides seemed to be this woman's primary mode of transport. I could picture her peering out her trailer's windows waiting, toadlike, for a car—any car—to pull up to the stop sign, then—*zap*.

Our hitchhiker settled herself on the backseat, elaborately straightening her wraparound denim skirt, then slammed the door shut. I waited for a lime-green Volkswagen bug to pass, then hung a quick left. Sophia and I had not spoken since we'd said good-bye to Lolita Lapierre; we were still living somewhere in her past.

"So, how's Her Highness?" our passenger asked, after a moment or two of silence.

"Her Highness?" It was almost five o'clock and traffic had picked up this Sunday evening, students heading back to campus after a weekend at home, tourists heading home after a weekend in the mountains.

"Yeah. Queen Lolita. How is she? You wuz in there long enough to find out."

Sophia and I exchanged puzzled looks, but my young friend left the talking to me. "Ms. Lapierre seems quite well." I settled the Subaru into the stream of traffic.

"She would. Always looking out for number one, that lady. What'd you girls talk to her about?" Curiosity vied with hostility in her tone.

"Oh . . . things." Small-town gossip could be useful, but I had no intention of sharing Lolita Lapierre's business with this harpy.

"You wuz talking about that Milly Deakin, I bet. Her that wrote that book that caused such a ruckus. Her that killed the newspaper fellow over in New York. You two don't fool me, you know, coming in here, talking so smooth." She suddenly fell silent.

Then she slapped her forehead with an open palm. I could hear the smack from the front seat. "Jeez. How stupid could I be? I bet you're reporters, too. Jeez Louise! I should get somethin' for putting you two on to Queen Lolita. How about it? I could sure use a twenty." In the rearview mirror, I could see the small eyes squinted in calculation. "And, who knows," she continued in a wheedling tone, "maybe I got more information the papers would like to know about, and maybe you got more twenties."

I resisted the impulse to stop the car and throw this woman out into traffic. "Sorry, lady, we're not reporters, and we don't have money to throw around. But I do appreciate you letting us know where Ms. Lapierre lives." I scooted around an old blue pickup and pulled up in front of Vinnie's Exxon in the center of town. "Now is this where you wanted to get out?"

Our passenger opened the back door and set her Reeboks on the asphalt, but she didn't get out of the car. "I'll bet Her Majesty didn't tell you nothin' about how her and that Gracie got so high and mighty all of a sudden? Them Lapierres never had two nickels to rub together, ya know. There was lots of talk around here, you bet, when Gracie Lapierre came up with the cash to buy that luncheonette. Why don'tcha ask Queen Lolita where that money come from, huh? See what she says." I revved the engine, and our passenger stepped hastily out of the Subaru with insufficient attention to the wraparound skirt. It billowed up around her, revealing a glimpse of flabby white thigh. She fussed the flapping

denim back into place. A hefty white-haired mechanic stood in the
open bay of the garage. Wiping a large wrench with a red cloth,
he turned to watch us, narrowing his eyes against the glare of the
late-afternoon sun.

"Good-bye," I said, and began accelerating before the car's
back door had quite closed. Then I felt a twinge of compassion. "I
hope you get home okay."

"Poor woman," Sophia said, as we pulled back onto Main
Street.

"Nasty, jealous bitch," I amended.

"That, too," Sophia agreed.

Lolita Lapierre had indeed told us where the money for the
restaurant came from. We'd talked for a long time about her
poverty-stricken childhood in Stallmouth, Sophia and I joining in
when Lolita's tale struck a particularly resonant note: shabbiness,
exclusion, shame. You'd think a person who's succeeded in making a good life for herself would get over the rough beginnings.
You'd think a mature, well-integrated personality would let go
of the run-down, outgrown shoes, the free school lunches, the
schoolyard catcalls. The low expectations of teachers. The never
having *anything*. You'd think . . .

Lolita had been six and a half years old when the letter came.
She remembered her mother puzzling over it, this official-looking,
thick, cream-colored envelope with the return address of a Manhattan law firm. Gracie had wiped her dishwater-wet hands on her
apron and sat down with the letter. Lolita, who'd just gotten home
from school, was drinking milk at the kitchen table across from
her mother. "More trouble, most likely," Gracie had said, and slit
the envelope with a table knife. "Whaaa?" she exclaimed at its
contents, and sat there blankly for "a gazillion years," as Lolita
recalled it, before she began to cry. Lolita remembered throwing
her arms around her mother and pleading to know what the

"trouble" was. "No trouble," Gracie had replied, tears turning into hiccups, "no trouble, Little Flower. Just some . . . unexpected news." But she'd kept the nature of that news to herself.

Very slowly, things got better for the Lapierre family. Gracie bought the luncheonette, and worked hard. Eventually they got a new mobile home. There was money for Lolita to attend the University of New Hampshire. The day of her daughter's graduation with a B.S. in business, Gracie sat her down at the same kitchen table and showed her the ancient letter and a bank-check stub. The New York lawyer had said only that an anonymous benefactor wanted them to have this twenty-five thousand dollars "to make their lives a little easier." The letter had come sometime after Mildred Deakin's disappearance in 1959, and Gracie had never had any doubt who her benefactor was.

After college, Lolita had come back to Stallmouth to live with her mother, and when Gracie died, she'd stayed on. Now she made "decent money," she said, in an administrative position in the Stallmouth College Bursar's Office. "People always ask me why I don't sell this trailer and get a house," she'd told us, "but I like it here. It was my mother's home, now it's mine. What would I want with a big house? I've got no husband, no kids. This way I'm free to travel—just pop the cat in a kennel for a month and take off. I love it. I've been all over—Italy, Greece, Australia, even China. And," she raised her eyebrows and smiled slyly at me, "I don't always travel alone—if you know what I mean." I'd nodded; I knew what she meant. "Plus, I've got money in the bank. That matters to me."

"Sounds like a great life," I'd said. Then I thought—*but she doesn't have Amanda.*

The September sun was low on the horizon as Sophia and I parked the Subaru in the Stallmouth College visitors' lot and crossed the campus to Stowe Hall where the English Department was housed. Call it morbid, but we were both so into the Lapierre story that—what the heck, we'd decided—since we were already in Stallmouth anyhow, we wanted to see the building where Bernice Lapierre had hung herself. *hanged!* As we approached Stowe Hall, late sunlight caught the tall windows, turning the glass opaque with gold.

"Do you really think we should go in there?" Sophia whispered, as we navigated around a touch football game on the lawn, and I pushed open the front door. "It's the weekend—and it's late."

As we'd come closer to the building, I'd begun to have qualms myself. Not only was this a morbid venture, it also felt a bit like trespassing. But, bulldozing ahead as usual, I brushed my misgivings away. "Department offices are always open," I said. "I work in mine at all hours of the day and night. And no one—"

"May I help you?" I started as the cultured male voice queried us from the recesses of the English Department office. An exotic figure stood outlined in the doorway of the darkened office, backlit by the light from an inner room, tall, slender, and wild-haired like some medieval wizard. Then he pressed the wall switch, and turned into the gray-haired jogger from earlier in the day.

"I . . . I . . ." Why couldn't I come up with a plausible reason for skulking in the Stallmouth College English Department at six P.M. on a Sunday afternoon?

Then Sophia spoke; she was beginning to show a real knack for getting me out of trouble. "Isn't this the dorm?" she asked, disingenuously. "My friend, ah, Gracie, said to meet her—"

"Sorry." The Merlin look-alike took off his gold-rimmed glasses and smiled at her in a manner that somehow managed quite inoffensively to acknowledge his appreciation of her fragile blonde beauty. How old was this guy anyhow? I wondered idly. The unruly head of gray hair threw me off. Was this theatrical-looking English-Department sorcerer in his forties? Sixty-five? Immortal? "The residence halls are on the back campus," he told us, pointing with the glasses. "Let me show you." He walked us out of the building and gave us meticulous directions. We thanked him and strolled in the direction of the dorms. When I turned around again to take a final look at Stowe Hall, the scene of Bernice Lapierre's suicide, the wild-haired wizard man had vanished. His image lingered in my mind. Where had I seen that man before?

On the trip home, a huge cinematic moon floated luminous and full behind snowdrift clouds. Sophia was silent, lost in thought. I was brooding over what I'd learned about Mildred Deakin and the Lapierre family. Lolita hadn't been able to tell me anything about the man in Mildred's life; she didn't even know who'd fathered her own cousin's baby. She'd been too young at the time to take notice of anything having to do with sex or romance. If Bernice and Gracie had known who Lorraine's lover was, they, like Lorraine, had taken the secret to their graves. Lolita had heard that there'd been a real hullabaloo in town at the time of the publication of *Oblivion Falls* about just who was who in the book. In particular, there'd always been a great deal of speculation about who the original was of the novel's Andrew Prentiss, the seductive young professor who despoils the fictional Sara Todd. And, since the novel's recent republication, that speculation had revived, to the discomfort of several distinguished professors emeriti. But, Lolita concluded, the scandal had happened so long ago, memories were hazy, people had died—and many professors had come and gone from the college over the decades. When it came right down to it, all she knew was the idle gossip of a few small-town layabouts, and she couldn't be bothered to repeat that.

Small-town layabouts: As I flipped the turn indicator for the Greenfield exit, I suddenly remembered the elderly ride-cadging woman. Someone like that—someone who was perhaps even a contemporary of Mildred and Lorraine—might prove to be a gold mine of information about the author's life. If you could believe a word she said, I thought, recalling the woman's nasty slurs against Lolita. But I'd keep her in mind if another visit to Stallmouth was warranted.

Oddly enough, I felt protective of Lolita. She was the Lapierre family member who'd had the least to do with the Deakin story, but she'd made a real impact on me—and for reasons that had nothing to do with Mildred Deakin. Here was a woman who'd come from a background similar to mine, and rather than cutting herself off from home and family, as I'd done, she'd settled into her hometown and made a success of her life. *But she'd had her mother on her side,* my prickly little superego argued. *Your mother was just as much a victim of your father as you were,* my wobbly little ego responded. *Yeah, but she should have been stronger and braver and more supportive,* shot back the prickly one. *Then she would have been another person entirely,* ventured the wobbly one. *Yeah. And that would have been a damn good thing.* Then I remembered the expression of regret and longing on my mother's face when she'd seen me last winter for the first time in fifteen years. A squishy feeling arose suddenly, somewhere in the region of my heart.

Sophia broke into my pained thoughts. "I really liked Lolita," she said.

"Yeah. Me, too." I pulled myself back to the present.

"And I *admire* her, on her own, like that, living her life. Not being ashamed of who she is or where she comes from. That's what really got to me. She's"—she gave me a sidelong look—"a lot like you."

"Oh, yeah?" There was that Mother Teresa look again. "Believe me, sweetie, I'm nothing like Lolita Lapierre; I got as far away from home as I could, as fast as possible, and I stayed."

"But Lowell isn't so far—"

"That's *not* what I meant."

Sophia glanced over at me, knowingly, her fine features bizarrely illuminated by the pink and orange lights from a

Dunkin' Donuts sign. "Well, anyhow, I'm really glad I came today. Now I have *two* good role models."

The visit to Lolita left me restless. I couldn't stop thinking about my mother. That night I called my sister's number. Connie didn't bother to hide her astonishment. "Karen. What do *you* want?"

"How *are* you, Connie?"

"Fine. What are you calling about?"

"I'm fine, too. Can I talk to Mom?"

"Karen? Honey? What's the matter? Why are you calling?"

"I just want to talk, Mom. How are things with you?"

16

The last thing in the world I expected to find in my Department mailbox on Monday afternoon was another letter from Mildred Deakin Finch. This time I recognized it immediately—the pinched handwriting and Hudson postmark. I snatched the letter up, took it into my office, and sat at the desk with the cheap envelope, still unopened, centered squarely in front of me. *Whaatheheck?* I hadn't responded to Milly's first letter because in it she'd ordered me to leave her alone. Now here she was, breaking her silence without even being asked to. I'd just slipped a long yellow pencil under the envelope's flap to rip it open, when Monica poked her head around my half-closed door.

"Karen," she announced in her stentorian tones, "you have a fax coming in. Eleven pages. From the New York State Police."

"The police?" I abandoned the letter and hastened into the main office before Monica could read the entire fax.

"The police?" Jake Fenton stood by the department information rack, leafing through the course offerings list. He grinned at me wickedly, gray eyes crinkling. "Karen, you naughty girl, what have you been up to?" Then he did the gun thing with his index finger, and I gave him a wan smile. How had I ever, I wondered, even for the most infinitesimal jot and tittle of time, found this womanizing narcissist attractive? My attention was drawn to his deep gray eyes, the square line of his jaw, the set of his broad shoulders. Well . . . maybe it was understandable.

"The police?" George Gilman's query was sober. "Is everything all right, Karen?" I nodded distractedly. I had no idea what George, a history professor, was doing in the English office, but was too preoccupied with my fax to ask. Brushing past Monica, I snatched up the three pages that had already printed out. A discreetly worded cover letter from Lieutenant Syverson asked me to look over *"the appended notes from the evidentiary records of a recent case"*—she was certain I would recognize their source—and *"communicate your findings to me as soon as feasible."* The faxed letter went on to say that the voice-mail message she'd left at my office number would tell me more. Page two of the fax consisted of a reproduction of a tall skinny page from a reporter's notebook, covered with cryptic journalistic shorthand. So did pages three, and four, and what had arrived so far of five. My God, I thought, these were Marty Katz's notes about his search for the missing Mildred Deakin! I rifled through the sheets and the words *Nelson Corners* jumped out at me from an otherwise illegible block of squiggles. I was so excited I could feel my heart thump. I was about to discover just exactly how the reporter had located Milly Finch. If I could decipher his shorthand, that is.

The Department's fax machine was transmitting very slowly, and, as I waited, tapping my foot impatiently, I fended off questions from George and Jake. Finally my curious colleagues left me alone in the office with the incoming fax, and I sat at Monica's desk, attempting to read the first pages of the dead reporter's notes. No sooner had I made out what looked like *stlmth,* no, *stllmth*—could it possibly be—*Stallmouth?*—than a sudden deathbed rattle from the machine let me know that all was not well in faxville. "Monica," I yelled, jumping up from the secretary's desk and speeding into the hall, but she was nowhere to be seen. Only Jake Fenton and George Gilman were visible—Jake entering his office next to the back stairs, and George exiting the Dickinson Hall main door carrying a massive book. Where the hell was Monica?

Back in the office, I hovered over the now-dead machine. PAPER

JAMMED, the electronic readout informed me. *Unh-huh,* I replied, and punched at the HELP button. Something chirped, and words rearranged themselves. Before I could decipher the new readout, Monica hustled into the office with a stack of photocopies.

"What are you doing?" she snapped. "I just spent the best part of an hour straightening that damn thing out, and now you go and screw it up again." She dropped her load on the desk, slammed out the fax paper cassette, then yanked a sheet from the innards of the machine and thrust it at me. "Now I'm gonna have to take this all apart again."

I glanced at the crinkled sheet in my hand: page eleven. "But this is only half-printed, Monica. Can you get the rest?—"

"Don't hold your breath, Karen. If you hadn't screwed around with—" Her mouth was pursed like a prissy schoolteacher.

"I didn't touch your damn machine, Monica!" Then I heard myself—shrilling like a spoiled duchess. But this nosy, bad-tempered secretary had that effect on me. I really should speak to Miles about her, I thought. The department needed someone more congenial than Monica Cassale. But right now, I'd have to work this out on my own. I took a deep breath. "Monica, I'm sorry I yelled like that. We must both be really stressed. Look, if the machine is giving you so much trouble, maybe you should call the service company. We do have a service contract, right?"

"Yeah." She seemed a little mollified. "But the technician they send is such a pain in the ass. He hates women. He's one of these guys who thinks that if it wasn't for affirmative action he'd be CEO of his company. And he can be real nasty." She twisted her lips, and it struck me how little power Monica had over her life. I happened to know that this low-paying, no-future job was just about all that kept her, her mother, and her young son, Joey, in food and shelter. Okay—so I wouldn't say anything to Miles. But *I needed the rest of my fax.* And I needed it *now!*

"Monica, listen. Why don't you call the service company and . . . and . . . let *me* talk to them."

"You? Talk to the service guys?" She squinted at me suspiciously. "Why?"

I shrugged. "Maybe I can help."

"Well, okay . . ." She started punching numbers with a stubby finger, then handed me the phone.

"Hello? Yes. Professor Karen A. Pelletier of the Enfield College English Department here." I swear I don't know how the British public-school accent crept into my voice. "It has come to our attention in this office that a representative of your company has been harassing our staff in violation of our institution-wide gender-equity policies. Now I imagine you have a fairly lucrative contract with the college, and that if I spoke to your president he would tell me he'd like to keep that contract. . . ."

Monica listened, bug-eyed, as I arranged for a different technician to be sent—and pronto.

"Thanks, Karen," she said, when I handed her back the phone. Then, reluctantly, "You're a pal."

I wouldn't, myself, have gone quite that far, but it's always nice to have the secretary on your side. "No problem, Monica. Now, about the rest of that fax?"

Nothing doing. The last half page of fax was digesting somewhere in the bowels of the constipated machine.

Then when I went back to my desk with the ten and a half faxed pages, the letter from Milly Finch was gone. I did a stunned double take. No letter. The yellow number-two pencil with which I'd been about to open the envelope was still lying slantwise across the desk pad, but—no letter. I looked everywhere: under the blotter, under the desk, in my briefcase, even under the edge of the green needlepoint rug. No. Letter.

Gone. Kaput. Dematerialized. Vanished.

. . .

Monica?" I could hear the anxious edge in my voice.

"What now?" She was at her desk, engrossed in something on the computer monitor far more momentous than any faculty inquiry. I peeked over her shoulder: a game of draw-three solitaire.

"A letter came for me this afternoon . . ."

"Yeah?" Monica clicked on the ten of spades, sending it flying home.

"And it disappeared off my desk before I could open it."

"Yeah?" She was on a roll now—jacks, queens, kings. Click. Click. Click.

"Have you seen it, by any chance? A small white envelope with a handwritten address—"

"You kidding? You have any idea how many letters come into this office every day? You think I have time to notice when you lose one? Ah!" She topped the queen of spades with the king, and the entire orderly rank of cards exploded.

Someone had taken Milly Finch's letter. That's what it came down to: I had not *lost* the letter; it had not been swallowed by any hostile machine; it had been *stolen*. But by whom? When I'd gone for the fax, I'd left my door open as usual. There's nothing worth stealing in my office. Except, it now seemed, letters from imprisoned novelists. I stood in the English Department hallway looking down at an impenetrable phalanx of paneled oak: All the office doors on the first floor were shut tight. Light spilled out from the transom above the door to Ralph Brooke's choice corner office. It was 3:35; other professors were either in the classroom or working at home. Jake, George, and Monica were the only people I remembered seeing after I'd left the letter alone on my desk, and each of them had been wandering around the building while I'd waited for that damned slow fax. I tapped at Jake's door. No response. Shoot. Like everyone else, he'd left for the afternoon. I clutched the thick fax to my chest, feeling that blank, uncomprehending emptiness that comes with losing something special, something serendipitous, something that, in the first place, you'd never expected to have.

Curled up in my green office armchair a half hour later, I struggled through Syverson's fax. Marty Katz's notes were basically incomprehensible: hooks, circles, squiggles, crosses. On the first page only *mdeakin* came across with any clarity. The second page offered *stllmth*, thereafter abbreviated as *stmth, lapierre,* abbreviated as *lp, edgemont tp,* something that looked like *tonicroft,* and an intriguing *prbrooke*. Brooke? As in Ralph Emerson Brooke, the POP Chair of Literary Studies? But before I had time to think that over, my attention was grabbed by an anomalous capitalized notation at the very bottom of the page: *LOLITA LAPIERRE!!!,* with a heavy arrow pointing back to *edgemont tp*. Huh! The reporter had found Mildred Deakin's foster sister . . . cousin . . . whatever. That didn't surprise me, of course. Marty must have visited Mildred Deakin's hometown—an obvious step on his part. What perplexed me was that Lolita hadn't mentioned seeing the reporter, and I didn't understand why not. Was she hiding something from me? If so, what was it? And would she tell me if I asked?

The crabbed shorthand of Marty's notes, the stale office air, and the unanswered questions had brought on a headache. I put the fax down and reread Syverson's cover letter. Then I went to my desk, picked up the phone and retrieved my voice mail messages. "*Professor,*" said the New York cop's wooden tones, "*since you are so interested in the Katz case, I'm faxing you Mr. Katz's notes. They were found in a notebook in the decedent's briefcase. We'd appreciate any input you might be able to give us.*"

Don't hold your breath, Lieutenant, I mused. *I'm no expert in ancient Sumerian encryption.*

I pushed open the casement windows. The cool air refreshed me, and I stood a moment, looking out at the activity on the common. A white panel truck was parked on the path by the front door of Dickinson Hall. Two overly thin women students leaned against it, smoking cigarettes and laughing at the sallies of a young man with straight blond hair parted in the middle and flopping down over his forehead. At the far end of the common, among a cluster of dark green oaks, a huge maple flaunted a single crimson-edged branch. I ran my hand over my forehead, then tucked a lock of hair behind my ear. *It's a beautiful day out there in the world, Karen. Such a day may never come again. Why are you sitting in this stuffy place, ruining your eyes over a dead man's scrawls?*

No sooner had I settled myself back in the vinyl chair with the fax, than there erupted from the Department office, a sound unlike anything I'd ever heard—the high, rusty screech of an out-of-control female voice. *Ohmigod!* I leaped up, dropped Syverson's fax on my desk, and raced across the hall to deal with whatever horrendous event had just occurred in the Enfield College English Department office. Hostage taker? Suicidal student? Mad gunman? As it turned out, there was no dire emergency. The screecher was Monica. She was talking to a dark chunky man in the striped shirt and navy pants of a service technician. She was laughing.

*I*n English class, Cookie slid into the seat next to Sara. "Sary," she whispered, "I'm sorry. My mother—" Then the bell rang and Miss Meserve began talking about Emily Dickinson. Sara took detailed notes.

After school Cookie waited for Sara outside the front door. "Listen, Sar, could you walk me home . . . well, partway home, anyhow?"

"I thought your parents didn't want—"

"They don't. I don't know what's gotten into them. The day after the party—the last time I saw you—they sent me to my grandmother's in Boston. I've been there ever since. Talk about boring! Grammy kept introducing me to 'nice, suitable girls' to be 'new friends.' But I don't want new friends. I want you." She squeezed her old pal's arm. "Oh, Sary, I missed you so much!"

"I missed you too, Cookie." But Sara couldn't keep the hurt out of her eyes. "What happened? What did I do? Why don't they like me anymore?"

"It must have been something at the party. The next morning my mother announced that she was taking me to Gram's, and that I shouldn't see you anymore. You were 'not a nice girl,' she said. She said she was afraid you were 'a little on the loose side,' whatever that's supposed to mean—that you would be a bad influence on me."

"Loose!" Sara gasped, and turned pale.

Cookie squeezed her arm. "Well, of course I know that's not true. You won't even let that cute Joe Rizzo anywhere near you. But, oh, Sary, I'm afraid we're not going to be able to see each other from now on!"

"I'm sorry, Cookie," Sara said, but she was walking and talking like an automaton. Loose, she was thinking, loose. A loose girl. A loose woman. She remembered the feelings Andrew Prentiss had aroused in her. Was it true? Was it inevitable? Was she destined to fall?

17

My office phone rang. Monica was on the line. I was in her good books now. Victor Perez, the new fax guy, was an absolute *doll*. And she didn't think he was married. At least, he wasn't wearing a ring. And, by the way, did I remember the last half page of that long fax? The page that hadn't finished printing out? That nice Victor had managed to retrieve it. Did I still want it?

Did I still want it? "Yes, please, Monica. Thank you."

I strolled across the hall to the Department office. Classes had let out, and things had picked up a bit in Dickinson Hall as students grabbed their last chance for the day to consult with professors. Mike Vitale, a sophomore now, gave me a jaunty little salute as I passed. I smiled at him; he was so adorable with his curly ponytail, little goatee, and general air of being too cool to live. I wondered who was fortunate enough to have Mike in class this semester, and almost wished I was teaching so it could be me. Stolen letters, unintelligible faxes, the pervasive sense of guilt over my inadvertent precipitation of the Katz murder and Millie Deakin Finch's arrest, all might be at least momentarily lightened by one of Mike's zany quips in the classroom.

I hated to admit it, even to myself, but this sabbatical thing had its down side. I felt isolated. I missed my students. I missed the teaching. I even missed the damn Department meetings—and I'd *gone* to one of them.

Closing my office door, I took the newly retrieved fax page to my desk. From the solid block of almost indecipherable notes at the bottom, one word instantly leapt out at me—a name: *Fenton*. Fenton? Yes, *thos & jnt fenton 13 elm kndhk ny*. Then a date *8/11/59*. Fenton?

Fenton?

How likely was it that Marty Katz would have uncovered a connection between Mildred Deakin and the only Fenton I personally knew—Jake Fenton? Not very likely, I decided, almost reluctantly. At least that would have given me some kind of solid lead to follow. Let's see what other info Marty had transcribed on this final page. *Scribble. Scribble. Scribble. Scribble.* Ah, here— just above the Fenton names—was something else legible—well, half-legible: *wldwd adptnag mnhttn*. I furrowed my brow as I stared at the cryptic abbreviations: *mnhttn* was easy—Manhattan. I scribbled it down on a yellow pad. For the first word—*wldwd*— worldwide seemed obvious, and I wrote it next to Manhattan; I was pretty damn good at this code-breaking thing.

Then my brain snagged hopelessly on *adptnag*. What could that possibly be? The name of some ancient Norse goddess, perhaps: Thor and Adptanaag? Not likely. Adopt a nag? Some kind of placement service for old horses? Hardly. I was focusing so hard, my eyes crossed. Then, suddenly, they uncrossed: adoption agency! That was it! Worldwide Adoption Agency, Manhattan! I grabbed the phone, dialed New York City Information. No Worldwide Adoption Agency listed, the Latina operator told me. *Oh.* I hung up. Wild goose chase. I stared at the faxed notes reproachfully. They stared back at me. Then *wldwd* reconfigured itself, and Wildwood sprang out at me. Worth a try. I pressed redial, and, unbelievably, got the same information operator. "How about Wildwood?" I asked, "Wildwood Adoption Agency?"

"Can't read your handwriting, no?" Then an electronic voice recited the phone number of Wildwood Family Adoption Services.

I wrote the number down, not quite certain why. I knew, of course, that all information about adoptions was, by law, strictly confidential. There was no way I could call Wildwood Family Adoption Services and ask them about *thos & jnt fenton* and the date August 11, 1959. I didn't even know if the agency had been in business that long ago.

And besides, how could I be certain that the two separate entries in Marty's notes had anything to do with each other? The *wldwd* agency note and the *fenton* note might simply have been juxtaposed by happenstance.

All the while, in spite of its wild improbability, a dark supposition was beginning to take root in my mind. Fenton. Fenton. Jake Fenton: forty-something year-old Jake Fenton, who could easily have been born—or adopted—in 1959.

No, Pelletier, I scolded myself. *That's simply too much of a stretch. You're letting your imagination roar down the track like a high-speed train.*

I called the Wildwood number. At least I could find out if the agency had been in business in 1959. In my most diffident telephone voice, I ventured, "Hello? This is Mary Smith? I'm a grad student in History at Columbia? Could you answer a question for me? I'm doing a paper on the history of adoption in New York, and I'm wondering . . . could you tell me, please, how long Wildwood has been in operation?"

The receptionist had been trained to answer in a reassuring and confident manner whatever anxious questions were thrown at her—and I'd bet she got a ton of them. "Wildwood is one of the oldest and most established of the city's adoption agencies. We've been helping happy families and children find each other for over eighty years. Now," her voice lowered solicitously, "is there anything I can do to help *you* . . . Mary?" This woman thought I was checking the place out for my own personal use!

"No, thank you," I said in my most demure graduate student manner and hung up.

You're twenty-one years too late, lady, to help me out.

Amanda's beautiful face flashed into my mind. Not that I would ever have thought about it. Not even for a millisecond.

On my way to the library to look up Jake Fenton's date of birth in *Contemporary Authors,* I ran into Ralph Brooke. Or perhaps it would be more accurate to say he ran into me. As I opened my office door, Ralph emerged from the Department office.

"Ah, Miss Pelletier . . . Karen? Am I right? It's going to take me a while to connect all these new names with all these new faces." Ralph gave a courtly little bow. "But in your case I don't think it will present a problem."

I smiled weakly. I wasn't in the mood for smarmy compliments. I wanted to get on with my sleuthing.

"Would you be free to take a cup of coffee with me?"

"Now?" Then I cringed at the inflection of dismay in my voice.

"Well, yes. *Seize the day,* you know." He seemed taken aback by my manner—and rightly so; I'd been rude.

I glanced at my watch, and shook my head. "Any other time . . . Ralph . . . but right now I have to go to the library."

"Ah, yes, class preparation. How clearly I remember my early days in the profession—scurry, scurry, scurry. But then, in my case, I was so very torn between the academy and the arts. Those late nights at the Village Vanguard with Jack and Neil—that's Kerouac and Cassady, of course." I nodded. He granted me a world-weary smile, but his gray eyes were shrewd behind the thick lenses. "Well, I mustn't keep you from your work."

Had the man's face ever been anything other than a polite mask, I wondered, as I scurried on over to the library. Thirty seconds later I'd forgotten about him.

Securing the heavy volume of *Contemporary Authors* that

contained Jake's bio, I took it to the nearest table. *Jacob Thomas Fenton,* I read, *(1959–   ).*

1959?

1959!

My dark supposition blossomed into a full-flowered theory: Marty Katz must have discovered that Jake Fenton was the out-of-wedlock child of Mildred Deakin given up for adoption in the summer of 1959! August 1959 would have been shortly after Deakin's disappearance from Manhattan, and not so many months before her mysterious autumn arrival in Nelson Corners.

All around me in the hushed Reference Room of the Enfield College Library, the business of dry academic fact-gathering was going on: the number of barrels of olive oil shipped from Roman ports to the savage British outposts in the year A.D. 79. The dates of the major battles of the Hundred Years War. The precise distinction between *metonymy* and *synecdoche* in figurative usage. All around me papers were being written for courses in Old English, History of Women in Ancient Greece, and Pre-Industrial Economics. All around me statistics were being gathered for scholarly monographs on the Peloponnesian Wars or colonialist appropriation of native resources in the late nineteenth-century Congo. And I—I had to uncover the heart-searing evidence of still-living, still-breathing, human tragedy.

Sitting at the long oak table with two unknown students, a red-haired guy in an Enfield T and an African American woman in a Muslim head covering, I wanted to tell someone about this . . . this *what?* Conjecture? Discovery? But *who? Whom* should I tell, I automatically corrected myself. Lieutenant Syverson? Most unsatisfactory. Like talking to a wooden bowling pin. Yes, I'd have to share my speculations with her, but Lieutenant Charlie Piotrowski? I thought, yearningly—that's who I really wanted to tell. He was so damn good to talk to. Smart. Articulate. Willing to listen to the far-fetched theories of a wild-eyed literary scholar. Willing to take risks.

But *no*. No. Piotrowski had nothing to do with this case. Marty Katz's death was a New York State homicide. And, maybe I'd wait before I said anything to Syverson. It wouldn't be fair to Jake Fenton to drag him into a murder case until I had ascertained with more than 100-percent certainty that he was indeed the adopted child of the *thos & jnt fenton* referred to in Marty's notes. Really, for all I knew, Jake might have been born to righteous missionary parents in, oh, say, Namibia, and brought up there among a dozen biological brothers and sisters. If I wanted confirmation that Jake was Mildred Deakin's love child, I would somehow have to get it from him.

If he even knew.

Monica?"

"What can I do for you, Karen?" The secretary flashed me a dazzling smile. I almost staggered back a step, her welcome was so effusive. It was, I thought, as if I'd delivered Victor Perez to Monica personally—in a gigantic pink birthday cake.

"Do you have Jake Fenton's address?" I pulled a little spiral notebook from the pocket of my khakis.

"You mean you don't know it by heart," she responded with a coy smile, gazing at me through slitted eyes.

Shit! That's right! Monica Cassale was the person spreading all those nasty rumors about me and Jake.

"Give me a break, Monica," I snarled.

She recoiled as if I'd slapped her. "Fine!" she snapped back. So much for any detente between us. She spun through her Rolodex, scrawled an address on an index card, ignoring my proffered pad, thrust the card at me, and swiveled back to her computer.

pulled into the wooded cul-de-sac where Jake lived. The neat white ranch-style house was half-hidden from the road by an overgrown lilac hedge. *Should I have called him first?* I wondered, as I shifted the gear lever into Park. But what would I have said on the phone? *Jake, if you don't mind, please divulge to me, a virtual stranger, the dark secrets of your parentage?* For that matter, what was I going to say to him in person?

It had been five o'clock—quitting time—when I swallowed the last bite of the Snickers bar I'd purchased from a machine in the Student Commons and pulled the Subaru onto Field Street in quest of Jake Fenton. As the sugar and chocolate hit my brain, reviving my sagging energies, it struck me that if Jake was indeed Mildred Deakin's son, that could have far wider ramifications than simply uncovering the poignant tragedy of a long ago mother-child separation. Wouldn't their relationship give Jake certain legal rights? Wouldn't it possibly make him an heir to the suddenly burgeoning royalties on his birth mother's runaway bestseller?

Two junior-high-school-age girls in matching magenta hair, corpse makeup, baggy black jeans, and lug boots, slouched into the zebra-striped crosswalk. I stopped and waved them across. The taller of the two automatically flashed me a polite, middle-class-girl thank-you smile.

I wished I could talk to Piotrowski about all this, I'd thought again, as I'd accelerated through the intersection. So many random possibilities were running through my solitary mind that I felt like a single sluggish rat in a maze. Two rats could at least go out for a beer and talk it over.

Late-afternoon sun slanted through the tall maples and oaks that isolated Jake's house from his neighbors and from the road. The shiny brown Range Rover was in the driveway, but Jake didn't answer my knock. I waited a good solid sixty-second minute and knocked again, five sharp raps. No response. Then I noticed a little white button secreted in the door frame. I pushed it, and a jarring three-note bell sounded so loudly that it startled even me. No answer.

Well—okay—so Jake didn't want to answer the door. Maybe he was writing. Maybe he was taking a hike. Maybe he was napping. Maybe he . . . had company. Maybe he was bombed out of his mind, on his own living-room sofa for a change. None of it was any of my business.

The tall multipaned French doors of Jake's living room were directly adjacent to the flagstone path that led back to my car. I could hardly avoid glancing in as I walked by. Jake Fenton was not lying bombed on the living-room sofa. He was sprawled on the living-room floor directly in front of the glass door, his handsome head centered in a spreading pool of blood.

I stopped in my tracks, frozen with horror. My first impulse was to throw the door open and rush to his aid. My second impulse, following so hard on the first it was practically simultaneous, was to get the hell out of there in case Jake's assailant was still hanging around. My third impulse, which I followed, was the most rational: Anyone who had *lost that much blood was beyond my help. Call the cops.* The Range Rover had a phone, I recalled. I threw open the driver's side door, jumped in, pressed the door lock, and frantically dialed 911. They'd get the cops and an ambulance here fast.

I jerked a glance in the direction of the French doors.

Not that an ambulance would matter to Jake. Not anymore.

Then, finished with the emergency dispatcher, I pulled a battered business card from my wallet and punched in Lieutenant Piotrowski's number. *This* homicide was definitely in his jurisdiction.

Then I huddled in the oversize chocolate-hued leather driver's seat of Jake Fenton's beautiful Range Rover and bawled.

I was crying for Jake Fenton; I was crying for the human condition; most of all I was crying for myself. Everywhere I went, it seemed, death and destruction followed me like an evil little goat.

His lips were hot upon her breast. He teased her nipple with his tongue. His hand caressed her ankle, slid slowly up her leg, slipped between her thighs. Sara gasped. "No, no," she whispered. "I can't. I shouldn't."

"It's all right, pretty girl. It's all right," he breathed. "You know you can trust me. I would never hurt you."

The sweetness of his kiss, the gentleness of him, his hard masculinity, it was all she had never known until this very moment that she had been wanting her entire life.

18

By the time Piotrowski's red Jeep pulled into Jake Fenton's driveway, I was seated in the backseat of a State Police car, dry-eyed and staring like a zombie at the mango-and-persimmon sunset that flamed the New England sky over the Berkshires to the west. I'd told my story twice, first, incoherently, to the flustered young town policeman who'd responded, within seconds it seemed, to my 911 call. Then, in more detail, to the first pair of state troopers who'd shown up in what now seemed like a major assault force of cop cars. In the thickening twilight, emergency lights flashed, searchlights glared, radios blared. A bat swooped down over the scene, then veered away, confused. I knew how it felt. I was confused, too, slammed into some phantasmagorical alternate universe composed of strangely hyper-real TV police-drama images.

Piotrowski stepped out of the Jeep and queried a passing trooper. The uniformed officer pointed toward me. Before I was completely out of the patrol car, the lieutenant was at my side, a solid presence in the lurid nightmare carnival of blinding blue lights and weirdly distorted radio-transmitted voices. I was expecting him to ream me out for being here in the first place. After all, he'd ordered me to *butt out* of the Katz homicide investigation. *But,* a little still-rational voice nagged, *how could he possibly know Jake had anything to do with Milly Finch? You just found out yourself a couple of hours ago.* And, anyhow, Piotrowski's expression wasn't angry. One look at the concern and compassion in his brown eyes, and I burst into tears again.

"Aww, now, Doctor," said this hardened homicide investigator, and patted my shoulder. I threw my arms around the cop's broad torso and hung on for dear life. He felt so solid, so strong, so—alive.

Then I deciphered the words the lieutenant was muttering in my ear. "I'm so *sorry*," he said. "I am so terribly sorry for your loss."

My loss? Reluctantly I loosened my death grip and pushed back far enough so I could see his plain, honest face. "My *loss?*" I queried, choking back the sobs.

"I know how much he must have meant to you." Piotrowski was gazing solicitously down at me. His big hands rested comfortingly on my shoulders, feeling as if they belonged there.

"Meant to me? Who?"

The policeman's broad brow furrowed. "The victim, of course. Er, Mr. Fenton."

"Jake? He meant nothing—" For some reason, I reached up and clasped one of Piotrowski's hands.

He shook his head slowly. "Poor thing. You're disoriented. Anyone would be . . . such a shock."

"Shock? Well, yes, it was a shock to find a colleague like that. But it's not as if I've never seen a dead person before."

"Tsk. Tsk. Doctor, you're clearly traumatized." His bright brown eyes reflected some complicated emotion. Pity? Sympathy? Concern? I couldn't tell.

Affection? Could it be *affection?*

"Trooper," he barked at a uniformed cop, one of three, I now noticed, who stood in a gawking semicircle, enjoying the spectacle of their superior officer being mauled by an hysterical woman. Suddenly embarrassed, I let go of Piotrowski's hand and pulled completely away. I was misreading a purely professional concern as something more personal. Even in the cool dampness of the autumn evening, I could feel heat rise into my face.

"Get this lady a cup of coffee. Black," the lieutenant demanded, and a tall, slim Asian trooper jumped to his command. I'd drunk a good deal of coffee with Piotrowski in the past, and was absurdly touched that he should remember how I took it—black, no sugar.

"And make it sweet," he added.

I gagged.

Then he took me by the arm, led me to his Jeep, and opened the door. "Look, Doc, I'm goin' in . . ." he gestured toward the house, "to take a gander at the scene, here. Then I want . . . need . . . to talk to you. I'll come back, get you out of here. Have you eaten?"

My stomach clenched. I felt my red face pale.

"Okay, well, maybe just toast or something." He patted my hand. "You sit here, pull yourself together. I'll be right back."

But he wasn't right back. Except for the glow diffused from the glaring police lights, the night sky was totally black by the time Piotrowski returned. I'd finished the sugary coffee, and it had helped. My tears had been replaced by numb detachment. I knew that all too soon I would begin feeling things again, and when I did, the memory of Jake Fenton lying sprawled on his living-room floor, blood gushing from his dark curls, would visit me with a case of the midnight horrors. Less important was the embarrassment I knew I was doomed to feel about the way I'd clutched the lieutenant when he'd offered me consolation, grabbing the man as if he were the last life preserver thrown from the *Titanic*. For now I welcomed the numbness.

When he returned to the car, Piotrowski was grim. Gone was the teddy bear of our earlier encounter. He took the wheel and backed cautiously past an ambulance and an emergency services truck without saying a word.

At a rear booth in the Blue Dolphin Diner he ordered for both of us—hot turkey sandwiches, Cokes, coffee. Then, with the waitress behind the long counter and out of the way, he sat back, gazed at me intently for a long ten seconds, pursed his lips assessingly, then sighed. "Doctor, you can't ever make a move without stepping right in it, can you?"

"Stepping in *what?*" Whatever I'd expected from him, this was not it.

Piotrowski retrieved from his jacket pocket a clear plastic evidence envelope and, unsmiling, slid it across the tabletop toward me. Inside the transparent envelope was another envelope, this one ordinary paper, letter-size, hand-addressed, stamped, postmarked. "You recognize this?" he asked, curtly.

"That's mine," I said, puzzled. It was the letter from Mildred Deakin Finch that had been stolen from my desk earlier in the day.

"I could tell that, Doctor: It has your name and address on it."

"But, but . . . where'd you find it?"

"In a wastebasket. In the victim's bedroom." He was studying me with cool cop eyes.

"Huh? How'd it get there?" Then I recalled that Jake had been hanging around the English Department office when I'd gone to retrieve Syverson's fax. When he'd left, the door to my office had been open, Milly Finch's letter unattended on my desk. . . .

"You don't know?" He smiled perfunctorily at the waitress as she set down a tray of Cokes and coffee mugs. "You didn't give it to him, maybe? Or leave it at his house?"

"Why would I?" I responded, slowly. "I hardly knew him. And I've never been in his house."

Piotrowski's forehead wrinkled again, a topographical relief map of puzzlement.

I was thinking hard, but I wasn't thinking about the envelope. I was focused on Charlie Piotrowski, putting two and two together, trying to read his eyes, his shoulders, his hands, trying to come up with some clue to this abrupt and unwelcome change of attitude. His earlier words echoed in my brain: *I know how much he must have meant to you.* I married those words to a memory: me standing with Piotrowski on the Dickinson Hall steps the first day of school, the day he'd called and told me Marty Katz was dead. In the memory, the attractive newcomer Jake Fenton emerged through the front door onto the broad landing, and I smiled at him and made a date to show him the town. Piotrowski must have put that incident together with my presence at Jake's house tonight and jumped to the conclusion that . . . *Oh, hell!* And now he'd found this letter in the dead man's bedroom wastebasket—a letter addressed to me! *Hell, damnation, and every single wailing circle of the eternally lost!*

"I did not have a relationship with that man," I blurted out.

Piotrowski's face froze for an instant—no longer—brown eyes still, lips immobile. Then he concentrated busily on stowing the evidence envelope in the pocket of his blue Red Sox jacket. "Is that right?" He looked up at me and repeated his question more deliberately. "Is. That. Right?" His tone had become one of detached professional assessment; I found it frighteningly unsettling.

"Yes. That's. Right," I snapped. "And I can't imagine where you ever got such a ludicrous idea in the first place." I ripped open a paper packet and dumped sugar into my coffee, stirred it vigorously, sipped it, then pushed the cup away.

"A *ludicrous* idea?" he replied, sliding his still untouched mug across the table toward me and taking my sweetened coffee. "Jake Fenton was a real good-looking man. Famous, too."

"Of course he was." I scalded my lips with the first sip of coffee.

"And I had a feeling he was attracted—"

"So? You think I put out for every nonrepulsive guy who . . ."

"Gives you the eye? No, I don't think that at all. Not at all." Then he said, oddly, "Believe me."

The sandwiches arrived, and I discovered that in spite of everything I had an appetite.

Piotrowski let me finish my meal without further interrogation. I knew he hated that word—*interrogation*—when it was applied to anything other than the proper context of an official, formal effort to extract crucial investigative information about a crime from a recalcitrant suspect or witness. Nonetheless, that's what it felt like: interrogation. Especially since the interrogator was so stupidly and blindly focused on extracting evidence about a love affair that had never existed.

When I'd sopped up the last of the gravy with the last of the soggy bread, I glanced up at Piotrowski and thought I surprised a fleeting warm expression in his brown eyes. No. Not *brown*, I mused. Chestnut, maybe. Or coffee. Or maybe a good rich chocolate. By the time I'd decided on a delicious toffee, any suggestion of warmth had vanished. He nudged his plate aside and said, "Tell me about the letter."

"The letter? Well, you must have read it. You tell me."

"There *was* no letter. Just the envelope. That's what took me so long in there. One of the officers snagged it outta the basket—which sorta puts you on the scene twice, I'm sorry to say. Then we did a search. No letter. So. Tell me about it."

He was a cop, first and foremost, and I was a witness.

I sighed. "You're not going to believe this . . . Lieutenant."

You have eleven messages," announced the robot voice on my home answering machine at 2:37 A.M. I pressed the OFF button, clicked the phone's ringer to MUTE, fell into bed in my wrinkled khakis, and slid into my exhaustion. I slept like the dead.

More than anything, Sara wanted to talk to Cookie about what was happening with Andrew, but outside of school she never saw her old friend anymore. And, besides, Andrew had insisted that their evenings at Oblivion Falls remain a secret, that their love was too precious to share with a crass and uncomprehending world.

One evening, late, when Sara was on her way back home from her lover's tryst, Joe Rizzo accosted her at the corner of Main and Winston, just outside the Marathon Ice Cream Parlor. It was after eleven P.M., all the stores were closed, and the street seemed empty. She shrieked when a hand grabbed her wrist and pulled her into the recessed doorway of the teen hangout.

"You little fool," Joe growled. "Do you have any idea what you're doing to yourself?"

Sara yanked her arm from Joe's grasp. "I don't know what you're talking about." Her wrist ached from his grip.

"Like hell you don't. I've been keeping an eye on you, Sara. Someone has to. Listen, Sara, you're a sweet kid. You deserve better than what that egghead jerk is doing to you."

"He loves me!" she protested.

"Like hell," he repeated. "You remember what I told you? People like that only want one thing from people like us—whatever they can get without paying for it. Listen to me, Sara, I care about you. Get yourself out of this before it's too late."

But she shoved him out of her way and ran the six blocks home, blinded by her tears.

19

The doorbell hadn't worked in months—it needed something complicated that I couldn't handle, something high-tech, like a new battery—and the pounding on my front door at 10:12 the next morning sent me bolting out of bed in a sudden cold sweat.

"I'm coming. I'm coming!" I yelled. I was dazed. I'd been dreaming about Tony. In the dream we'd been lying in the big bed in our Upper West Side Manhattan apartment, and he'd been chopping firewood: *thunk—thunk—thunk—thunk*. At least, I *think* he'd been chopping firewood; the details were vague, but I know I'd felt warm. Now the chairs and tables in my real house seemed far too solid and shiny after the dreamy furniture of the night.

I peered out the front door's glass panel. A severe-looking young woman with a scrubbed face, cropped brown hair, and a green wool jacket that bulged under the arm peered back at me. Sergeant Felicity Schultz, Piotrowski's partner. She'd probably been at the scene of Jake's death last night, but sequestered in the Jeep as I'd been, I hadn't seen her.

When she glimpsed my groggy face through the glass, Schultz seemed relieved. I opened the door and she greeted me, "You're not answering your phone these days?"

I shoved a lank clump of hair out of my face and rubbed my eyes. "You thought maybe I'd done a bunk?" I muttered.

"A *bunk*, Professor? A *bunk*? Now just what kind of edifying books you been reading?" She scanned me, head to toe, and grinned at my disheveled state—bare feet, matted hair, sleep-mussed shirt and khakis. Then she got serious. "No, we knew you were here, but, Ms. Pelletier, I gotta tell ya, when we have an individual that's so close to a homicide, and she doesn't pick up the phone, we—the lieutenant, that is—gets a bit antsy."

The lieutenant! That's who I'd been in bed with in the dream, the lieutenant, *not* Tony. And he hadn't been chopping wood. I hoped the hot blush wasn't spreading to my face.

"I turned the ringer off," I said, sharply. "I needed to sleep." I tucked my wrinkled cotton shirt in at the waist. Traces of the dream seemed to cling to my body. "What's up, Sergeant? You want some coffee?"

"Nah, I'm coffeed out." But she trailed me through the kitchen door, then wandered over to the plant stand by the window. She poked at a wilting ivy in a cracked yellow pot. "This needs water."

"So, water it, then." I measured out beans, dropped them in the grinder. Surprisingly, the sergeant did not react to my gibe. Neither did she water the plant. Moving to the counter, she lifted a chef's knife out of the block. "Nice knife," she commented, balancing it in her hand.

"Thanks." It was one of a set Tony had given me on our first Christmas. "You taking a forensic interest? I thought Jake Fenton was shot, not stabbed."

"Real funny, Professor." She slid the big knife back in its slot. "No, I'm just in the market." She pulled out the carving knife, tested it on her forefinger, winced.

I pressed a button, and the coffee grinder sprang into earsplitting action. "You're in the market for *cooking knives?*" I asked once the beans were ground. Somehow I couldn't envision Schultz functioning domestically.

"And other things," she replied and fluttered her left hand in the air. On her fourth finger, Felicity Schultz wore a gold ring with a tiny diamond, the size I always imagined when I heard the word *microchip.*

"Oh, my God, Sergeant! You're engaged!"

She blushed. I couldn't believe she was capable of a blush. I oohed and ahhed over the ring, asked all the expected questions. Schultz's pink face glowed.

Then, female bonding accomplished, she sat with me at the round oak table while I drank my coffee, and got down to business. "So, you want to know what's up, huh? Two things, Ms. Pelletier. The lieutenant wanted me to ask you if you ever noticed anything . . . unusual in Professor Fenton's office at the college?"

"He wasn't a professor," I replied automatically. "He was just a writer."

"*Just* a writer?" Schultz queried, breathing on her ring, then polishing it on her sleeve. "Is that inferior to a professor? I thought English professors *studied* writers?"

But they've got to be dead, was the response that sprang, unbidden, to my mind. Then *Ouch!* Jake *was* dead.

"Well, of course we do. I didn't mean that the way it sounded." It's creeping up on me, the intellectual ossification I'd sworn a blood oath to avoid when I became an academic. "And . . . I don't think I was ever in Jake's office. He'd only been on campus for two or three weeks. Why do you ask?"

"Because"—she drew it out for dramatic value—"because in the drawer of the desk in Mr. Fenton's office this morning we found a Colt thirty-eight Commando Special." She waited for my reaction.

"Wow!"

"That's exactly what I said—*Wow!* Tell me, Ms. Pelletier, is possession of handguns customary on a college campus?"

"A gun in a college teacher's desk drawer? No, I wouldn't say that was customary at all. It's not like he was teaching high school. . . ."

She nodded; that went without saying. "You ever have any reason to think that Professor . . . ah, Mr. . . . Fenton was *afraid* of someone?"

I thought about it. "Looks like he had good reason to be, doesn't it. But, knowing him, I wouldn't be surprised if it wasn't just part of the macho image, carrying a gun, I mean."

"He was like that, huh? All balls?"

"You ever read any of his books?"

She gave me a flat look, *You think I waste my time with that crap?* "Nope."

"He was like that."

"Oh." She slitted her eyes. "Well, he was a bit of a stud muffin—at least, from the picture on his books. And speaking of *knowing* him, how well *did* you?"

I groaned. Here was Piotrowski's misconception raising its ugly head again. "Not well at all, for your information, Sergeant." I dropped two slices of rye bread in the toaster and slammed the lever down. "No matter what Lieutenant Piotrowski thinks."

"Really?" she replied. Her eyes were slitted. "That surprises me. Word at Enfield College this A.M. is that you two were an item."

"Monica! That bitch!"

"Monica? She's your Department secretary, right? She wasn't around when I was on campus. Too early. I got that information from . . . someone else."

"Who?"

"Now, Ms. Pelletier, you know I can't—"

"God"—I dropped my head onto my folded arms—"it's all over campus!"

"So, there's some truth—"

"Goddamnit, no!" And I told her the story of my disastrous night on the town with Jake Fenton.

When Schultz and I walked into the anemic green conference room at the Western Massachusetts B.C.I. headquarters, Lieutenant Piotrowski met my eyes only briefly—

probably, I thought, because of the way I'd clung to him the night before. I gave him a hedged look—that damn dream wouldn't trot itself off to wherever it is inappropriate dreams go to die—and returned his curt nod. Was I never going to be able to meet this man again without wondering what it would be like to go to bed with him?

It was 2:34 in the afternoon, and five of us sat around the long table: the New York visitors, Lieutenant Paula Syverson and Sergeant Rudolpho Williams; the home team, Piotrowski and Schultz; and the football—me. Except for Schultz, who was virtuous with some no-name bottled water, we all sipped from plastic coffee cups.

Syverson was doing the talking. The soulless white fluorescent lighting rendered her thin lips the hue of peeled cucumber. "You seem to be the linchpin for this entire sequence of events," she said. "Can you tell us why?" Sergeant Williams and Sergeant Schultz each wrote a single word in his or her respective notebook. Probably *linchpin*.

Schultz's second directive from Piotrowski that morning had been to roust me out of my coma and get me down to the B.C.I. meeting. I'd showered, washed my hair, donned a teal-colored wool pantsuit in deference to my dignity. If I was going to be interrogated by cops, I wanted to look like someone they should think twice about before threatening with truncheons. Whatever truncheons were. On the way out of the living room, I pressed the button next to the telephone answering machine's blinking light. The readout window now noted fourteen messages. The first call was from George Gilman. I didn't get beyond his first shocked words—*"Karen, I just heard the most appalling thing about Jake Fenton. Are you all right?"*—when the sergeant barked, "No time for that, Ms. Pelletier, we gotta hit the road."

So here I sat, at the business end of a battered conference

table, sweaty in my too-hot wool suit, my too-thick hair damp and frizzy, my too-taxed brain reluctant to slip into gear. The table was inscribed with the historical record of the room—coffee stains, mug rings, ragged gouges, tight, nervous doodles. This table had seen so much horror that misery practically shrieked from its surface. Except for an elaborate penciled maze toward the foot, complete with princess and fire-breathing dragon, nothing resembling the transcendence of the human spirit was in evidence here.

Syverson's comment had sent me into a tailspin. She was right; I was a jinx. A linchpin and a jinx. I wanted to go home, and crawl into bed, and never get up again. The New York cop snagged me with her cold blue gaze. Or, maybe, crawl *under* the bed. I shivered.

"She didn't mean that the way it sounded, Doctor." They were the first words Piotrowski had spoken since the interview began. "Nobody thinks you actually caused any of this." He cast a reproachful look at the New York lieutenant.

Good cop; bad cop, I thought, cynically. But I knew Piotrowski was sincere, and his empathy unsettled me.

"Except me," I squelched the tears before they started. "I can't get out from under the guilt. If only I'd kept my mouth shut in the first place."

I'd already told the investigative team the entire story—everything I could conceive of as being relevant to either Marty Katz's or Jake Fenton's murder: my casual comment to the reporter about *Oblivion Falls;* my casual date with Jake and the way in which it had been misconstrued by all and sundry (I gave Piotrowski a level look); my not-so-casual trip to Nelson Corners, and what I'd learned about Mildred Deakin Finch's mysterious arrival there forty years ago; my visit to the novelist in jail; what Sean Small had told me about the birth of a child out of wedlock; the two letters from Milly Finch, only one of which I'd gotten to read; my call to the Wildwood Adoption agency; even my visit to

Stallmouth, and meeting the niece of Mildred Deakin Finch's girl-hood housekeeper. "And if that isn't a stretch," I'd concluded, "I don't know what is."

Now I repeated my *mea culpa:* "If only I could learn to keep my mouth shut."

"So," Syverson said, ignoring the self-pity, "in a nutshell, this is what we got. The article in the *Times* revives the popularity of this *Oblivion Falls* book. It starts selling like hotcakes. Marty Katz plays investigative journalist and tracks down the author, who we know as Milly Finch. She's pissed at being located. She shoots him—"

I protested. "We don't know that for sure! Doesn't this second killing throw her guilt into doubt? After all, she was in custody when it happened."

Piotrowski exchanged glances with Syverson. I wasn't the first to come up with that idea.

Syverson shrugged. "Katz *gets shot*. Okay? We finger Finch for the killing. Okay? She claims innocence. Then—outta the clear blue ozone—this Jake Fenton gets nailed. And now, according to your speculations about the significance of the reporter's notes, he turns out maybe to be Milly Finch's son—"

Piotrowski interrupted his colleague brusquely, sliding a Xeroxed sheet across the table at me. "What can you tell us about this?" I glanced at the paper: a page from a date book: *Tuesday, August 31, NYT——Katz.*

"What *is* it?"

"A page from Jake Fenton's appointment book."

"My God! You mean, *he'd* met Katz? They'd talked?"

"Seems so. Whaddaya make of it?"

"Nothing. I'm baffled."

"You think maybe Katz confronted Fenton with being Deakin's son?"

"Could be. Do we . . . do you . . . know that for sure? *Was* Jake the child Mildred Deakin gave up for adoption?"

Syverson snatched the photocopy from my hand and gave it a close perusal. It seemed this was the first she'd heard about this particular piece of evidence, and she didn't look happy. Interstate cooperation was not going quite as smoothly as the New York investigator would have liked. "We're following up on adoption records right now," she said, absently, staring at the Xerox. "That can take a while." She frowned over at Piotrowski, then abruptly turned back to me, resuming charge of the interview. "Okay, now, Professor, let me ask you this, in literary terms—right?—after all, that's why *you're* here—right?—for your *literary expertise. . . .*" She glowered at Piotrowski. "So, then, *literarily* speaking, what connections might you possibly posit between these two homicides?"

"Literary terms?" I mused. Then I sat straight up in my hard wooden chair. "Money! Jake Fenton was killed for money! Find out who gets the royalties from *Oblivion Falls* and you'll find the killer!"

Piotrowski leaned forward, his meaty hands clasped on the table in front of him. "Run that by me in a little more detail, Doctor."

"It's obvious. Anything published since about 1925 is still in copyright. And as Lieutenant Syverson says, *Oblivion Falls,* which appeared in 1957, is selling like hotcakes. The royalties must be enormous. Somebody is going to come into a great deal of money."

Syverson, erect and watchful, was leaving the interview to Piotrowski now. "But wouldn't that be Mildred Finch?" he asked. "After all, she's the author."

"Yes," I said, my hot theory colliding with cold reality. "Yes. But . . . well, what if she doesn't *want* the royalties. After all, she walked away from the novel in 1959. And she's leading a very simple life—by choice." I produced Milly Finch's initial letter, which I'd had the foresight to snatch from my desk at home as Schultz hustled me out the door. Evading Syverson's outstretched hand, I passed it over to Piotrowski. Perhaps I imagined it, but for the millisecond the envelope remained in both our hands, it was transformed into a conduit for some vital force—electrical? emotional? sexual? I released the thin paper instantly, as if it were radioactive. The lieutenant fussed with the envelope, clumsily extracting the folded letter. Sergeant Schultz, seated next to him, looked up from her notetaking and glanced from Piotrowski to me, then back to Piotrowski again. A glare from him caused Schultz to lower her eyes immediately.

Without comment the officers read Milly Finch's words. *There is nothing to do in this place from sunrise to sunset except to think.* . . . "Well, Professor," Syverson said when she'd finished, "this is all very . . . ah . . . touching . . . the bit about the goats is especially nice. But it's been my experience that nobody but a saint says *no* to a shitload of money. And there ain't no saints. If there's a monetary motive behind these killings—and if Milly Finch isn't the perpetrator—then she's the individual whose safety I'd be most concerned about."

That was a sobering thought.

On a yellow pad, Piotrowski was doodling a pattern of vines and flowers so elaborate he couldn't take his eyes off it. "Tell us more about this, Doctor. Who stands to benefit most from the success of this book?"

As an academic, I'd had only the most illusory brush with literary profits. "The author, of course, her heirs, if she's deceased—"

"—or if her whereabouts have been unknown for forty years," Piotrowski added, "and she's presumed dead."

"Well, of course. Then, let's see, um, her agent would receive a percentage and the publisher would profit. This is a reprint edition, of course; I don't know if the original publisher would have a claim to anything, but the reprint house would have." I watched Piotrowski add a trellis to his vines. "That's all I can think of. I don't know much about commercial publishing."

Syverson jumped in; she'd had enough of sitting on the bench. "Let's begin with the obvious. Who are Milly Finch's heirs?"

"Jake Fenton, possibly. Or do children not inherit if they're given up for adoption?" I glanced around the table. All four cops shrugged.

"Does she have other children?" I asked.

"Not that I know of," Syverson replied. "But there's her husband—"

"Her *husband!* Of course!" I was jolted by a flash of inspiration so palpable that it practically knocked me off my chair. "Listen, *this* is how it happened. Gotta be. Mildred Deakin left Manhattan soon after the birth of her child, the baby boy who became Jake Fenton. Fleeing from a disastrous love affair, racked with guilt and remorse, Deakin boards a northbound train and rides to the end of the line. Blind with grief, she stumbles off the train in a remote upstate New York village, struggles through an autumnal storm, collapses on a winding country road, is rescued by a handsome young farmer, marries him, renounces her fame, fortune, and superficial life in the city, and settles down to live happily ever after with her doting husband and a herd of dairy goats. Forty years later, a reporter sniffs her out, encounters the husband, reveals Millie's true identity and the existence of a previously unknown child. Threatened with the loss of his idyllic marriage, the husband shoots Marty Katz down in cold blood, then seeks out Millie's son and guns him down in order to protect his wife's spotless reputation. That's it! Don't you see? It all fits."

Piotrowski looked straight at me for the first time that afternoon. He grinned, his brown eyes warm. "I always enjoy it when you do that."

"Do what?" I frowned.

"Make up these wild stories from the flimsiest bits of evidence." He shook his head admiringly. *"Guns him down.* Whoa!"

Syverson watched this byplay with pursed lips and cold eyes. "Only one problem with that scenario, Professor."

"Yeah," Piotrowski agreed. "It's fiction."

The New York cop laughed. "Damn right. And if Jim Finch was so concerned about his wife's reputation, why'd he let Milly go to jail for a homicide he committed in order to protect her?"

"Oh." I really *should* learn to keep my mouth shut.

Syverson glanced over at Piotrowski and raised her eyebrows inquiringly. He stared at her, then nodded. She turned back to me, intertwined her thin, bloodless fingers, reversed her hands, stretched her long arms in front of her, rolled her head on her neck. Then she centered her folded hands on the table in front of her. "Ms. Pelletier, we been thinking—there may be something you could do to help us out, after all."

Cookie was combing her hair in the girls' bathroom when Sara entered with Joni Creed. Sara was sweaty and trembling, and Joni supported her with an arm around her shoulders. Sara ran into the stall and bent over the toilet, gagging. "Just let it all come up, Sara," Joni said. "It'll make you feel better."

Cookie could hear the thin spew of vomit as it hit the water. "Sara . . . Sary. Oh, what's the matter?"

Joni noticed her for the first time. "She got a little sick in gym class. That's all."

"But she should see the nurse. I'll go get her—"

"Oh, no you don't." Joni blocked the way to the door. She was a strong girl, stocky, with cropped bleached hair. She wore skirts so short they showed her knees, as much makeup as the school would let her get away with, and big gold hoops in her pierced ears. "Turn that water on," she commanded. She twisted the taps on two of the sinks, directing Cookie to the other three. "We don't want anyone to hear her out in the hall."

Cookie acquiesced, and the streams of water splashing in the sinks covered the sound of her friend's gagging. "But why not? Everyone gets sick sometimes."

Joni gave the younger girl a disgusted look. "You don't know anything, do you, kid?"

Cookie gaped at her. Slowly, she began to realize the true nature of Sara's affliction. She pushed past Joni and put an arm around her friend. "Oh, Sara, tell me it's not true . . ."

20

"Y ou're messing in my life again."

Milly Deakin Finch looked perceptibly older than when I'd visited her two weeks earlier, and even thinner. Lines radiated from the corners of her eyes and across the soft weathered skin above her cheekbones. In the glare from the fluorescent lights overhead, the vertical grooves between her eyebrows seemed etched by a satiric artist's engraving tool. The high, barred windows, the hefty blond prison guard slouched by the door of the visitor's reception room, both seemed absurd in the face of this sparrowlike woman in her oversize prison drabs.

"I . . . I . . ."

"Don't deny it, Miss Pelletier. Lolita Lapierre came to visit me." Milly's attempt to eradicate all emotion from the announcement lasted only until her voice quavered on the final syllables.

"Oh." I *had* been messing in her life, and I was here to do more messing. But I was surprised at Lolita's visit. She'd given no indication that she intended to get in touch with Milly. "Well, then you know I've been to Stallmouth."

"Yes!" She spat it at me.

"I'm only trying to help you, Mrs. Finch." In actuality I wasn't here on my own initiative, but at the request of Lieutenants Syverson and Piotrowski. And just as when I'd misled Lolita at her home, I felt terrible about misrepresenting myself to this woman.

But Milly wasn't interested in assuaging my feelings. "Last

time I saw Lolita, she was just a little girl," she mused. "But now . . ."

I waited for more, but when it wasn't forthcoming, I asked. "What did she want?"

A stone-wall stare.

"Ah, well, she seems to have done quite well for herself." I paused. "Thanks to you."

Milly's head shot up. Her dark eyes bored into mine. "I don't deserve any gratitude. For anything. Do you understand, Miss Pelletier? And, *you*, didn't I tell you I never wanted to see you again?"

"When I received two letters from you, Mrs. Finch," I responded drily, "I thought you might have changed your mind."

"Both letters stated explicitly that you were to leave me alone."

"Did they?" A single unprovoked demand for solitude might strike me as convincing; two sounded a bit more like an invitation to the dance.

"You read them, of course." She shot me an anxious little glance from the corner of her eye. She wanted me to have read them.

"Well . . ." I glanced back to where Lieutenant Syverson was waiting unseen, outside the door. "Actually, that's why I'm here. Your second letter went missing before I—"

"Went missing? What do you mean, *went missing?*" One small sallow hand fluttered to the other, squeezed, the fingers paled.

"Someone took it off my desk." I followed Syverson's instructions precisely: that I attempt to find out what was in the second letter without mentioning to Milly Finch anything about Jake Fenton, either his putative relationship to Milly, the probability that he had been interested enough in her to run the risk of stealing her letter, or his death. "And," I continued, "I thought I'd better talk to you, just in case you had something urgent you wanted to tell me."

"Urgent? I have nothing urgent in my life anymore except getting out of this place and back to my goats." The hands had a life of their own, like nervous, etiolated birds. "Jim takes good care of the goats, but he doesn't pay them the kind of attention I do. They're sensitive little creatures, you know," she asserted, challenging me to deny it.

"I'm sure they are," I acquiesced. *Sensitive? Goats?*

"And affectionate."

"Right."

"And they miss me." Her eyes seemed suddenly wider, refracted by contained tears. "They don't understand why I'm not there."

If I thought she would have tolerated it, I would have taken her hands, soothed them into . . . quietude. "How many do you have?" If she wanted to talk goats, we'd talk goats.

"Twenty doe—they're the dairy goats—and two bucks. Daisy and Petunia are both with kid, and . . ." The tears overflowed. ". . . I won't be there for the births."

"I'm sorry," I said, and meant it.

She blinked, and the tears vanished. "But you didn't come all the way from Enfield, Massachusetts, to talk about goats." She controlled her fluttering hands, pushed her glasses down on her nose, and peered at me over the rims. "I don't know why you *are* here, unless it's about that biography."

"I'm not writing a—"

"Because if it is, don't think you're going to pry any deep, dark secrets out of me."

"That's not it. Really. I'm merely curious about what you told me in the letter you wrote this week."

"I didn't reveal any deep, dark secrets, that's for sure." She was lying. I could tell by the way her anxious hands went perfectly still until she finished speaking.

"I understand. Now, Ms. Deakin—"

"Mrs. Finch!"

"I'm sorry. Mrs. Finch. I was extremely touched by your first letter, which I *did* read, and with great interest. What you said about the wild strawberries struck such a . . . a resonant note with me—*the sweet stains . . . the tart intensity . . . the glory of each bright jar on the shelf.*" I paused, searching for the right words to express my empathy. "To experience the physical world like that, genuinely through the senses, *gloriously,* unmediated by intellect or language, that's a pleasure most people are denied." The words sounded stuffy, exactly like something an English professor would come up with. *Unmediated by intellect. Jeez!* But how *do* you get the physical world into language?

"Humph." The glasses went back to the bridge of her nose.

I kept trying. "I know exactly what you mean about the glory." And I did. "One day last fall I was shopping at a green market in Northampton, when I turned a corner and . . . and I was stunned. There, right in front of me, was the most beautiful thing. . . ." I let the words trail off, feeling foolish.

"What was it?" Her tone was skeptical, but curious.

"Potatoes."

"Potatoes?"

"Potatoes. A whole heap of *glorious* potatoes—firm, brown, plump. It almost blew me away—the way they looked and smelled of the earth. The way they filled out their skins. The plentifulness of them. The . . . the *thingness* of them."

Her gaze traveled inward, it seemed, through a dimension compounded of memory without words, into the long-ago past when language had dominated her life. "*Thingness,*" she mused. "What James Joyce calls *quidditas.*" Her voice was hesitant, as if it were no longer accustomed to articulating abstract nouns.

"Yes!" I said, "*Quidditas!* Of course. From Latin." And we had moved already from talking about potatoes to talking about language.

I'd first read *Portrait of an Artist* in my freshman literature course at North Adams State. I was working nights at the truck stop and taking classes during the day. I'd come home after midnight from the late shift at the diner and picked up the novel, which was scheduled for the next morning. At six A.M., when four-year-old Amanda padded into my bedroom in her Dr. Denton's, I'd just closed the book, stunned by the awareness of having finally found my spiritual home—the capacious, welcoming world of the written word.

"I haven't read Joyce," Milly said softly, "in almost fifty years." She was silent then, toying with the gold band on her ring finger. Then, "I don't read much at all anymore."

"Mrs. Finch," I inquired, after a long minute's wait, "what did you tell me in your letter?" I sensed her conflict. There was something she wanted me to understand, but fear . . . or pride . . . or decades of reticence . . . kept her from communicating it to me in person. "I'd truly like to know."

She snapped back from wherever she had gone in her reverie. "Next time, take better care of your mail."

If I'd forged a momentary connection with this woman, I'd lost it now. But I didn't give up. "Could we talk about *Oblivion Falls,* Mrs. Finch? I've read it twice. I truly enjoyed it."

"Did you?" she said, in her dry, unpracticed voice. "That's why I'm in this mess, isn't it? Your enjoyment. I don't want you here anymore." She stood up. "Guard! This person is leaving now."

On my way back over local roads to the Massachusetts Turnpike, I stopped at the Homestead Restaurant in Chatham for supper, and was startled to walk into the busy restaurant and find Professor Sean Small there. The plump scholar, his balding head anchored by its long, reddish ponytail, was sitting in a window booth conversing intently with a burly, white-haired man, while an entire high-school football team crowded the tables around them. The minute I walked in the door, Sean recognized me and popped up from his seat. "Karen Pelletier," he exclaimed, "good God, what are you doing here?"

"Getting something to eat. How about you? You're pretty far from home, yourself."

At the sound of my name, Sean's companion had turned around, as if curious, and I recognized the man I'd seen during my first visit to the Homestead—the hunky white-haired man who'd been flirting with the young waitress. "Jim Finch," he said now, rising and studying me through slitted eyes. "So you're Karen Pelletier? Care to sit and have some supper with us?"

It was just after seven P.M., and the sun had already begun to set. From Milly Finch's goat yard, the view to the west was . . . well . . . glorious: a series of rippling hills and valleys, wooded inclines and smooth green dales. In the far distance loomed a hazy blue mountain range that Milly's husband informed me was the Catskills. As the red sun approached the horizon, dense layers of crimson and peach alternated with ridges of puffy gray cloud to cast a magical pink glow over the distant mountains—and over this storybook setting of red barns, green goat pens, and pristine white farmhouse. Jim Finch, the man I had earlier that day, in the presence of four police officers, denounced as the killer of two men in two states, showed Sean Small and me around the prosperous dairy farm where Milly had spent the last forty years.

Sean was in Columbia County for a tour of the Finch farm, he'd told me at the restaurant, background for the biography of Mildred Deakin Finch he was planning. I'd cast a glance at Jim Finch: Why, when Milly was adamant against anything to do with publicity, was her husband allowing a biographer to traipse all over his farm? I couldn't come up with an answer, but decided I might as well take advantage of his hospitality. As casually as possible, I asked if I could go along on the tour. Sean's lips formed an immediate *no*. "Sure," Jim Finch replied. It sounded like *shurr*. "The more the merrier." The *merriment* of a visit to this place that so recently had seen blood shed eluded me. But I thought if I could learn just one thing about Milly's reclusion—and the secret history behind it—perhaps I could help the police investigators identify the real killer, perhaps I could begin to right the wrong I'd done to her and help bring Milly Finch back home to her goats. Jim's blue Ford pickup traversed the hilly road I'd previously driven with the loquacious realtor. In a mini caravan, the Skidmore professor's red Ford Escort and my maroon Subaru followed him.

From the moment I set foot on the sunset-drenched farm, I was in love: in love with the sprawling white house, with the neat, well-maintained barns, with the black-and-white cows, with the goats, with the green rolling hills, with the idea of a simple life close to the land. Even—for a moment or two—with Milly's husband, Jim Finch, a solid, sixty-year-old man of medium height whose muscular body and tanned, weathered features spoke of heavy work done daily in direct proximity to the sun, wind, and rain. Bucolic bliss, agricultural ecstasy, uncomplicated harmony with the land and the elements: for a moment I bought the beautiful myth, even though I knew it was nothing more than that. As with any other romance, I knew the infatuation would wear off with direct exposure to its object, in this case, long hours, hard physical labor, financial uncertainty, mud, sweat, tears, and animal excrement. But following Jim around his farm and listening to him talk about Milly's dedication to the rural life, I found it all too easy to get carried away with the notion of myself as some sort of idealized milkmaid out of eighteenth-century pastoral poetry.

"We're mostly a dairy-cow operation," the farmer said. "Holsteins. But Milly has her goats. She sells the milk to a dairy-goat farm down county that supplies cheese to the city markets. *Artisanal* cheese, they call it," he said sarcastically, with the countryman's disdain for city pretensions. The farmer yanked off his Blue Goose Feed cap and rubbed his head. In spite of his sixty years, this man radiated physical strength and energy. Freed from the cap, his thick hair, bleached white by age and by exposure to the same sun that had darkened his skin, sprang up with a raw vitality of its own. "With only twenty goats, Milly don't bring in a heck of a lot of money, but it makes her happy." He shrugged. "As long as she's happy, it's okay with me."

Sean and I were trailing Jim through a small, exquisitely clean barn where brown-and-white goats with funny little beards and wattles were kneeling on straw, ready for their night's rest. The curious animals followed us with amber eyes. What did this unexpected human intrusion into their usual routine portend? An extra mouthful or two of hay?

"Can I touch one," I asked, enticed by the small, oddly deer-like creatures.

"Sure." *Shurr.*

I reached down tentatively and stroked a white head. The goat bumped against my hand: *More. More.* I scratched her under the chin, joggling her wattles. She nipped my fingers playfully.

By the time I caught up with the men, Jim was standing by the barn door with his hand on the light switch. Sean and I followed him back to our cars, parked next to each other in the ell formed by the driveways to the house and the barn.

"Has Milly been farming goats ever since she arrived in Nelson Corners?" I asked, as I reached for the Subaru's door handle.

"Pretty much. Course she was sick for a while when she first come here. Couple years." He shut his mouth on the words. He'd said too much.

"Sick?" Sean asked quickly, ever the biographer. "Physical ailment, or psychological?"

"She wuz sick. That's all." He thrust his broad, scarred hands deep into the pockets of his denim jacket. "We got her healthy again, me and my mother. She's been fine since then." The words were abrupt and defensive. He donned his cap again, stuffing the recalcitrant hair back into its confinement.

"Look," Jim continued, "I know Milly won't like it that I talked to you and let you see the place. She don't like people poking into her business. But I figure you two'll be writing about her, and folks around here have been saying some pretty nasty things, so I know what you been hearing. I want to set the record straight. Milly's not a . . . an easy lady to live with. Never has been. And I can't say as I been a saint. . . ."

I recalled my first sight of Jim Finch; he'd been flirting with the young waitress at the Homestead. No, not a saint.

". . . But she's a good woman, and I don't want her to go down in the books wrong. I thought if you could see what her life is like, you'd understand a little better." Then he frowned and added, as if to himself, "But, mebbe it was a mistake to bring you here. . . ."

It was full dusk now, with rose-madder cloud remnants. In the relentless hard-edged clarity of motion-sensor lights, the barnyard suddenly appeared less welcoming than it had in late sunlight—a domain of sinister, clinical light and abrupt, impenetrable darkness. My infatuation with the farm was vanishing with the sun. In spite of my wool suit, I shivered. I was glad not to be alone with Milly Finch's husband in this place of suspicious white illumination and sharply demarcated shadow, stupidly thankful for even the company of the pudgy, out-of-shape Sean Small.

There was more I wanted to ask Jim Finch, but Sean had taken the hint, and was making ready to leave, slipping his notebook into the pocket of his leather jacket, thanking the farmer for the tour. He got into the red Ford Escort and turned the key. The melancholy tones of R.E.M. engulfed us along with the roar of the motor.

"Mr. Finch," I asked, giving it one more shot as I opened the Subaru's driver's side door. "Did you know . . ." I hesitated, then plunged on, "did you know before the . . . the homicide, that Milly, er, Mrs. Finch, was a famous novelist?"

"I didn't know she was a writer of any sort, famous or not. She never said." He examined his close-clipped fingernails intently, then looked up at me. "Threw me for a loop to find out she's been keeping that from me all these years." He paused for a second or two, then muttered, "Of course, now it's starting to make sense why she never got rid of that old typewriter. . . ."

Still standing by the car, I eased the door shut. The interior light clicked off. My heartbeat accelerated. "What old typewriter?" I checked over my shoulder. Sean's Escort had already pulled out of the driveway, carrying the depressive music with it. I didn't know whether to jump in the Subaru and take off in pursuit of his dubious masculine protection, or to secretly hug this new piece of information to myself until I'd teased out its significance. If it *had* any significance. Wendy, the realtor, had mentioned a typewriter, but I didn't know until now about Milly's continued attachment to it.

Jim hesitated before he answered. "One a those portable jobs they used to have. In a blue case with a handle. She had it with her the night I found her."

"Really. A carrying case, huh?" Instantly I fantasized a stowed-away manuscript, the salacious sequel to *Oblivion Falls*. "Is there anything else in the case? Did you ever look to see?" Maybe Piotrowski was right; maybe I do suffer from hyperthyroidism of the imagination.

Jim Finch jerked his head up to look straight at me. "Of course not. Why would I? What else would be in there besides an old typewriter?"

"I was thinking . . . maybe some writing—"

He was quick. "You mean—another book, mebbe one like . . . *Oblivion Falls*?" He bit one side of his lower lip.

"Maybe." Sean's taillights had vanished in the distance. I took a quick, deep breath and glanced toward the farmhouse. "Could I take a look?"

Milly's husband hesitated again. The harsh barnyard lights revealed his total lack of expression. When he spoke, it was with an absence of the vitality that had infused his voice earlier in the evening. "I don't think Milly'd like that, Miss Pelletier. I don't think she'd like that at all."

Cookie knew her mother would never allow her to help Sara. Her father, however, was altogether a more worldly and compassionate person. He might know what to do. After school that day, she barged into Professor Wilson's office at the college without knocking on the closed door. "Daddy," she gasped, "there's something terribly wrong—" Then she noticed that she had interrupted a sober conference. Her father and three other full professors—the colleagues her father always referred to as the "senior men in the department"—sat at one side of the long mahogany table with that handsome young Professor Prentiss across from them. All five appeared strained—and shocked now by Cookie's intrusion. An aura of crisis, she sensed, hung heavy in the air. She could not help but think that they had been castigating the younger man.

A moment's awkward silence ensued as Cookie hovered in the doorway. Then she whispered, "Sorry, Daddy, I'll come back later, when you're not busy."

But something about the scene she had interrupted haunted Cookie for the rest of the day. She never did speak to her father about what she had on her mind, and he never asked.

21

The thing that was so different about dealing with modern literature, I mused, strolling down Columbus Avenue in New York City two mornings after my visits to Milly Finch and to her dairy farm, was that so many people were still alive. In my usual study of the mid-nineteenth century, I could be assured that all concerned were safely tucked away in their little beds of clay, as Emily Dickinson might have put it. Even though her "Life had stood—a Loaded Gun," Dickinson herself was securely stowed in a plot in Amherst, Massachusetts, beneath a good solid stone inscribed with the reassuring words "Called Back." She wasn't about to surface in some remote barnyard with a thirty-thirty Winchester and blow any newspaper reporters to kingdom come.

But Mildred Deakin was another story. Not only had she herself been resurrected live and in person, with lethal consequences, but other participants in her long-ago literary drama were beginning to surface. Evelyn Sackela, for instance—Milly's 1950s literary agent.

After my disappointing "interview" with Milly Deakin Finch in the Columbia County Jail, Lieutenant Syverson had decided to forgo any further investigative assistance. But Piotrowski had called me the next morning, all brusque and businesslike. The suits, he said, in his most formal manner, had recalled "how useful my specialist consultation had proven in previous cases" and wanted to offer me the usual deal to look into Milly's literary background. I'd sighed at the lieutenant's distant manner, but, since the "usual deal" was seven-hundred-and-fifty dollars a day for the kind of research I found fascinating enough to do for free, I jumped at it. I got right to work with the sources at hand, i.e., the materials mentioned in Sean Small's bibliography of Mildred Deakin.

In the Enfield College Library periodicals archives, I'd found a microfiched copy of a January 1958 *New Yorker* biographical profile of Mildred Deakin. The article summarized the details of the young writer's childhood in New Hampshire, her education at Eden College in New Hampshire, the publication of *Oblivion Falls* and its instant popular success, the rumors of a hot new sequel to that novel, and the author's presence as a *"glamorous star in the firmament of modern Manhattan nightlife."* Most helpful, however, had been the mention of Evelyn Sackela, named as *"the high-profile Manhattan literary agent"* who'd *"discovered the luscious Miss Deakin"* and propelled her to literary fame. I'd leapt up from the antique microfiche machine in the periodicals room and headed for the library reference room, where I'd scanned the shelves for the current volume of *Literary Market Place.* To my astonishment, an Evelyn Sackela Literary Agency was still listed on West 84th Street. *Gotta be her daughter,* I thought, as I dialed the number from my office phone, but the ancient voice had answered in person and was more than delighted to accommodate a visitor.

Passing a Starbucks on Columbus, I glanced at my watch. *Early.* Might as well get a coffee. I ordered a half-caf, short, skim latte and carried it past the revolving book rack with its brightly colored paperbacks to the counter by the window. Seated next to me, a graybeard in blue sweats was engrossed in a copy of *Oblivion Falls.* The latte was scalding hot, and I peered through its steam at the thronged sidewalk. As usual, the passersby were heterogeneous in every possible way: multi-ethnic, multi-generational, multi-sexual-oriented; multi-wealthed. Well-groomed, well-toned guys and gals in suits lugging laptops and talking on cell phones. Middle-aged artsy types in jeans and, on this brisk day, windbreakers or leather jackets. Students studded with gold in every conceivable body part.

A stout middle-aged Indian woman in a turquoise sari executed an undignified side step to avoid an African American bicycle messenger, who had veered cursing onto the sidewalk, cut off by a speeding white Mercedes with a blaring horn. An eleven-year-old baggy-pants white boy with a bleached Mohawk who should have been in school, swerved easily past on his state-of-the-art skateboard. An elderly street musician accompanied this little drama with a riff on his clarinet.

Street vendors with books. Street vendors with fruit. Street vendors with bagels and coffee. It was too early in the morning for the pretzel and hot-dog carts.

The Upper West Side of Manhattan was my old stomping grounds. For six years Amanda, Tony, and I had made our home there, and I knew its bustling neighborhoods well. After calling the literary agent yesterday afternoon, I'd left Enfield in the early evening and spent the night at 102nd and Broadway with Sandy Glazier, a friend from graduate school who was now teaching at CUNY. This particular Starbucks, at the intersection of Columbus and 86th, was way the hell out of my way in getting from Sandy's place to Evelyn Sackela's at 72nd and West End Avenue. But—so what? So Tony, my old boyfriend, lived only a half a block away? I'd had a good healthy walk—and I needed coffee. I glanced at the clock over the coffee bar. It said 9:34. If Tony still worked downtown, he might possibly be passing this corner right about . . . now.

A slim blonde walked by pushing a stroller. I wondered if that could be Tony's wife Jennifer, with their little Colin. I'd never met her, but Amanda had, and she'd described this interloper to me: *Blonde. Skinny. French braid. What else you need to know?* A million other people passed by, but I watched the blonde intently until she was out of sight. *Hmm,* I thought, if that *was* Jennifer, and if Tony was still home, he would be alone. It had been a long time since I'd talked to him.

I slipped a quarter and a dime in the coffee-house pay phone and dialed the familiar number.

"Gorman residence. Jennifer speaking."

The receiver settled back into its bracket with a clumsy clunk. Another slim blonde passed by pushing a stroller. Then another. Then another.

Get a life, Pelletier, I admonished myself. *Mooning around over a man you walked out on three and a half years ago, a solid family man with a wife and child, a man you haven't seen or heard from since that chintzy Christmas card last year, that sappy stable scene featuring a gold-metallic holy family and a donkey. Get. A. Life.* An evanescent image superimposed itself over the bustling crowd outside the plate glass: Charlie Piotrowski's broad face, his warm brown eyes and shapely lips.

Then another slim blonde with a stroller turned the corner of 86th. Maybe *that* was Jennifer.

Evelyn Sackela was a twig of a woman in a tree of an apartment on the top floor of a 1950s co-op. The tiny foyer was jammed with oversized potted plants—rubber trees, ficus trees, a long table crowded with gigantic cacti. Any contribution the resultant carbon-dioxide overload might have made to healthful respiration was offset by the cigarette dangling from Evelyn's carmined lips.

Evelyn was in her eighties, chic in black, parlor-tanned, and desiccated. If she told me she weighed as much as ninety pounds, I wouldn't have believed her any more than if she'd told me the bright hair teased and styled into a mid-sixties flip was its own natural blonde. "Professor Pelletier," she rasped, her voice not so much smoky as smoked. "How *intriguing* to hear from you. You've quite made my day."

She led me into a living room overlooking the Hudson through an extravagant set of windows that wrapped around a corner of the room. I sat on a forest-green velvet couch next to a side table featuring a free-form orange ceramic ashtray heaped high with cigarette butts. The smoky fug in the room slammed me back in memory to my childhood home where hazy carcinogens were as much a part of the atmosphere as the scent of onions frying with cheap meat. I coughed automatically.

"I don't get many visitors," the fragile-looking elderly woman said. "So I'm tickled pink that you've come." She'd gone all out. The glass-topped coffee table was set with a platter of bagels, plates of cream cheese and lox, a carafe of Mocha Macadamia Nut coffee, and a pitcher of mimosas. My hostess stubbed out her cigarette in a lime-green twin to the orange ashtray. "And with news about Milly Deakin! Fabulous! I'm dying to hear all about her. Tell me, how does she look?" She picked fastidiously at a half bagel topped with a schmear and a single slice of Nova.

Not, *how's her health?* Or, *where has she been all these years?* Or, *what's her emotional state in this moment of crisis?* But, *how does she look?*

I'd come to New York to find out everything I could about Mildred Deakin's life here in the 1950s. Increasingly I was convinced that she hadn't killed the reporter, and of course she'd had nothing to do with the murder of Jake Fenton. If the roots of these crimes did lie, as I suspected, in her early literary career, Milly's agent might unknowingly hold the one piece of information that would untangle everything. Love, lust, hatred, anger, ambition, greed—from everything I'd heard, the Manhattan literary scene of forty years ago had been a hotbed of homicidal motivations.

"Milly doesn't look very well," I temporized, spreading cream cheese thick on a pumpernickel bagel, then loading it with lox.

"Hmm." Evelyn's green eyes slitted in their thick mascara fringes. "And she used to be such a glamor puss."

I tried to accommodate the term *glamor puss* with the plain, weatherworn woman I'd met in the Hudson jail. The two images simply didn't compute.

I bit into the bagel. Heaven. "As I said on the phone, Ms. Sackela, I'm pursuing the possibility of writing a Deakin biography, and I'm delighted to locate someone who was actually acquainted with Mildred Deakin ... Milly Finch, as she's now known." I took another bite and chewed, considering the best approach to this conversation. Evelyn knew that Milly had been charged with homicide—she'd trilled and clucked over it on the phone—but I'd kept mum about my connection to the investigation. And I hadn't told either of my police minders that I'd located the agent or that I was coming here today. I'd decided that a long-time pub-biz player like Evelyn Sackela would be far more likely to open up to a literary biographer than to a cop. The intellectual mystique of the pure disinterested scholar would get me the best gossip, then Lieutenants Syverson and Piotrowski could send in their investigative cleaning ladies and vacuum up the crumbs. I began in my driest academic tones.

"Ms. Sackela, I'm convinced that in-depth research into Mildred Deakin's life will not only afford compelling life-narrative material, but will also provide the key to understanding the psychosocial and textual ambiguities of *Oblivion Falls.*" It's not easy to form polysyllabic words between mouthfuls of cream cheese and smoked salmon. "In particular, I wish to deconstruct the sociobiographical circumstances that caused its author to vanish so precipitously." I'd misused the term *deconstruct,* but the word was a surefire way to impress a layman, and very few outside the academy understood what it meant. "And who would be in a better position than you, her literary agent, to know just exactly what was going on in her life at the moment of her disappearance?" I felt so smarmy misleading this elderly woman that I wanted to excuse myself and go take a shower.

"Well, Karen—it *is* okay, isn't it, if I call you Karen? You seem such a girl to me it's difficult to think of you as *Professor.*" She wriggled in her chair, as if she were settling in for a good long titillating gossip.

"A *girl?*" I almost choked on the last bite of bagel. "Ms. Sackela, I'm almost forty."

"It's Evelyn. And forty's a *baby.*" She selected a cigarette from a leaded glass box on the coffee table, leaned back, and lit up. The first drag was so long and languorous, I half expected the agent to morph into Lauren Bacall right before my eyes.

"If you say so." It felt good to be thought of as a girl again, even if by an octogenarian, even if only for an hour.

"Karen, *nobody* ever knew 'just what was going on' with Milly Deakin." The avid glint in Evelyn Sackela's eyes let me know that encouraging her to talk about her former client wasn't going to be a problem. "Milly kept herself very much to herself. She was strange that way."

"But you must have some idea why she left Manhattan so suddenly in November of 1959?"

"November? It wasn't November. She took off sometime in the summer—early. I remember calling her several times about a Fourth-of-July get-together at Lillian's on the Vineyard, but she never answered her phone. And I hadn't seen her for months before that. She'd been getting odder and odder." She shook her head; not a hair shivered in the platinum flip. Something told me the elaborate hairdo was special for my visit. "She broke lunch dates, just left me sitting there at 'Twenty-one'—twice! Got extremely evasive about the new book. Said it was going to be steamier than the first one. Maybe so, but I never saw a word. She kept making excuses for not showing it to me, then started calling at odd hours, soused and crying. Then she just vanished. Poof!" She waved her cigarette between two withered ringless fingers.

"And you don't have any idea—?"

"Not an inkling." Evelyn took another drag. Smoke curled from pursed lips. "Could have been anything. She was living that crazy boozy life we all lived back then. God knows how anyone survived it. And the *men!* We all slept around, of course, but Milly was like a bitch in heat. Couldn't get enough. Then there was the dope—"

"Milly was on drugs?" My eyes popped wide open.

"Who wasn't?" She shrugged. "The stuff was all over the place—pot, horse, coke. . . ." She shook her head again. "The good old days," she said wryly. "It's a wonder I'm still alive."

I'd been thinking the very same thing.

Evelyn laughed abruptly. "Karen, you're gaping at me like I'm some sort of debauched fossil that's just unexpectedly hiccuped back into life!"

I closed my mouth. "Sorry, Evelyn. I'm afraid I'm a product of a much more prudent generation."

"And with good reason, I'd say. At least *we* didn't have AIDS to worry about."

"Speaking of sex—"

"Were we?" she asked coyly.

"You mentioned AIDS," I responded dryly. "I made the leap. So . . . speaking of sex, was there any one man in particular in Milly's life?"

"Aside from my husband, you mean?" She slammed the cigarette into the ashtray, viciously, as if she wanted to kill it.

"Oh." I was getting in over my head here. "I'm sorry to hear that."

"Fred Sackela—may he rot in hell—had an eye for a pretty girl, and Milly was that. But unfortunately she didn't take him with her when she did her bunk. Fred hung around for another decade before he absconded with some twenty-year-old flower child for a summer of love in Haight Ashbury. He never came back. Overdosed on LSD."

"Oh, my." I felt as if our roles were reversed, that I was the eighty-year-old and Evelyn was some hot young thing set on scandalizing me with her dissolute life.

She hefted the pitcher of mimosas and glanced at me. I held

my hand over my glass. She filled hers. "The only time I ever knew Milly Deakin to be less than casual about her conquests was with some guy from Columbia."

"Colombia? You mean the country?" I visualized some handsome Central-American diplomat. He was dressed like a gaucho. I don't think they have gauchos in Colombia.

Evelyn barked with laughter, then began coughing and snatched an inhaler from a half-open side-table drawer. When she'd caught her breath, she continued. "No, not the country—the university. Some professor. I used to see them together at the jazz clubs. Milly was starry-eyed around him, like an infatuated schoolgirl."

"Really?"

"And he was a *doll*. Tall, curly-haired, with that gaunt, hollow-cheeked look intellectual men used to have back then—Kerouac, Cassady." She coughed three ghastly hacks, and resorted once more to the inhaler. A couple of puffs left her still wheezing. Under the thick makeup, her complexion grayed. Age and illness vied with loneliness and the desire to talk. She slumped, exhausted, back in her chair. "Sorry I'm not more help with Milly's disappearance, Karen. What else can I tell you?"

I knew I should leave and let Evelyn rest, but I had so many questions only she could answer. "What's going to happen with *Oblivion Falls*? Are you still handling it?"

"Yes, I am." She wheezed. "I still do rights and royalties for a few of my old clients. And I do keep up with the business." She gestured toward a pile of *Publishers Weekly* stacked on a Naugahyde ottoman within reach of her armchair. Then she levered herself up off the low chair. "My office is right down the hall. Come on. We'll look at Milly's file, see if anything there will help you out."

I followed the agent down the narrow hall to a good-sized room filled with gray filing cabinets and surprisingly up-to-date computer equipment. "I've got most of the current data on disk,"

Evelyn said, "but not Milly's. I don't think anything's come through for her since I got computerized. That reprint request for *Oblivion Falls* was a few years back. Let's see . . ." She pulled out a file cabinet drawer labeled A–E, selected a thick file, and slapped the folder down on a dusty library table. We both coughed.

"Okay, the reprint permission is the most recent action on Milly's account. I am . . . was . . . her literary executor, so I signed the contract myself. The publisher was a small feminist press, and they didn't offer an advance. I didn't push it. Who the hell else would have wanted the book? But now—thanks to you, my dear—now, it's a different story. Let's see . . ." She plucked a half-dozen recent-looking newspaper clippings from the file and set them aside on the table. I recognized my interview with the *Times* from the picture of the young Milly Deakin that accompanied it.

Evelyn rifled through the folder, separated the top document from the rest, studied it intently, then looked up at me. "Come October first there should be a humongous royalty payment. And—will wonders never cease?—after forty years of being dead, Milly Deakin herself will be around in person to receive it!" She laughed, then hacked twice. Her makeup was a vivid mask over the gray complexion.

I knew I was pushing my luck—and hers—but I had one more question to ask. "Evelyn, who would have gotten those royalties if Milly's whereabouts hadn't been discovered?"

The agent started to respond, then stopped and glanced at me through narrowed eyes. "I shouldn't be telling you this financial stuff. It's confidential. Does Milly know you're here? Do you have her permission to ask these questions?" She wheezed again and looked around for an inhaler.

My tongue wouldn't let me lie. "No."

A half dozen conflicting impulses flitted through her eyes, but the urge to gossip won out over professional discretion. She shrugged.

"The royalties would have been paid to her estate, of course.

But at the moment I can't remember who her heirs were. I do know that when Milly's father died, she told me she had no further living relatives." Evelyn pulled a molded plywood chair up to the table and sat. "Let me do an archeological dig in this file and see if she ever designated anyone else as her heir." She grimaced wryly. "Like my respiratory system, my memory's not what it used to be, and this was all a very long time ago."

The agent began sorting through documents. A letter on fine cream-colored stationary caught her eye. It was attached to a matching business-size envelope that caught mine. The envelope seemed familiar to me, not as if I'd actually seen it before, but as if I'd read about it somewhere, or had had it described to me. Cream laid paper. Green three-cent stamp. I peered over her shoulder. Elegant engraved return address: *Anthony Parton, Esq. Attorney at Law, Madison Avenue, New York.* Recipient's address neither handwritten nor word-processed, but typed in the old-fashioned way—on a manual typewriter. Something about this envelope was pecking at my brain like a nervous sparrow. Where had I heard about a business letter from a Manhattan lawyer?

"Ha," Evelyn Sackela barked, then half choked on the resultant cough. "This is it. This letter is the last communication I ever received from Milly Deakin, and it's directed to me through her attorney. Looks like Milly won't be collecting her own royalties, after all. Her final instructions to me before she vanished some forty years ago were that all future royalties from *Oblivion Falls* were to be paid to a Mrs. Grace Lapierre in Stallmouth, New Hampshire. My records indicate I sent checks to Mrs. Lapierre for, let's see, eight years. But the book went out of print in 1967, and there haven't *been* any royalties since."

Mrs. Grace Lapierre? *Gracie Lapierre!* It was all I could do to keep from snatching the attorney's letter out of Evelyn's frail hand: this letter was surely the mate to the one Lolita had told me about—the letter that had arrived one weekday afternoon and changed the Lapierre family's life.

"Grace Lapierre was the sister of Bernice Lapierre, Milly's father's housekeeper," I said, slowly, putting it all together. "Bernice brought Milly Deakin up. She was like a mother to her. But after her daughter Lorraine died, Bernice committed suicide. So Milly must have left the royalties to Bernice's sister in memory of her foster mother." I was moved by the writer's benevolence.

"Isn't that lovely?" Evelyn rasped. "Well, now that the reprint edition has been so very successful, Mrs. Lapierre is in for a nice little surprise. If she's still alive, that is. Otherwise, the proceeds are payable to her heirs."

Gracie Lapierre had been dead for years. This windfall of *Oblivion Falls* royalties would be paid to her daughter, Lolita Lapierre, who was still very much alive indeed.

*T*he evening *after she'd finally told Andrew about her condition, Sara waited and waited on the granite ledge, but Andrew never came. It was a chill November night with a misty rain in the air. Below her the cataract roared, fifty feet of deadly foam breaking on fractured, jagged rocks.*

The next morning Sara skipped school. In English class, while they read e. e. cummings, Cookie fretted. She had never known Sara to be absent before. When school was over, she followed the worn path to the ledge overlooking Oblivion Falls and found her friend huddled there in a too-thin coat. Sara looked terrible—pale and sick.

"Sara, you'll freeze to death. Just look at your lips—they're almost white! Here, take my parka." She stripped off her warm jacket and placed it around Sara's shoulders. "Are you trying to kill yourself?"

"That might not be such a bad idea," the shivering girl sobbed. "I don't know what else to do. My life is over, anyhow."

"He won't . . . ?"

"No."

Cookie sat down next to her friend and huddled close to share body warmth with her. "At first I thought it must be Joe Rizzo," she said, "but he'd marry you in a minute. It's not Joe, is it?"

"No."

"Who is it, then?" She thought she knew.

"I won't tell. It's . . . it's not his fault. I . . . wanted him so much, and he couldn't help himself."

"Sara, don't be ridiculous. Don't you remember, Mrs. Batten told us in Hygiene class that the man is just as responsible as the woman?"

"But it would ruin *him if word got out. He told me so."*

"So you're going to let it ruin you instead?"

The girl pulled away from her friend. "Cookie, you're a virgin. You can't possibly understand anything about love."

Far below them the cataract raged.

22

So you see, Lieutenant," I said to Piotrowski in his cluttered office. "Ah, *Lieutenants,* that is," I amended and nodded toward Piotrowski's desk, where Syverson was listening in on the speakerphone. "Here's yet another suspect in the killings of Marty Katz and Jake Fenton. I hate to say it, because I liked Lolita Lapierre when I met her, but if we're . . . ah . . . if *you're* going to take into consideration anyone who has a monetary motive for these two killings, Lolita fits the bill."

"Just explain to me in a little more detail how that works, willya, Doctor," Piotrowski requested. He hardly seemed to be paying attention, playing as he was with a thick rubber band, pulling it out perilously to its farthest length, letting it snap back on his fingers.

"It's obvious—or, at least, it's quite possible," I said, trying to keep this a little more in the realm of pure conjecture than my previous fevered proposal of Milly's husband Jim Finch as the killer. "Marty Katz had Lolita's name in his notes. Am I right about that, Lieutenant Syverson?"

A disembodied agreement came over the wires from New York.

"Katz was a high-powered investigative reporter. Certainly he would have gone to Stallmouth sometime this summer and interviewed Lolita. He *must* have—the trailer-park address was in his notes. But Lolita never said a word to me about it. We talked about Milly being arrested for killing the reporter. I named him by name. But nary a word from her about having met him. Don't you think that's . . . suspicious?"

Silence from both investigators.

I took another tack. "Look, Marty Katz would have told Lolita that *Oblivion Falls* had become a bestseller again—if she didn't already know. Let's say she realized that she, herself, would be in line to get the royalties. Lolita Lapierre is a savvy business-woman and money means a lot to her. She told me so. Wouldn't it be in her best interests to eliminate the reporter who threatened to drag Mildred Deakin back into the limelight? The last thing she would want is to have Mildred Deakin found, because, who knows, the novelist might change her mind about renouncing the proceeds from *Oblivion Falls*—"

"This is all beginning to sound pretty convoluted," said the disincarnate voice from the telephone speaker.

I glanced over at Piotrowski, but he was silent, wearing the cop face, flat, expressionless. There must be a shop where they buy that thing, or maybe it's issued as part of the standard equip-ment, like handcuffs and a .38.

"And what about Jake Fenton? Why kill him?" Syverson per-sisted.

"Obvious, again. Wouldn't she want to eliminate a Deakin child who might contest the Lapierre family's rights to a fortune in royalties?" Suddenly an image of Lolita's cozy trailer home came to mind. The rocking chair. The pumpkin-colored cat on my lap. Just as suddenly my homicidal conjectures seemed absurd. "This is, of course, all pure speculation, all based on the . . . ah . . . unlikely supposition that Lolita Lapierre is a cold-blooded killer." I didn't want to be accused of blatant fictionalizing again.

But Syverson wasn't willing to let it drop. "Only thing is, Ms. Pelletier, how would Lapierre know that Fenton was Milly Finch's love child? And he *was,* you know. The adoption records finally came through. Mildred Deakin's male child was adopted by Thomas and Janet Fenton in upstate New York in 1959."

"So, I was right—"

"But," she repeated, "how would Lolita Lapierre know that?"

"Uh, beats me. I don't see how she could have."

"Well, there you are," said the phone voice. Piotrowski was still silent, stretching the rubber band out to its farthest length, letting it go. *Ouch!*

"She did visit Milly in jail, though," I said, half to myself. Piotrowski's head snapped up. I had his attention now.

Syverson also heard me. "I remember you told me that," she mused. "It didn't mean anything to me at the time."

Why was I pursuing this? I wondered. I had nothing against Lolita Lapierre. I didn't want to get the woman in trouble. "But I *liked* her, you know. She's good people. She wouldn't kill anyone." I heard how lame that sounded. "Just forget I said anything."

"Right," Syverson said, dryly.

Snap, went Piotrowski's rubber band.

I t had been a long day: first Evelyn Sackela's apartment in Manhattan, then Piotrowski's office. Hell—it had been a long two weeks since Piotrowski's first call. Driving home through the supper-hour traffic, I got caught in a tie-up on I 91: cars stopped as far ahead as I could see. Lowering the sun visor to keep the glare out of my eyes, I slipped a Neil Young cassette in the tape player, sat back, and tried to process the various bits of information I'd gathered during the day. Milly's avid pursuit of men during her sojourn in New York, her drinking, drugging, "hysteria." The fact that she'd vanished from Manhattan months before she showed up in Nelson Corners during the autumn of 1959. Where had she been all that time? Who was the father of her child? Why had she renounced the profits from *Oblivion Falls*?

We'd been sitting stock-still on the Interstate for at least twenty minutes. People were getting out of their cars now, craning their necks, talking to other drivers, trying to get a fix on what lay ahead. I stayed put. After all, I was doing the same thing, only I was trying to get a fix on what lay in the past. On the tape player, Neil Young wailed about loneliness.

Piotrowski had been maddeningly taciturn during our meeting, and he'd hardly looked me in the eye. The only sign of life he'd exhibited was adding yet another suspect to the roster of potential killers: Evelyn Sackela.

I'd laughed. "Lieutenant, the woman is so sick and frail, it's a wonder she can walk to her hairdresser, let alone travel to remote towns to commit murder."

He'd treated me to a cool stare. "Mightn't she have someone in her family who'd do it for her, Doctor? Or mightn't she pay off a handyman or someone else who could use the money?"

Mightn't she? Huh?

"All I'm saying is that this lady would of had as much of a monetary motive as anyone else to commit these homicides. The agent gets a percentage of the royalties, right?"

"Probably ten percent."

"Which, from what I understand about how well this *Oblivion Falls* book is selling, would not be peanuts, right?"

"Right."

"And if you, a perfect amateur at investigation—"

I sputtered, indignantly. *Amateur, indeed! I had a Ph.D. in literary research. If that didn't constitute a type of investigative expertise, what did? Not to mention all the work I'd done for him in the past!* Piotrowski held up a hand to forestall interruption. "If you—an amateur—could find this agent, Katz probably got there first. Did she say anything to you about that?"

I shook my head.

"So—what if he went to see her and let on that Deakin was still alive and that he was close to locating the writer? What if she—this Sackela woman—started thinking maybe this recluse is gonna do something to screw up her royalties windfall—withdraw the book, or something? Or . . ."

"Or, what?"

"Didn't you say the Deakin woman had been playing around with Sackela's husband?"

"That was forty years ago! Talk about far-fetched!"

"What's good for the goose is good for the gander," the lieutenant had muttered obscurely, then retreated back to silence. *Maddening!*

The car behind me honked. Traffic was inching forward. It was time to come back to the real world.

The next morning I met George Gilman for breakfast at the Blue Dolphin. When I'd gotten home after my visits to Evelyn Sackela and Lieutenant Piotrowski, I'd found three messages from George on my answering machine. He had something he wanted to tell me, was even willing to come all the way out to my house right then. But I was exhausted and stressed, and I put him off until morning.

The Blue Dolphin's customary aroma of onions, bacon, and coffee drew me irresistibly to a booth near the grill. After a meager supper of Wheaties with overripe banana, I was primed for a bounteous breakfast. When George didn't arrive by 9:25, I ordered my cheddar-and-bacon omelet, and was half finished with it by the time he rushed in at a quarter to ten, forty-five minutes late.

"You're still here!" He plunked himself down opposite me. "I thought for sure you'd have given up on me."

"I did give up," I said, spreading marmalade on a slice of toasted rye, "but I hung around because I was hungry."

The weather was sunny, but September crisp. I'd been overly cool in my light denim jacket, thankful for the efficient heater in the car and the aromatic warmth of the diner. George wore a red windbreaker with a blue collar. He shrugged out of the jacket, and placed it neatly folded on the seat next to him.

"Sorry to be so late, Karen," he said. "The phone rang, just as

I was leaving the house, and it was a call I had to take." There was a suppressed excitement in my little colleague today. His gnome's face seemed alight with anticipation. As he studied the menu, I studied him. His intelligent brown eyes, large nose, thin lips, and receding chin made up the same less-than-harmonious array of features as always. But what was left of George's fly-away brown hair was neatly trimmed, for a change, and he was dressed with far more care than usual in a pair of neat khakis and a navy-and-white striped polo shirt.

As the waitress delivered his mug of tea, George kept talking—babbling, actually, the words were spilling out so fast. "Karen, did you ever get the sense that life was passing you by?"

Who? Me? "Well—"

He didn't wait for a response. "That's a stupid question. Probably not. You're so attractive, and you've got your daughter and a bunch of friends—"

"Uh—"

"But *me,* all I've ever done is work. Then one day this summer, my birthday, actually, it hit me—something's missing. Seriously missing. It hit me hard. Here I am forty years old, and I've been in school in one capacity or another for thirty-five of those years. Schoolwork—my scholarship and teaching—is my entire life. Now don't get me wrong, Karen. I love what I do. But there's got to be something *more.*" He spooned the tea bag out of his mug, twisted the string around the bag, and squeezed. Then he deposited the dead bag on my empty toast plate. It was an elaborate operation, and George seemed momentarily incapable of looking directly at me. "You remember that day at Greg's when I told you, uh, how I . . . uh . . . felt about Jill . . . ?"

He poured milk into the mug and stirred, concentrating hard on the difficult procedure.

"Ah—" So that's what this was all about.

"Yes, *ah.* I went home and, when I sobered up . . ." He

glanced at me tentatively, then his gaze skittered away. He seemed to think better of what he'd been about to confide.

"What?" I prompted.

"Well . . ." It wasn't easy, but he choked it out. "I bawled like a baby, okay? All night. In the morning I went to the gym—"

"The gym?"

"I'm in lousy shape, okay? I haven't been there in years, but I had to let off some steam. And, then, while I was pounding the punching bag, I had an inspiration—hit me like a bolt of lightning, just like I was in some revival meeting or something. Just because I can't have Jill doesn't mean I can't have a better life. That I can't have . . . a home and family."

"Well, of course not—"

"So, I decided to take charge."

George's breakfast arrived, carried by Glenda, my favorite waitress, a prototypical diner beehive-blonde. She slapped the bowl of steaming oatmeal in front of him. "Good for what ails ya," she proclaimed.

It was the first time I'd seen my plump colleague face-to-face with such a healthy meal. It looked as if George had started taking charge already.

He poured 2-percent milk on his cereal. "I'm adopted, you know."

"You told me that." I pushed away the remaining omelet. The cheese had congealed unappetizingly on the cold plate.

"And I don't know anything about my birth family."

"Oh—"

"So, that morning in the gym, I developed a plan. It all came to me when I was in the sauna. First I'm going to find out where I came from. Then I'll decide where I'm going."

"What do you mean, George? Where you've come from? And, where you're going?"

"Step one." He raised an index finger, as if he were lecturing to a classroom full of students. I wouldn't have been surprised to see him look around for the blackboard. "Step one," he repeated, "search for my birth parents."

"Whoa!"

"Step two." A second stubby finger. "Begin proceedings to adopt a child. Probably a hard-to-place child from a third-world country."

"Wowzer!"

"Step three." A third finger. "Place a personal ad in the classified section of the *Enfield Examiner.*"

"Jee-zuz Christ, George. A *personal?* You don't do anything by halves, do you?"

He stirred his oatmeal and took a spoonful. "That call just now? The reason I was late? That was from a private investigator who's looking into my sealed birth records."

"Whew! Isn't that illegal?"

"Maybe. But it's not immoral, and that's what matters to me. Anyhow, she . . . the investigator . . . thinks she's got a line on the location of my birth mother."

"Oh, George, how exciting. Where is your mother? What have you found out about her?"

He paused. "I'd rather not say anything more until I see if the investigator actually finds her—and how well the reunion goes." He was silent for a few seconds, contemplating the possibilities. Then he shook his head suddenly, like a dog emerging from a river. "Well, anyhow, that's not what I wanted to see you about."

"It's not?"

"Only tangentially. I'm really here to talk about Jake Fenton." He abandoned his spoon, reached out, and squeezed my hand. "You're so brave about his death, but I know how devastated you must be."

"George! I told you—there was nothing between Jake and me!"

He'd retained my hand, and now he patted it comfortingly.

"So you've said, Karen. So you've said. But I know you're not the type to . . ."

"What type is that?" I was so irritated, I wanted to smack someone. Preferably Jake Fenton. This pernicious rumor was going to live far longer than he had.

George looked at me, hesitantly. "The type to screw around . . . unless you have feelings for someone, that is."

"Listen to me." I raised a forefinger. Now he had me doing it. "One: I do not now have, nor have I ever had, any 'feelings,' amorous or otherwise, for the late, oh so great Jake Fenton. Two"—I raised a second finger. "I did not 'screw around' with Jake. He got drunk and passed out, and I didn't know where else to take him other than my house. That's why Monica Cassale saw his car there so early in the morning. Three"—A third finger popped up. "Everyone on this goddamn nosy little campus needs to learn to mind his or her own goddamn business." The angrier I got, the more precise I became with my grammar: *His or her.*

George gazed at me steadily with those intelligent eyes, and decided to believe me. He reclaimed his spoon. "Well, good, Karen, then you wouldn't be interested in what I was going to tell you about Jake's search for his birth mother." He began to eat.

But, of course, I was interested. And this is what George told me: After his epiphany in the gym, he had joined a semiunderground adoptee's support group. The group was clandestine because, in order to tease information from sealed court records and the confidential records of private and county adoption agencies, many of its members would be forced to collude in breaking the law. Jake Fenton had been a member of the group, George said. Jake had been adopted at birth by an upstate New York high-school principal and kindergarten teacher who'd told him nothing about his origins. After the death of his adoptive mother the year before, he'd begun the search for his birth mother, and at the last meeting of the group, he'd said he was close to finding her.

"It was all hush-hush, very confidential. He even said he might have some news that would probably *make* the news." He paused and thought for a few seconds. "I wouldn't be telling you all this if Jake were still alive. But I remember that I warned you against him rather forcefully, Karen. Now that he's gone, I wanted to leave you with some insight into his softer side. But, if you didn't really care for him—"

But I was thinking about the police investigation into his death, and I was thinking out loud. "Maybe Jake's search for his mother set something in motion that proved fatal to him. Could it be . . ." But as I was engaged in some semiclandestine snooping myself, I decided belatedly that discretion was the better part of staying alive. I changed the subject back to George's three-step plan for better living, and, now that he had started, he was only too happy to keep on talking.

Together Cookie and Joe Rizzo found the wherewithal to get Sara to the doctor down in Burlington known to help girls who'd gotten in trouble. Joe had "borrowed" a big Packard from the garage where it was in for some work on the radiator, and he'd contributed the entire contents of the coffee can he'd been filling with fives and tens to save for a Chevy truck. Cookie had found the bankbook for the account her grandmother had opened for her on her first birthday to teach her the habit of thrift.

During the entire long trip to Burlington, Sara sat silent, white as a bed sheet. Cookie held her hand in the backseat, while Joni Creed showed Joe the way through the dark, silent city to the back-street tenement where the doctor had his office. Joni had proven unexpectedly knowledgeable as to how a girl set about "fixing" a problem like this.

They pulled into a narrow alleyway behind a brown-shingled house. "Oh, Sara, are you certain you want to do this?" Cookie asked, as Joe opened the car door.

"What other choice do I have?" her friend responded. "Tell me that—what choice do I have?"

23

"*You bitch! You set the cops on me.*" On my office voice mail, Lolita Lapierre's fury came through loud and clear. I cringed as the crash of the slammed receiver reverberated against my eardrum. The police had been busy since I'd talked with them yesterday. I wondered which team had trekked all the way up to the hinterlands of New Hampshire. Syverson and Williams, most likely. Lolita was connected to Milly Finch, the suspect in the New York killing, not to Jake Fenton, whose death lay in Piotrowski's jurisdiction.

It was noon, and the life of the college swirled around me. My neighbor Ned Hilton was holding office hours, and the hallway swarmed with his students. Out the window I could see a student club fair in progress. Tables lined the walkways around the Common, identified by computer-generated signs: the African American Club, the Latino/Latina Club, the Gay and Lesbian Alliance, the French Club, the Womyn's Alliance, the Student Investors Club. Student recruiters hawked their organizations as rock and rap blared from competing speakers. Everyone had a sense of purpose except me. All too abruptly it seemed that I had nothing better to do than to meddle in other people's lives. My major scholarly project had just been yanked out from under me.

On my desk sat a memo from Avery Mitchell, the President of Enfield College. Replacing the phone in its cradle, I read the note again. Once again I was stunned by its contents: *I regret to inform you that the legal proceedings involving the estate of Dr. Edith Hart have entered a new and more complicated phase. It now looks as if significant time will be required to resolve the differences between the claims of the Brewster family and Dr. Hart's stated intention to bequeath Meadowbrook and ten million dollars to the college. . . .* Across the bottom of the memo, in his bold handwriting, Avery had scrawled: *Karen—I'm sorry!*

Edith Hart was the great-granddaughter of Serena Northbury, the nineteenth-century popular novelist whose biography I had planned to write. Upon her death, Edith had left the bulk of her estate, including her home, Meadowbrook, to Enfield College to found a research center. The institution was to be called the Northbury Center for the Study of American Women Writers, and I was to serve as its director. In this memo Avery was telling me not to hold my breath, either about the Northbury Center, or about research access to the multitude of Serena Northbury's manuscripts and personal papers that had been stored at Meadowbrook. Quite effectively, this lawsuit would derail my plans, not only for the center, but also for the biography, since now the papers I needed to research it would be unavailable: maybe for years; maybe for decades; maybe for millennia. I'd been afraid that this might happen, but the certainty communicated by Avery's memo numbed me. My immediate scholarly future was suddenly as blank as a newly erased blackboard.

At a loss for what to do next, not only for the next five years, but in the next two-and-a-half minutes, I looked around me. On the left side of my desk were piled a half-dozen social histories of mid-nineteenth-century America, background material for the proposed biography. On the right side sat three literary histories of the 1950s; I'd planned to plunder these book-length histories for any mention of Mildred Deakin's literary career.

I reached to the right, and the phone rang. It was Piotrowski. "Doctor, you're a better investigator than I gave you credit for."

"Huh?"

"The way you threw Lapierre in our laps yesterday—that was real smart. Turns out she's the missing link."

"She's the *what?*" I resisted the image of a Cro-Magnon woman in a double-wide that came lurching into my mind.

"She's the link between the two homicides. We knew there had to be a connection, and she's it. Ms. Lapierre is gonna have to answer some hard questions. She probably knew both victims, Katz and Fenton, and she definitely knew one of them well. *Real* well. If you get my drift."

"Piotrowski, what are you talking about?"

"The Lapierre woman. She and Fenton had a hot thing going. They spent the month of August together on one of those Greek islands. Paros. You know it?"

Piotrowski had more than a nodding acquaintance with the circumstances of my life. I couldn't imagine why he thought I would know anything about Greek islands other than that there were some. But my untraveled status was not foremost on my mind.

"Lolita Lapierre and Jake Fenton!" My voice rose an octave with each word.

"Don't screech at me, Doctor." His tone was acerbic.

"Sorry." I settled back into my normal alto range. "But are you sure?"

"Of course I'm sure. It's my business to be sure. It's all written down here in this big, fat diary we found in Fenton's bedroom. Pretty hot stuff. I looked it over a couple days ago, but it didn't mean anything to me then. Fenton referred to his . . . er . . . companion as Lolly—ya know, like the pop. Could of been anyone. Then you input that stuff about Lolita Lapierre and got me thinking. *Lolita. Lolly.* Ya get it?"

"Yeah, I get it. But it doesn't make any sense. Are you sure it's the same . . . ah . . . Lolly?" *Like the pop? I didn't even want to think about it.* "And, by the way, *input* is not a verb."

He ignored my grammatical fastidiousness. "How many Lollies could there be? But, yeah, *it's the same . . . ah . . . Lolly.* I don't go around making unfounded accusations—you know that. A few calls up Stallmouth way ascertained Lapierre's whereabouts during the month of August. According to her boss, she was in Greece. On the island of Paros."

I recalled Lolita telling Sophie and me about her travels—and that she didn't always travel alone. "But . . . but . . . how did Jake know Lolly . . . ah . . . Lolita?" Then it hit me. "Oh!"

"Oh, *what?* Don't stop talking now, Doc. You're on a roll."

"Well," I mused, "these elite New England colleges provide a sort of writer's circuit. A teaching job for a year or two at Yale, one for another year at Amherst. It keeps poets and novelists solvent when their published books don't pay the bills. And—I remember now—someone, Miles Jewell, I think it was, mentioned that Jake spent a couple of years at Stallmouth before he came to Enfield. *That's* how he would have met Lolita."

Three seconds passed as Piotrowski processed this information. "Hmm. So that's how those two got together. You're being real helpful here, Doctor. Of course any connection of Lapierre to the homicides is purely circumstantial at this point. She knew both victims. You provided us with a possible motive. But we gotta have evidence . . . or maybe a confession. Syverson's up there now. . . ." His words trailed off, as if he were mentally speculating on the effectiveness of Syverson's interrogation techniques.

I recalled Lolita's furious imprecation on my voice mail. "Ah, Lieutenant?"

"Yeah."

"Somehow I don't think you should count on a confession."

I called Sophia. "Hey, kid, how ya doin'?"

"Terrific! Just got a poem accepted by a little magazine in Seattle. The editor said she was *enchanted* by it!" I could hear the hum of excitement in Sophia's voice. "Can you imagine? *Enchanted!*"

"That's great, Soph!"

"And she paid me a whole seventy-five bucks!" She laughed.

"Don't quit your day job, kid." I winced as soon as the words came out of my mouth.

"That's a sore point, Karen!" But she was too buzzed to be angry.

"I know. Sorry. I'm an insensitive jerk. Which poem was it?"

We talked about her poetry for a minute or two, then I got down to the purpose of the call. "That day we went to Stallmouth, Sophia? I was wondering . . . do you remember whether or not Lolita Lapierre said anything about Jake Fenton?"

"Jake Fenton? Noooo. We talked about Mildred Deakin's book, but nobody mentioned Fenton's."

"Not Fenton as a writer, but Fenton as a person. A friend, maybe?"

"A *friend?*"

"A . . . *boyfriend?*"

"You kidding? Like we both wouldn't have been right on top of that if she'd dropped even the teeniest hint!" A silence. "I *do* remember, however, I got the distinct impression that Lolita had no shortage of men in her life . . ."

"Yeah, me, too. Not that *I* haven't got a shortage. What I mean is, I got the same impression. No shortage of men in Lolita Lapierre's life. No shortage at all."

On the way to lunch, I checked my mail. Monica took the opportunity to bend my ear about the virtues of her new boyfriend, Victor Perez. The evil fax technician had been fired and then had threatened Monica for costing him his job. The two men had engaged in some kind of a violent altercation, and Victor had been heroic. I was half listening to her as I sorted through the day's offerings. I saw the envelope addressed in Milly Finch's pinched handwriting and gasped, effectively terminating Monica's monologue.

"Karen?" the secretary queried, "you okay?" Now that I was so tragically bereaved, the Department's designated mourner for Jake Fenton, Monica had become sweetly solicitous of my welfare. "You poor thing, you went all pale just now, like you mighta seen a ghost. Maybe the ghost of Jake Fenton."

"Monica, I've told you—Jake and I were *not* in a relationship."

"So brave." Monica patted my hand; she had seen what she had seen.

I shook off my annoyance and her hand, clutched Milly's letter to my chest, and recalled Jake's fate all too vividly; he'd been the last person to possess one of Milly Finch's communications. *No ghosts, Monica. No grief. Just a missive someone might find dangerous enough to kill for.*

The English Department office was busy. Miles, our chairman, sat at a long conference table collating a set of poems he'd photocopied for a class. It took more courage than most of us possessed to request that Monica undertake such a menial task as preparing teaching materials. "Donne, Keats, Whitman, Eliot," Miles muttered as he sorted. Then, *thwack,* he hit the stapler. He had a rhythm going. *Donne, Keats, Whitman, Eliot, thwack. Donne, Keats, Whitman, Eliot, thwack.* The copy machine was, of course, programmed to collate and staple, but that procedure involved the sophisticated technical skills of reading electronic directions and pressing electronic buttons. Miles simply wasn't up to it.

By the office door, a student in jeans and a black cotton crewneck ran a finger down a list of professors' office hours taped to the wall. Tall, thin, and stringy-haired, the boy looked wasted, as if he hadn't slept in a week. That did not bode well for his semester; it was still only September. A compact blonde in khaki shorts and hiking boots searched frantically through the course offerings booklet. If she was looking to transfer into a new course, she was out of luck; the offerings listed there were now three weeks underway, well beyond the tolerance of any professor for the admission of a new student. In the recessed window seat Ralph Brooke paged through the latest issue of *The Chronicle of Higher Education*. He had switched from seersucker to tweed, and today had augmented his gray jacket with a black turtleneck. Through the tall windows, the midday sun cast a luminous glow on his freckled pate, then passed over him, and bathed desks, file cabinets, computers, and Monica's uncannily lush begonias with a buttery yellow light.

Harriet Person bustled into the office, then halted in the doorway and gaped at me. She seemed transfixed by the sight of Jake Fenton's designated mourner bravely undertaking such a mundane task as collecting the daily mail. Anything so petty as sexual jealousy was forgotten. "Karen," she breathed, "I am so sorry about your . . . friend's . . . untimely demise."

I sighed, shoved the letter from Milly Finch deep into my jacket pocket, and headed for my office.

I wanted to live beyond words . . . the epistle began. I had locked, then bolted, my door. Then I had slit the envelope open with a nail file. As she often did, Emily Dickinson provided apt words for my experience: *The Way I read a Letter's—this—/ 'Tis first—I lock the Door.* What, I wondered, could I expect to find behind the locked door of Milly Finch's life?

I had no more story to tell [Milly wrote]. *But I was wearing my "authorship" like a too-tight skin. I wrote one book and it was what they call a success. I was trapped in it, that success. Everyone expected a second novel, but the words simply were*

not there. I was so young. Everywhere I went, the smiles, the
adulation. The men. The booze. Flashbulbs! Oblivion Falls *made*
so much money, made me so visible. It was as if I were living in
a skin of words. My editor, my agent, my readers—everyone ex-
pected a second book, and I expected to write it. Being a writer
was my only purpose in life, my only identity, but I couldn't get
anything on paper. My brain was dry. I tried to escape. The sex.
The gin. I lied about another book. I lied and lied. Then I got
pregnant. I went away for a few months. Saw how easy it was to
slip out of my skin. Saw I could slip out of my life just the way
that child slipped out of my body. It was easy. Easy. I never had
to see the child again. I never had to see my life again. So—I
went away. And you know the rest. Jim Finch and his family
saved me, and little by little I slipped into their life. It was easy.
So easy. And I've never been sorry. Ever.

A postscript was appended: *This is all I have to tell you. Don't*
come snooping around here again.

The missive wasn't signed. It was as if the writing of it were
signature enough.

My hand went immediately to the telephone, but I sat for a
long minute before I lifted the receiver. What exactly was I going
to tell Piotrowski? That I had received a third letter from the novelist? That it brought us no closer to a motive for the two murders? I'd been working on the assumptions that the homicides
stemmed either from someone's monetary self-interest or from
some deep dark secret in Milly's writing life that I could convince
her to tell me. But it seemed as if we were dealing with nothing
more criminal than writer's block here. How could writer's block
provide a motive for murder? Could what was *not* written be
worth killing for? Should I ask her?

. . .

Monica," I said, after a brief telephone conversation with the lieutenant, "if another letter like this . . ." I showed her the envelope, pointing out the pinched handwriting, the Hudson postmark, "comes for me, would you do me a favor?"

"Sure thing, sweetheart," she replied, with a beatific smile.

"Would you lock it up in your desk and give me a call? I can't tell you why right now, but I wouldn't want it sitting around in my mailbox."

"Okay." She patted my hand.

"Thank you," I said, uncertainly, not quite knowing how to deal with this new, nicer, Monica. "I really appreciate your help."

She beamed at me. "It is *so* not a problem."

I kept thinking about Mildred Deakin's typewriter. The typewriter that she had held on to so assiduously in spite of her desperate flight from a life of words. The typewriter that I now knew concealed no book manuscript in its blue leather case. When I got home that evening with Milly's letter, I called directory assistance and asked for Jim Finch's phone number.

"Funny, I was just thinking about you," he said.

"Oh, yes?"

"Yeah. I got to considering about whether, like you said, there might be another book kicking around that Milly wrote before she came here. So I been looking for that old typewriter I told you about, but I couldn't find hide nor hair of it. Was afraid maybe she'd got shet of it. Then I went up in the attic and found it stuck way back under the eaves."

"Really?"

"No book—whaddya call it, *manuscript?*—in the typewriter case, though." It sounded as if Jim was talking around a mouthful of potatoes. I must have interrupted his dinner.

"Umm." I already knew that.

"Nothing but that old machine. Still works. Sitting there for forty years, and the keys just as quick to the finger as if it was brand new. Funny thing, though. It's not her typewriter."

"No?" *Not her typewriter?*

"No. Got a slot inside for the owner's name. Doesn't say Mildred Deakin at all. Name card in there, though. Handwritten. Owner was a guy named Brooke. You know anybody by that name? Ralph Waldo Emerson Brooke?"

24

The name **Ralph Brooke** mean anything to you?" Piotrowski and I sat face-to-face with Mildred Deakin Finch across a long metal table in a Columbia County jail interview room. Milly Finch cringed at the lieutenant's abrupt query, and I glanced pleadingly at her interrogator. *Take it easy on her,* I wanted to say, but I knew I couldn't, and I knew he didn't intend to.

I'd called Piotrowski again as soon as I got off the phone with Jim Finch. Ralph had been Jake Fenton's colleague only briefly, but the long-ago connection of his name to Milly Finch raised some intriguing questions—such as, given the nature of human nature, might Ralph Brooke possibly be Jake's father? Might that relationship have been the occasion for the odd vignette I'd observed during the Department meeting, when Jake had whispered something to Ralph, and Ralph had turned pale? Rank speculation, but, because I had "developed a rapport"—as the lieutenant phrased it—with Milly, he'd brusquely asked me to accompany him to his interview with her. *Some rapport!* I thought. *She writes me letters telling me she never wants to see me again!*

Piotrowski picked me up at the college at 8 A.M., and on the trip across the Mass Pike he'd cued me in advance that he intended to press Milly Finch hard. "It's for her own good, Doctor. If she didn't do the Katz killing, she shouldn't go down for it. And you—God knows what kind of a game she's playing with you.

Jerking you around. Teasing you with bits and pieces, then putting you off. She's got something preying on her mind, something she wants to tell you, but she's kept it quiet for so long she can't get it out. If it involves this Professor Brooke of yours, there might be some connection to the . . . er . . . Fenton homicide." He sounded as if he still wasn't convinced that Jake and I had not been involved. "You did say there was bad blood between Fenton and Brooke?"

I nodded. "It looked that way. But he's not *my* Professor Brooke." I shuddered. "The man makes my skin crawl."

"Now *that's* interesting." He gave me a brief glance. "You don't strike me as a lady who's easily creeped out."

"No?" I'd been *creeped out* ever since Marty Katz was killed. "It's just that I've never met anyone who was as concerned with— I don't know—with reputation, I guess . . . as Ralph Waldo Emerson Brooke is. He's constantly putting himself forward as some kind of heavy-duty fifties intellectual. But when it comes right down to it, I suspect there's not a heck of a lot underneath that facade."

"Except maybe another facade," Piotrowski suggested.

I laughed. He was so good at getting right to the point.

"I'm serious," he continued. "That's usually the case with these blowhards—whether they're high-watt intellects or low-life gangsters." We were in the early stages of the trip, just zooming past the big green sign for the Westfield exit. "You know, Doctor, what you said to Syverson a while back? Something about this Finch woman having some deep, dark secret? I think you might be right about that. And I think she's got *you* marked as the one she's gotta tell—the mother confessor. Only, when it comes right down to the telling, she can't do it. She just can't get it out. Ya gotta feel sorry for the poor old thing, so confused she don't know her ass from her elbow—if you'll pardon my language. So, we'll go in there together. I'll be the heavy. Right? And you'll be the confessor."

"Piotrowski," I'd queried, after a few moments' reflection, "do you think it's possible that Milly Finch's writer's block is what's been keeping her alive all these years? I mean, if she knows something that someone will kill to keep from having revealed. . . ." I couldn't bear to take the thought to its logical conclusion.

But Piotrowski had no problem with that. "Could be. She could be the next victim. Maybe prison's the best place for Mrs. Finch. She's safe there. Maybe now she's surfaced, someone's afraid she's gonna get loquacious."

"*Loquacious?*" I grinned at him.

"What?" His expression stiffened. "It's a perfectly good word."

"I know," I teased him.

"Then don't patronize me," he snapped abruptly, and tightened his very nice lips. A broad hand flashed out and clicked the radio on to an all-sports station. *Fordham tops UMass, 56–47.*

His words stunned me. I stared at the big man next to me, his eyes hooded, mine wide with hurt. "I . . . I didn't mean to . . ." I reached over and touched his hand. "I was only—"

But he turned the radio's volume up and ceased to acknowledge my existence. *UConn over* . . . After thirty or so interminable seconds, I removed my hand; an angry Piotrowski was a formidable sight. We passed over the Pike, the staticky sports show fading in and out, reception blocked by the increasingly impenetrable mountains. He drove very fast, but it was a long, long trip to New York state.

Mrs. Finch, you'll feel better if you tell us." The lieutenant and I had been talking to—or, more accurately, talking *at*— Milly Finch for over thirty minutes. She had relinquished the right to have her lawyer present, so it was just the three of us at the table. The more Piotrowski pressured Milly or I cajoled her, the more she withdrew into some emotional locked ward—some psychological cellblock—where she could protect herself from whatever menace she was threatened with by the utterance of her own knowledge.

"Mrs. Finch," I pleaded with her, "I . . . uh . . . we . . . know you're hiding something that could help us find the murderer of Marty Katz. And the lieutenant's right. You'd feel a lot better if you'd only share it with us."

Her eyes grew even more inwardly focused. Her resistance seemed palpable, a solid field of invisible unyieldingness that felt almost as if it could be weighed and measured, chopped and stacked like cordwood.

Then, after a long, agonizing, period of silence, Piotrowski abruptly sat back in his plastic chair, sighed mightily, and turned to me. "All right, Doctor, I didn't want to have to do it this way, but I guess we'll have to tell her."

"Tell her?" This wasn't part of the scenario, and I wasn't certain what he had in mind.

"About the Fenton homicide."

"Oh." I felt myself blanch. The police had not yet informed Milly Finch that a second murder had been connected to the killing of Marty Katz, and that the victim of that homicide was her long-ago relinquished child. "I don't think you sh—"

But he did. Mildred Deakin Finch's eyes grew wider and wider as he spoke. She sat, dead white and unresponsive, for perhaps fifteen seconds. Then, suddenly, she slumped in her chair, leaned slowly to one side, and before either of us could reach her, toppled unconscious to the hard tile floor.

"Shit," Piotrowski muttered, as he knelt beside her. "I never meant— Guard! Guard! Get a doctor in here *now!*"

I t was a quiet ride back to Enfield. On the trip out, Piotrowski hadn't been talking to me. On the trip back, I wasn't talking to

him—at least not after I'd finished giving him hell for psychologi-
cally brutalizing Milly Finch. Our parting was so cold, I had no
idea whether or not Piotrowski wanted me to keep looking into
Milly's past, but I didn't care. I'd continue to investigate for the
writer's sake. In the college parking lot, I slammed out of the Jeep
without saying good-bye. Then the sight of the big man's face in
profile, staring straight ahead as if he were a bus driver letting off
an anonymous passenger on a particularly troublesome stretch of
road, gave me pause. "Wait—"

But the red Jeep kicked up gravel as it roared away. I didn't
know if he'd heard me.

A bad night's sleep—waking, staring at the ceiling, pacing,
drowning myself in camomile, dreaming short, intense, restless
dreams—left me in a correspondingly bad mood, restless like my
dreams. How had I gotten myself in such a mess? And why did I
give a damn what Lieutenant Charlie Piotrowski did—or what he
thought of me? And what *was* it that had happened in New
Hampshire some forty-odd-years ago that could, only today—yesterday?—cause Mildred Deakin Finch to collapse in a state of
shock?

Sunday I brooded all day. Even a long talk on the phone with
Amanda didn't cheer me up. Monday, I got up at dawn, showered,
pulled on jeans, a red cotton sweater, and a yellow rain slicker
against the gray drizzle, and took off in the Subaru for coffee and
a bagel. By the time I reached the main road, it had begun to rain
hard, and the windshield wipers were ticking hypnotically. I
turned the car in the opposite direction from Enfield. If I went to
the Blue Dolphin or Bread & Roses, I'd probably spend half the
morning fending off condolences. Somehow, I ended up traveling
north on the Interstate. Two and a half hours later, I found myself
getting off the highway four miles outside of Stallmouth. Still
hungry. As yet uncaffeinated. Determined to solve the mysteries of
the past.

The clock over the counter at Gracie's luncheonette read 8:47.

The place was bustling with factory workers and hungry students. Lolita Lapierre's trailer-park neighbor—the stout woman to whom I'd given a couple of rides—was once again ensconced at Gracie's rear table. Yes! I'd pegged her for a Gracie's regular. She'd been there a while; the hooded camouflage rain jacket draped over her chair back was dry. I sat down across from her, feeling ridiculous about the twenty-dollar bill poking out between my fingers. The woman looked at the bill, then glanced up at me, then looked at the money again. "I knew you was a reporter."

I shrugged.

"That skinny guy gave me forty." *She had talked to Marty Katz!* I found another twenty in my wallet. She snatched the bills. I had her full attention. "So, waddaya wanna know?"

"Were you by any chance in school with Mildred Deakin and Lorraine Lapierre?"

"Maybe I was . . . by some chance. What about it?"

"I have a few questions I need to ask you."

After dropping Toni Croft off at Edgemont Trailer Park, forty bucks richer, I stopped at Vinnie's Exxon, and took Vinnie Russo, the seventy-year-old proprietor, out for coffee. Vinnie remembered Lorraine Lapierre very, very well.

The gray-haired, ponytailed man behind the chairman's desk in the Stallmouth College English Department office was Professor Richard Graves. Today instead of skimpy running shorts Professor Graves wore a sand-colored linen suit and a blue-checked oxford-cloth shirt. Gold-rimmed glasses lay in front of him on the thick green blotter. "We've met before, haven't we?" he asked, after I'd introduced myself.

"We might have run into each other at the MLA," I replied. I didn't want Professor Graves to think I made a habit of lurking around the Stallmouth campus. "I do American. Nineteenth-century. How about you?" I was quite clear on my previous sightings of this man. He had long, lean, muscular legs, I recalled, and moved like a racehorse when he ran. Also, he'd been at Jake Fenton's book signing, arguing heatedly with the writer.

"I do British," he replied. "Eighteenth-century revenge tragedy." Scholarly identities satisfactorily established, we exchanged social smiles. The Stallmouth chairman picked up his glasses, clicked the earpieces open, then closed them with another click. He sat back in his big leather chair and gazed at me curiously. "How can I help you, Karen?"

I f some cultural critic of the late twenty-first century attempts an analysis of mid-twentieth-century American society based solely on the 1950s Stallmouth College yearbook, the *Stalwart,* he or she would come to the conclusion that all twentieth-century Americans were Caucasian, male, and monochromatically gray of hair, skin, and eye.

In the 1952 *Stalwart* I found what I was looking for. For fifteen minutes I brooded over it, then swallowed my pride and called Piotrowski. Sergeant Schultz took the call. "Yeah?" she said. "That's interesting." She listened some more. "Okay, I'll run all this by the lieutenant when we get hold of him. He's . . . well, he'll . . . well, one of us will get back to you." She paused, then added, "You take care, now, Professor." The little sergeant sounded quite solicitous.

The Italian Delight was a pizza-and-pasta restaurant in a strip mall on the outskirts of Stallmouth. As I headed for home, it caught my eye, and I stopped for a quick sausage-and-mushroom slice. I entered the restaurant, my eyes adjusted to the dimness, and I saw Professor Richard Graves seated in a back booth, conversing with a woman whose face was turned away from me. But I immediately recognized the precision-cut blonde hair as belonging to Lolita Lapierre. I hovered uncertainly in the doorway. Then Richard Graves noticed me, tapped Lolita on the hand, and spoke urgently to her. She swiveled around and stared. Damn! I ducked out of the restaurant. The trip home was a long, hungry, and anxious one. What was the gray-haired wizard man's relationship with Lolita Lapierre? Had he been talking to her about me? What had I initiated by going to Graves for information about the past?

Blood was everywhere, all over Sara, all over Cookie, all over the gray plush of the Packard's wide backseat. When the doctor had hustled Sara out his side door and into the car he'd thrust a wad of towels in with her and told Cookie what to do with them. Then he slammed the car door and took the odor of gin away with him. Cookie jammed the towels between her friend's legs in a vain attempt to staunch the flow.

"Faster, Joe. Faster," Cookie pleaded. "If we don't get her to the hospital, she'll bleed to death!"

But it was already too late.

25

It was late when I pulled into the driveway after the trip to Stall-mouth, one of those vast, clear nights when the little house seemed pinpoint-centered under a transparent bowl of stars. I stood by the car, stretched to relieve my cramped muscles, gazed at the sky, and tried to think about something other than Milly Finch, her ancient secrets, and their murderous modern consequences. But what else was there to think about? Oh—my life. I could brood about my life. Okay. So I was alone; so I had antagonized and alienated a man who was beginning to intrigue me; so Amanda was growing up and away, and would most likely be heading off to God-only-knew-where for graduate school; so my mother and sisters found my world as alien as if I'd been transported to some distant galaxy on one of those UFOs they read about weekly in the *National Enquirer*. So? So what? There was always this, the cool, crisp September darkness and the luminous bowl of stars.

I squinted at my watch as I climbed the front steps to the house: a blurry twelve-something-o'clock. Time to brew a cup of camomile tea, pick up the latest volume of *American Quarterly*, tuck myself into my warm bed, open the scholarly journal—and fall asleep. I got drowsy just thinking about it.

But Monica's voice on the answering machine jolted me awake. "*Karen, you know that letter you showed me? The one you didn't want me to put out in your box? Another one of those came in today's late mail. I'm leaving for home now, but I locked the letter in my desk drawer like you said. The desk key is in my pencil cup. I put the cookie key on your desk so you can get into the office after hours.* " A brief silence. " *I wish to hell you'd tell me what this is all about.* "

Within seconds, I was back in my Subaru. The night had shrunk down to me and Milly Finch's fourth letter. As far as I was concerned, nothing else existed: no big cop with hurt feelings, no cup of camomile, no scholarly journal, no warm bed, no firmament of stars. Just me and the missive that I was now certain would—finally—solve this mystery—would cue me into whatever it was that had occurred in the 1950s that carried its lethal energy smack to the cusp of the twenty-first century.

At that time of night, with no traffic and no traffic cops, I made the twenty-minute trip to campus in less than fifteen, the autumnal trees that arched the narrow country roads blurring past my speeding car with kaleidoscopic velocity. I pulled into the Dickinson Hall parking lot alive and undamaged in spite of my insane speed, and let myself into the darkened building. Dimmed hallway sconces provided sufficient illumination to guide me to my office, where I clicked on the overhead light. At the unconventional hour of—I glanced at my watch—12:22 A.M.—I'd rather not draw the security guards' attention to my presence here, but I hadn't thought to bring a flashlight in from the car. The cookie key—our department's passkey clipped to a ring with a grubby plastic chocolate-chip cookie—sat in plain sight on my deskpad. I scooped it up, doused the lights—they must have been on for all of seven seconds—and headed for the main office. Up and down the wide hallway, doors were solidly shut, sconce lights at their lowest settings, no security guard in sight: all was as it should be.

I inserted the key in the lock, heard the click, pushed the door open, slipped inside, and closed it. Damn! Complete darkness, except for a pale glow from the pole light just outside the window. I groped toward Monica's desk and fumbled for the pencil cup that held the desk key. Crash! Pencils, pens, coins, and other secretarial detritus rolled across the desktop. The toppled cup clunked to the floor. I froze and listened for reaction from . . . anyone or anything. A faint hum from the electric wall clock. The distant whir of a car passing on Field Street. A boozy whoop from somewhere in the direction of the dorms. The usual creaks and groans in the walls of the old building. No storm-trooper-like stomp of Security descending on me in force. I took a relieved breath, and suddenly the absurdity of the situation struck me. I giggled at the thought of how ludicrous I would appear to any chance observer, standing here by Monica's perfectly ordinary secretarial desk in this perfectly ordinary departmental office, paralyzed with terror about the possibility of being discovered on a perfectly ordinary professorial errand. Sheesh! I clicked on the lamp. This clandestine stuff was stupid! There was no reason whatsoever for me to slink around the office like some lowlife burglar: I worked in this department; Monica knew I was coming; she'd even made arrangements for me to be here. The buzz of the fluorescent bulb was comforting. So was the round, safe island of light that created its own little illuminated world.

That world—the desk cluttered with computer monitor, keyboard, telephone, piles of papers, stacks of folders, sponge-filled plastic dish for dampening postage stamps, Lucite-framed school picture of Monica's son Joey, carved-wood hand-flexing gizmo for preventing carpal tunnel syndrome—was now strewn with a half-dozen pencils and pens, a balsa-wood letter opener, and a quarter that balanced precariously on the very edge of the desk. I didn't see any key. I retrieved the red ceramic pencil cup and turned it upside down. Nothing. I tapped the cup. No key fell out. I peered inside. No key was stuck to the bottom with spirit glue. Whatever spirit glue might be. I sorted through the mess on the desk. No key under the piles of papers, the stacks of manila envelopes, the phone, the keyboard. I sighed and checked again around my feet. That far from the lamp, nothing but two sturdy brown walking shoes could be seen. It wasn't until I got down on my hands and knees and groped around on the carpeted floor that I found the tiny key lurking underneath one of the wide chrome balls of the wheeled chair.

Ah! I plucked the key from the floor between my thumb and forefinger, rose, rolled the chair away from the desk, and inserted the key into the small lock in the narrow central drawer. The letter wasn't immediately visible. Front and center I found two rubber-banded stacks of neatly labeled computer disks. I felt farther back in the drawer. Scissors. Scotch-tape dispenser. Stapler. Monica was known to guard her personal office supplies with the ferocity of a pit bull. I felt even farther back. Plastic stamp box. Then I noticed the envelope, right up front, anchored by the stacks of computer disks. As I pulled my hand back to retrieve the letter, my fingers brushed against something hard and heavy and cold that I was in too much of a hurry to identify—yet another piece of office equipment Monica habitually locked away from marauding professors, no doubt. My eyes were all for the envelope. I slid it from under the disks and positioned it in the center of the lamp-light circle. Hudson postmark. Pinched handwriting. *Professor Karen Pelletier, English Department, Enfield College.* Eureka!

"Miss Pelletier, whatever are you doing here at this hour of night?"

In the suddenly blinding overhead light, a bulky male figure stood in the abruptly opened office door. My hand fluttered melodramatically to my heart. I caught my breath with an audible gasp. "Jeez, you scared the sh—. You startled me."

"So it seems." No apology. In his damp navy raincoat and black beret, Ralph Brooke filled the doorway. Why do men have to be so goddamned big? He squinted at me from behind his thick glasses. "What are you up to in here?"

"Me? Oh, I just . . ." This was *not* the person I wanted to see right now. I smiled sweetly. "How about you, Ralph? You habitually prowl the ivy halls after midnight?"

"I couldn't sleep," he replied. His frown let me know I'd failed to insert any feminine charm into the situation. "Remembered a book I wanted." He cut it off sharply. The Palaver Chair does not explain his actions to an assistant professor, the lowest of the low. Now, if it had been Monica he'd disturbed, the elderly scholar might have been more polite; Monica he needed things from.

Ralph noticed Milly's letter on the desk. I noticed him notice it. His magnified gray eyes fixed on the hand-addressed envelope as if he recognized the letter for what it was, a missive from the past. We grabbed at the same moment. I was closer, but he slid the unopened envelope from my suddenly nerveless fingers, and studied the handwritten address. The lines of his rubicund face were fixed and unreadable. Then he glanced up at me. "For someone who hasn't written a word for decades, Milly Deakin has turned into quite a correspondent, hasn't she?"

I had no response. The various levels of Milly's story, past and present, had come together for me. I said: "You're Andrew Prentiss, aren't you?"

His level gaze hardened, told me he knew I knew. But he shook his head. "Andrew Prentiss? No, not me. There never was an Andrew Prentiss. Andrew Prentiss was merely an imaginative projection, the overheated fantasy of a maladjusted schoolgirl. The product of an overly repressed sexuality." Surely Ralph Brooke knew that the Freudian psychobabble of the fifties was long passé; even if he had never been a scholar on the cutting-edge of any of the various postmodern intellectual discourses, he was a sophisticated academic. Yet at this moment of crisis, he slipped back into the familiar jargon of his youth.

I ignored his denial. "And *you're* the one who stole Milly's second letter from my desk."

He smiled, as if I'd let something slip. "Was it her *second?* I only saw the one. No, Miss Pelletier, you can't blame me for stealing your letter. Not that I haven't held it in my hands. Not that I haven't read it—while it still existed in readable form, that is. But did I take it from your desk? No, not I. That theft was the unfor-

tunate—and unfortunately fatal—misdemeanor of your . . . your
. . . dear friend Jake." A pause allowed the momentary softening
of his adamant expression. "Too bad about Fenton," he mused.
"A true loss . . ." I held my breath. Was I about to learn—at long
last—the truth about Jake's parentage? Brooke sighed. "A fine
strong, virile writer. A true loss to the literary world."

I don't quite know how the gun got into his hand; he must
have been packing it in his raincoat pocket. It was a good-sized revolver, gray and steely, and glinted in the harsh overhead light as
if it contained an independent luminosity. "And too bad about
you. You'll be a loss, too." The hard-boiled expression on the elderly professor's face—eyes slit, mouth a hard straight line—was
right out of film noir.

Me? A loss?

"You're really quite decorative, you know."

Decorative! I scowled. Women's Studies 101, lesson number
one, the pernicious aesthetic objectification of women.

"Now, what am I going to do with you?"

I shrugged, but my mind was racing. I was a healthy, agile,
not-yet-forty-year-old woman—and a feminist!—and he was an
elderly man. The bulky gun collapsed the age differential, but,
still, there must be some way I could overpower—or outwit—this
man. I surreptitiously checked the desk top for some potential
weapon or distraction. The heavy wooden hand-flex gizmo? No.
Neither big enough nor weighty enough. The keyboard. No. Too
clumsy to clobber him with, and besides the cord was too short.
Something in the drawer? I took a rapid memory inventory of its
contents. Scissors? Scotch-tape dispenser? No. And no. My hands
tingled with the need for a weapon. Then, without warning, almost independent of my brain, those very same hands identified
the shape of the puzzling object they'd brushed against in the back
of the drawer. The awkward shape. The object that was hard and
heavy and cold.

"I had plans for Milly," Brooke reminisced. "She was supposed to be at Dash and Lillian's for the weekend. A drowning accident would have taken care of the problem, and none of this would have been necessary. A neurotic, vengeful woman would have vanished, and without yet another no-talent lady writer the world would have been a better place."

No-talent lady writer! A powerful rage surged through my fingertips. Women's Studies 101, lesson number two, the misogynist trivialization of the female literary tradition! Professor Brooke had gone too far! His gun terrified me, but his smug condescension infuriated me even more. *Decorative! No-talent lady writer!* No goddamned, sexist, superannuated son-of-a-bitch was going to—

"Milly had a psychological complex about me. A twisted sexual fixation," said the goddamned, sexist, superannuated son-of-a-bitch. "She was a vicious slut, even when she was a scrawny kid. . . ."

Slut! Twisted sexual fixation! Women's Studies 101, lesson number three, the masculine terror of female sexual aggression. The Vagina Dentata—the vagina with fangs.

". . . vengeful. Spreading lies. Besmirching my good name—"

"There's another one," I said. The words popped out of my mouth, surprising even me.

"Another *what?*"

"Another letter. From Milly Finch—Mildred Deakin, that is."

Ralph's eyes narrowed. "Another letter? Where is it?"

"In here." I gestured toward the desk drawer.

"Get it," he said, motioning imperiously. The old goat seemed to like bossing a woman around at gunpoint. I shuddered as I reached into the drawer and fumbled through its contents.

"Well?"

"I can't seem to find it." And I couldn't, dammit!

"Do you have it?" He waggled the gun.

No! Then—*wait! Hard. Heavy. Cold.* My fingers clutched.

"Yes," I said, and shuddered again. I had it.

"Then give it to me."

"If you say so," I replied, clicked the safety catch off the small handgun I'd found secreted in the far reaches of Monica's desk drawer, swiveled around, aimed squarely for Ralph Emerson Brooke's chest, and pulled the trigger.

Years ago, when Tony had insisted on giving Amanda and me shooting lessons, he'd told us to aim right for the target's torso. "If you're ever in a position where you have to fire a gun—and, God willing, you won't ever be—don't putz around with trying to wing someone. If the situation is dire enough that you have to shoot some son-of-a-bitch, then, for Chrissake, aim straight for the heart. Shoot to kill."

Luckily my aim had never been terrifically good, so I didn't end up with the death of an éminence gris on my conscience. I'd aimed for Ralph Brooke's heart, but I'd winged him in the shoulder. Winged him well enough to drop both him and his gun. He fell to the hardwood floor. I kicked his big gun away; it skittered across the polished floorboards into the hallway and came to rest with a clunk against the recessed base of the Xerox machine. Suddenly the little automatic with which I'd shot him seemed to scorch my fingertips. I hurled it out into the hallway after the larger gun. I didn't know if Ralph was alive or dead; I just wanted to get the goddamned lethal weapon as far away from me as possible. Within thirty seconds, alerted by the gunshot, a campus cop was on the scene, a pair of town police joined us within a handful of minutes, and then, as I huddled in the window seat in a state of shock, a stream of officers that seemed to go on and on.

*C*ookie skipped school to attend Sara's funeral. It was a simple ceremony at the small Baptist church in Satan Mills— Sara's mother, the youngest of her three brothers, and a couple of elderly neighbors. Her father, furious at Sara for humiliating him "in front of the whole town," stayed home and got drunk. The only flowers were a vase of gladioli provided by the church and the dozen perfect white roses Cookie had purchased, defiantly demanding a ten-dollar bill for the purpose from her father.

During the service, Cookie sat in the back with Joni Creed while the preacher droned on about sin and salvation. Joe Rizzo wasn't there. He was in jail, charged with auto theft, destruction of property, and contributing to the delinquency of a juvenile— three counts. A charge of manslaughter had been considered, but dropped at the intercession of Professor Wilson.

At the grave, Cookie tossed the roses on top of the coffin, all twelve of them, one at a time. Then she went home to bed and didn't get up again for ten days, causing her loving parents no end of concern.

26

When's Piotrowski going to get here?" I asked Sergeant Schultz. She showed up at 1:37 A.M. in the company of a tall, thin uniformed trooper with a hawklike beak of a nose. The first troopers on the scene had called the homicide squad even before the ambulance had arrived to transport Ralph Brooke to Enfield Regional. Schultz had responded with surprising alacrity in spite of the lateness of the hour. Since the English office had been taken over by scene-of-crime technicians, we had been seated in my office catty-corner across the hall for the half hour it took to give the cops my story.

"The lieutenant's not coming," Schultz replied.

"Not coming?"

She cast me a sideways look. "No." The sergeant looked especially youthful tonight in jeans, a baggy yellow sweater, and scuffed white Nikes. Reddish highlights glistened in her cropped brown hair.

"Why not?"

Schultz exchanged glances with the tall, saturnine trooper. Both remained irritatingly expressionless. "He's taking care of a personal matter," the sergeant replied.

"Oh." An inexplicable bleakness invaded my heart: Piotrowski must be out with a woman. What did I know about the lieutenant's personal life, anyhow; maybe he was out with a *dozen* women.

Schultz studied my face with that disimpassioned manner all

cops learn—as if they themselves have somehow been exempted from the messier exigencies of the human condition.

"You know, Professor, we oughta have a talk, you and me. We're almost done here, that right, Lombardi?" The trooper cast his sergeant a cryptic glance, then nodded. Schultz returned his stare, equally enigmatic. Then, abruptly, she turned back to me. "So, Professor, you just sit here in your office for, oh, say, ten minutes, while I . . . uh . . . take care of some business. Then we'll go get coffee. That okay with you?"

I nodded. I could use coffee. I was cold, shaky, and definitely disoriented; it's not every night I shoot a senior colleague.

Obediently I slumped into my green vinyl chair. Ten minutes lengthened into fifteen, then twenty. I was nodding off when I heard the scene-of-crime team lug their equipment back to the van. The slam of the vehicle's doors jolted me awake. Where the hell was Schultz? Did she think I wanted to hang around here all night? And, besides, I had to go to the bathroom. Bad.

The Dickinson Hall corridor was now brightly lit by overheads. Except for a round-faced red-haired officer on duty at the open front door, the hallway was empty, and the sergeant was nowhere to be seen. From the main office, a staccato male voice participated in a telephone conversation. "Right. Right. Right. Right. Got it. Right." I headed toward the dim alcove under the stairway where the women's room—an afterthought in this once all-male college—was located in a former broom closet. At the sight of the embracing couple sequestered in the shadows of the staircase, I skidded to a halt. "Oh!" I gulped.

Felicity Schultz's startled face emerged from behind the gray mass of Lombardi's uniformed shoulders. "Uh, Professor, I, uh, I thought I told you to wait in your office."

"That was a half hour ago." While I'd been waiting in good faith for this supposedly consummate professional to return, she'd been making out underneath the stairs.

"Uh, we were just . . . well . . ."

I grinned at her. "I know—taking care of business."

She grinned back, sheepishly. "Lombardi here is my fiancé, Professor. It's been a few days since we saw each other."

Trooper Lombardi towered over both of us. In a sallow face, his expression was perfectly impassive; he was letting the sarge handle this. I nodded at the trooper. So this was Schultz's fiancé? Funny, the plain little officer had told me she was engaged, but somehow I'd never thought of there being a real man involved, a rather prepossessing man with that dark complexion and beak of a nose, and not unattractive.

I gazed at the sergeant with new eyes. A blush pinkened Schultz's cheeks, and her lips were soft from kissing. I sighed with envy.

At the Blue Dolphin, Schultz bubbled about her plans. Big wedding. Catholic church. Holiday Inn reception. Swing band. Dancing.

Sounded like fun. Sounded like my kind of scene. If I wasn't shell-shocked from almost killing a colleague, I'd want to boogie right now.

When my coffee came, along with Schultz's Sleepytime tea, the sergeant got serious. "Ya know, Professor, I gotta say, for someone in your business, you sure got smarts."

I started to protest: someone in *my* business! Why, *smart* was the very *essence* of my business!

"Yeah, yeah, I know. You got a Ph.D. and all. But *smarts* is something different from head knowledge. That scene in there tonight coulda ended bad." She shook her head. "*Real* bad. But you pulled that trick on Brooke about the letter . . . That was *smart*. And . . . how'd you learn to shoot like that, anyhow?"

I told her. She flashed me the look of reluctant affirmation I remembered from Tony and his pals: Civilians related to cops are somehow not quite as totally clueless as other civilians.

"So," she said, "just so's I get this right for the record, let's go over it one more time. Tell me again exactly what the hell was going on in there."

"Well, Sergeant, this is how I see it." And I told her about Ralph Brooke's early professional life at Stallmouth College and his seduction of Mildred Deakin's friend Lorraine Lapierre. "According to *Oblivion Falls*—that's the novel Deakin wrote about Lorraine—"

"I know. I read it. I didn't know they wrote such hot stuff back then."

"Umm. Well, according to the novel, Lorraine—who was the Sara character—died during an illegal abortion. Now, this is what I think: Ralph Brooke, on whom the Andrew Prentiss character was based, was responsible for Lorraine's death—after all, he was the one who got her pregnant—and Milly knew it.

"Marty Katz was doing deep research on Deakin, and he picked up the connections between Deakin, Lorraine, and Brooke. When he approached Brooke, my dear distinguished colleague must have feared his reputation—which seems to have been his most cherished possession—was threatened. That old scandal connecting him to the dead girl was going to be dragged up again. Instead of being immortalized for his intimacy with the great Beat writers, he would end up with his memory tainted by some sordid story about what he clearly thought of as a mere youthful indiscretion. Then, when Brooke learned that Katz had actually located Mildred Deakin in Nelson Corners, he was terrified. Who knew what she'd say now? Maybe she'd even publish a sequel to *Oblivion Falls* and openly reveal his part in that old story. And here he'd just gotten this prestigious little sinecure at Enfield College—"

"Sinecure?"

"*Sinecure:* a cushy job requiring little work. Brooke thought he was set for the rest of his life. Not only did he have his pension from all those years at Chicago, now he had this named professorship at Enfield. Money *and* status. But, whereas, in the 1950s the death of a pregnant townie might easily have been brushed aside, not so in this more equalitarian age. A revived scandal would destroy him professionally. When Katz threatened to drag Mildred Deakin back into the public limelight, Brooke must have followed him to Nelson Corners and killed him before he could talk to her, hoping the whole nightmare would end there."

Schultz scowled. "But, then, why kill Jake Fenton?"

"Weeell," I said. "That's harder. Maybe it has something to do with Jake being an adopted child. A colleague told me Jake had been engaged in a search for his birth mother. It turned out he was Mildred Deakin's child. And, who knows, maybe Ralph Brooke was his father? Maybe in the process of searching for his mother, Jake uncovered Ralph and the Stallmouth scandal, and was threatening him with exposure."

Schultz twisted the diamond-chip ring on her left hand. She looked unconvinced.

"And then, when it seemed as if I was about to drag it all up again, Ralph—" I shivered.

She reached out and patted my hand. "You did well, Professor. You did *real* well."

Out the diner's wide window, a few pale pink rays were beginning to light the sky above the low eastern hills. It was well past time for me to be in bed, but there were a couple of other things Schultz wanted to bring me up to speed on.

Number one: the guns.

Of course, Forensics would determine if Brooke's gun was the identical weapon used to kill Jake Fenton. Meanwhile, we knew it was the same caliber—a .45. Now, what a seventy-four-year-old English professor was doing strolling across a college campus after midnight packing a big Colt revolver, she couldn't for the life of her say. As for the . . . er . . . actual shooting weapon—she meant the gun I'd fired at Ralph Brooke—she'd been on the horn with Monica Cassale about what the hell that weapon was doing in the secretary's desk drawer anyhow. It seemed that . . . let's see . . . did she have this right? . . . it seemed that there was this *fax technician* that had made some threats to Ms. Cassale after a complaint from the Enfield English office had cost him his job. Then some boyfriend—also a fax technician—had supplied Cassale with a Smith & Wesson .38 for protection. It was all pretty muddled—they'd woken Monica up when they called, and the guy was confusing things by giving advice in the background. So—did any of this make any sense to me?

It made good sense, and I told her why. Because I'd made the call for fax service, the nasty serviceman had gotten fired. Because he'd lost his job, he'd threatened Monica. Because he'd threatened Monica, Victor had supplied her with protection in the form of a gun. Because Victor had supplied her with a gun, I . . . Again I shivered. Not only had I casually set into motion the chain of events that had ended in two homicides, but I'd also, just as offhandedly, initiated another sequence of events that had allowed me to apprehend the killer and save my own life. A prime example of dramatic irony if I'd ever heard one, providing what I might have called in a pedagogical context a *teachable moment*.

There was a silent interlude while Schultz sipped her herbal tea pensively, and I stared out the window. The entire eastern sky was now shot through with Easter hues, pink, yellow, white. "*Then* there's the matter of the lieutenant," Schultz ventured.

At the sound of her voice, I started. In my exhausted state, the sunrise had almost hypnotized me. "The lieutenant? You mean—Piotrowski?"

"Yes." Schultz's diction suddenly veered into the formal. "This is something I'm hesitant to speak about, Professor. But, all things considered, I think maybe—for his good and yours—I oughta tell you."

He's engaged, I thought. *No. Not engaged. Married. He's on his honeymoon. That's why he didn't show up tonight.* I clamped an iron expression on my face.

The little cop shot me an owlish look. "Lombardi and me, we

been talking this over. But you gotta promise you'll never tell the lieutenant I said word one about this because if he knew . . ." She paused and twisted her lips. "If he knew, he'd ruin me. He'd run me through the wringer and hang me out to dry. Why, he'd stomp me into the ground and use my bones for fertilizer. He'd . . ."

I vowed lifelong silence. *Married,* I decided, *and expecting a child.*

Schultz leaned over toward me, her gray eyes wide with sincerity. "Since we're talking personal here, all right if I call you Karen?"

"Sure . . . Felicity." *No. Not one child. Twins.*

"Karen, we think, Lombardi and me, we think Charlie Piotrowski, big and tough as he is, is scared stiff." Her gaze was searching. "God, I hope I'm doing the right thing here!"

"Scared? Piotrowski?"

"Terrified."

"Of *what?*" I was utterly baffled.

She gnawed her lower lip. "Of—you."

"Me?" A mouselike squeak.

With her spoon Schultz dipped the drowned tea bag up and down in her mug. "Not that he's ever said anything about it, you understand. But I got eyes in my head. And that poor man has got such a thing for you."

"Piotrowski? He hates me!" I blurted out. "He's been so damned—"

She shrugged. "Like I said, he's terrified. His wife walked out on him, oh, five–six years ago. He took it real hard. The only woman I've ever seen him look at since was some social worker from down in Springfield. But that didn't work out—she couldn't take the heat of being with a cop. It's just as well, anyhow, she . . ." The sergeant let it trail off. An entire chapter of Piotrowski's life would remain prudently unspoken. "And then *you,* and you're way out of his league, a professor and everything—"

"Bullshit!"

"Well, he's *gotta* be thinking that."

"Bullshit! Bullshit about a professor being 'out of his league.' Nobody's out of Piotrowski's league, for Chrissake! And bullshit about his having a . . . *thing* . . . for me, anyhow. The whole damn thing is bullshit! I'm sorry, Schul—ah—Felicity, but you are dead wrong here. Charlie Piotrowski thinks I'm a pretentious, condescending, effete-intellectual snob. And, look," I cinched my argument, "I almost get killed, and he doesn't even show up!"

Schultz passed a stubby-fingered hand through her short hair. Suddenly she looked very tired. "Karen, the lieutenant's father had a stroke yesterday afternoon. Piotrowski's been in the hospital with him ever since. He doesn't know anything about the incident with you and Brooke 'cause I didn't call him—and I'm gonna catch hell for that. But if he did know, you'd better goddamned believe he'd a been there."

"Bullshit!" I slammed the empty coffee mug down on the table. Hard. The handle broke off in my fist. I stared at the curved piece of white ceramic, stupidly tried to fit it back on the mug, then laid it carefully on the edge of the table. At last I glanced up at Felicity Schultz and gave her a level look. "And besides, Sergeant, I've lived with a cop. It's no kind of life. I'll never do it again."

"Umm. Too bad," she said. "A couple of nice people. And both lonely."

"Lonely! I'm not—"

"Lombardi and me think—"

But I didn't want to hear it. Felicity Schultz was in love, she was in the mood to be romantic, and she was oversentimentalizing everything. I was out of the booth in a half second, shrugging into my denim jacket, bolting for the door.

*P*rofessor Andrew Prentiss *survived the tongue-lashing administered by the senior members of his department, but the humiliation rankled. He began to grow restless under the constant scrutiny of the prudish college community. Reports of "hip" urban scenes began to filter through, even to New England. He made plans to get away.*

As for Sara, she had been a particularly flamboyant specimen of the hardy summer roses that push their way into evanescent bloom in this otherwise unyielding northern soil. When Prentiss thought of her, if he thought of her at all, it was with the vague regret one feels for the passing of such a common flower.

27

For two and a half weeks I stayed away from campus. National headlines about the Case of the Killer Professor were bad enough, but they would die down soon, and until then I could simply avoid reading the newspapers. The local publicity was what I dreaded—that, and the titillated glances, the prurient questions, the horrified commiserations I was bound to encounter at the college. And to tell the truth, it was almost impossible to get out of bed in the morning. Not only had my life been threatened at gunpoint, not only had I been forced to shoot an elderly man, but I'd also, damn it, alienated the one man who intrigued me in the slightest—and he was the one man the Professor Priss who operates my left brain insisted I'd be better off having nothing to do with. *With* whom *you'd be better off having nothing to do,* she corrected me. I sighed: she was right, *with whom.*

Somehow the world had turned a dull, flat, disembodied gray. I had no love life; the crimes had all been solved; I wasn't teaching; I'd had my major scholarly project yanked out from under me: What was there to get out of bed for? Every time I turned my eyes from the suddenly all-engrossing television set, I could see Ralph Waldo Emerson Brooke's big gun pointing directly at me; I could feel the jolt in my shoulder when I'd pulled the trigger of Monica's .38; I could hear the thud as the elderly man fell—the thump of his body, the crack as his head hit the hardwood floor.

September eased into October. Maples and sumacs flaunted their annual reds and golds, but not even the flamboyant foliage and the prospect of a brisk autumn walk could entice me out of the house. When I remembered to eat, I ate stale bread and canned soup. Phone messages from everyone but Amanda went unanswered. Word got out that I was not in the best of shape. One Wednesday afternoon Sophia, Earlene, and Jill showed up unannounced with little Eloise and a tea party—ham sandwiches, scones, and a big pot of Ceylon tea. It was almost worth turning off Oprah Winfrey for.

When the phone rang late that Friday afternoon, the last voice I expected to hear was Charlie Piotrowski's. Since our acrimonious trip to the Columbia County jail three weeks earlier, I'd had no word from the lieutenant, and expected none. Felicity Schultz had handled all paperwork related to the shooting of Ralph Brooke and his subsequent arrest for the murders of Martin Katz and Jake Fenton. Something had occurred to render her once more as stiff and formal in her dealings with me as when we'd first met. No more girls together: I was *Professor* again, and she was *Sergeant*. Most likely Piotrowski had raked her over the coals for not immediately notifying him about Brooke's shooting. Also, I knew she must have regretted her impulsive late-night confidences. In any case, Trooper Lombardi made no further appearances, nor was any reference made to him, and neither of us breathed a word about the lieutenant.

But here, at 4:39 on an October Friday, was Piotrowski's abrupt bass on the telephone. I could hear his deep voice loud and clear over Oprah's alto tones. *"Doctor? We need to talk. Meet me at Bud's in a half hour."* He hung up.

I half-considered not going: nobody orders me around, etc. etc. But if I didn't show up at Bud's Diner, Piotrowski would surely materialize at my front door within the hour, and the last thing my Professor-Priss rational self wanted was that big cop in my house. I clicked off the television, took a hard plastic brush to my less-than-pristine hair, climbed into a clean pair of jeans, donned a leather jacket against the autumn chill. Then I glanced at myself in the oval mirror by the front door and grimaced: long, lifeless hair, eyes puffy and shadowed, pallid skin. A touch of makeup, perhaps? But, no, I didn't have time. I fired up the Subaru for the first time in days and drove the ten minutes to the diner located on a country highway outside Greenfield, next to an abandoned gas station with a green shingled roof extending out over old-fashioned pumps.

The first time I'd met Piotrowski, as obnoxious as I'd found this overbearing police lieutenant in every other way, I'd nonetheless admired the sharply indented bow of his upper lip, the deep, full curve of the lower. Now, seated in his customary back booth facing the door, he pursed those nice lips disapprovingly when he saw me enter the small diner. "There you are," he said, glancing ostentatiously at his watch as I slid into the seat across from his. Then he did a quick double take. "You don't look so hot, Doctor."

"Thanks, Lieutenant." I gave him the chill, professorial stare, the one guaranteed to drop impertinent undergraduates trembling to their knees. "What's up?"

A dull red suffused his complexion. "Not that I mean to say you look *bad*."

"Did you get me all the way out here just to insult me, Lieutenant?" I can't tolerate feeling as vulnerable as this big lug of a man made me feel.

His eyes went blank for five seconds as he processed my jibe. Then he sighed, and raised a hand to the waitress. It was a large, strong hand, not aristocratic in any way, but the mere gesture was elegant. "Of course not, Doctor. We've had another communication from Mrs. Finch and I thought you'd want to see it. Two coffees," he told the heavyset redhead who showed up to take our order, and turned back to me. "I dropped by your office earlier, but Ms. Cassale said you haven't been there for a while." It was half an indicative locution, half interrogative. *I hadn't been there; why hadn't I been there?* I could confide in him if I felt so inclined.

But I didn't. "The letter?" I queried.

He slid two faxed sheets across the table. The first was a copy of an envelope addressed to Lieutenant Paula Syverson and posted in Nelson Corners. The second wasn't really a letter. It was just a brief note: *Get that professor out here and I'll tell you what really happened to Lorraine Lapierre.* I glanced up at Piotrowski. "Milly Finch has been released, of course?"

He nodded. "All charges dropped."

"But she still wants to talk to me?"

"Seems so." He shrugged.

"I should do it," I mused. "I should talk to her while she's in a talking mood." Not that it mattered, now that the police had Brooke in custody, but there were still large holes in what I knew about Stallmouth, New Hampshire, in the 1950s. I wouldn't call myself nosy, exactly: let's just say it's my fine scholarly diligence about getting the details precisely right.

Piotrowski tilted his head. "Go if you want to." He could care less.

I gazed at him, the plain, honest face with its beautiful lips. Schultz's words came back to me: *A couple of nice people, and both lonely.* Then a thought hit me like a bomb. "You know, Piotrowski, you really didn't have to come all the way out here with this note. You could have read it to me over the phone."

"I could of." He stared at me. Big brown eyes you could drown in.

After a long, dry-throated minute, I swallowed and said, just to be saying something, "How's your father?"

He shook his head as if to clear it. "Better. Uh, he's better. But he's not gonna be able to come home. He's down in Springfield. It was a hard call, but we decided to put him into a . . . whaddya call it . . . a skilled nursing facility."

"Sorry to hear that. Who's *we*?"

"My brother and me." He cast me a quizzical glance. "It's for the best. Dad hasn't been himself for a long time." A pause while he examined the pink and white packets in the sugar bowl. Then without looking up at me, he said, "How's your mother?"

"Okay." I ran my fingertips over the embossed border of a paper napkin. "I'm thinking of asking her to come stay with me for a while."

"Oh." The big round clock over the door ticked monotonously, as if it were chewing time without savoring it.

The coffee came, and we sipped. After a while, Piotrowski paid the bill—two coffees, a dollar-fifty plus tax, less than half of what I'd paid for *one* at the Columbus Avenue Starbucks—and walked me out to the Subaru. The sun was low over a vista of mountains and more mountains. Rows of evergreen trees fronted the two-lane road, oddly regular in shape, all about eight-feet high. *Christmas-tree farm,* I thought.

Bud's dinner crowd was just pulling in. Two grizzled men in green work clothes climbed out of a black pickup with a smashed-in passenger door. A heavy young woman with twin toddlers hefted them one at a time out of their car seats. "Jason, stay right there while I get your brother. Jason? Jason! *Stay!*" Piotrowski scooped up the speeding toddler, lugged him back to his mother.

I unlocked my car door. I felt stupidly bereft at the thought of leaving Piotrowski and going back to my empty house. It was Friday night. We could go somewhere. Have dinner. Hear some music.

It's for the best, Professor Priss intoned. I turned around to say good-bye. He was right behind me. Big, strong man. Those brown eyes. Those lips.

"Goddamnit all to hell, Karen," Charlie Piotrowski said. "*This* is why I came all the way out here." He gathered me up in his arms and kissed me.

This is a really, really bad idea, Prissy carped. I ignored her and kissed him back, really, really hard.

28

Milly Finch's kitchen was green and cream. A worktable held center place, its enamel surface cream-colored with a light-green tinge at the edges. A large enamel cookstove, half wood-burning, half gas, held a fire this crisp October morning. We sat at a maple dining table by the front window overlooking the porch, the low Berkshire foothills crimson and gold in the distance.

"I don't want you to think that since I left New York—since *Oblivion Falls*—my life has been a failure, nothing but . . . but epilogue," Milly said, glaring at me in spite of my reassurances that I *still* was not planning to write her biography.

"Nobody thinks that," I protested. Mildred Deakin Finch was a different woman in her domestic surroundings, her raddled face—so emaciated when I'd seen her in prison—beginning to fill out now, her color heightened in the warm room. She wore loose khaki slacks and a long-sleeved cotton shirt with a heather-gray sweater vest, so resolutely out of fashion she looked as if she'd come fresh from a Ralph Lauren outlet. A different woman—but she still had her crotchets.

"Ha! You intellectual types! It's all *words* with you. You think words are more important than reality." She waved a dismissive hand, directing our attention to the spacious kitchen with its crackling stove, the towel-covered loaves of bread dough rising on the worktable, the glass-fronted cabinets with their rows of green dishes, the worn, but immaculate, green-and-cream linoleum. "This has been my life for the past forty years. Does it all look like . . . *epilogue?*" Lieutenant Paula Syverson and I exchanged mystified glances and shook our heads simultaneously: *No, not epilogue at all.* I bit into one of the cinnamon buns Milly had taken from the oven five minutes earlier. It was still too hot, but the pungent spice was irresistible. I took another bite and burned my mouth again.

"It's been a good life," Milly insisted.

"A very good life," I agreed, glancing around me. "I'm envious." And at that moment I was. Three long nights with Charlie Piotrowski had put me in the mood to savor the physical world.

Piotrowski hadn't come today because he knew his presence would intimidate Milly Finch, especially after he'd bullied her into a state of shock at the Hudson jail. I still couldn't think about that episode without a sense of unease. How he could be so . . . unfeeling . . .

I was here in Milly Finch's kitchen with Lieutenant Syverson, who'd come along in case Milly told us anything relevant to the case against Ralph Brooke. From reading *Oblivion Falls* we thought we knew the story we'd hear: Sometime in the early fifties Brooke had seduced Lorraine, gotten her pregnant, and then abandoned her in her hour of crisis. She had died following an abortion—illegal at the time—a victim of the sexual double standard and primitive medical conditions. And of Ralph Waldo Emerson Brooke's selfish lust.

In graphic detail Milly retold the tale, focusing on Brooke's role. "He was a cad. Wouldn't even come up with money for the . . . the doctor. Vinnie Russo and I, we put together whatever we could get, and Toni Croft got the name of a doctor over in Rutland. Then Vinnie borrowed a car from Halper's Garage where he worked, and we all took Lorraine over there." Milly clutched a yellow quilted potholder fiercely, as if it were all that stood between her and the chaos that was her youth. Her eyes grew wide—in *Oblivion Falls* she probably would have written *her eyes grew wide with unshed tears.*

"And she died on the way home." Tears burned my eyes.

"Died on the way home?" Our companion jerked out of her reverie. "She did not. The . . . termination . . . went fine. It took a couple of weeks, but she recovered."

"But . . . but . . . in *Oblivion Falls* you wrote—"

"That was Sara, the character, not Lorraine, the person. That's your problem, you professors, always mistaking literature for life! No, what happened to Lorraine was worse."

"Worse than death?"

"Worse than *that* death. And that's why I wanted you over here—you and the lieutenant both. To tell you what really happened to Lorraine Lapierre."

No storyteller could have wished for a more attentive audience. Syverson and I were riveted.

"Lorraine got better, but she didn't go back to school. Wasn't allowed to. Word got out about the abortion, and the school board in those days had a policy—they wouldn't let a . . . bad girl . . . contaminate the morals of all the chaste young women of the town. You girls now—you have no idea what it was like back then. No, Lorraine stayed home and brooded over what had happened to her. Of course my father wouldn't let me have anything to do with her after that, but I used to sneak out some nights when I was supposed to be in bed. Sometimes, Lorraine and I, we'd go up to Oblivion Falls and just sit there. She'd cry and cry. Then, after a few months, she began to get angry. Why the hell should she be the only one to be punished. She'd had such big dreams for herself, college and everything, and now she couldn't even finish high school—all because she'd had sex with some guy who didn't suffer *any* consequences. Something was wrong with that. Something was goddamned wrong.

"One night she arranged for Profess . . . Ralph Brooke to meet her at the Falls. She was going to make him help her, help her at least to get out of town, get set up somewhere else where no one would know her, and she could get work. Maybe Providence, maybe Boston. I was worried about her being up there alone with him, but she told me not to be silly. Anyhow, when she went up, I hid down at the bottom of the path behind some bushes. Five minutes later that . . . that *animal* showed up. After a half-hour he came back down the hill. I waited for Lorraine. She never showed up. Three days later her body surfaced ten miles downriver—all battered."

I was speechless. Paula Syverson's pale eyes had gone steely. "Why didn't you inform the authorities?" the lieutenant asked Milly.

"I did. Oh I did. I told the police and I told them and told them. I told my father, my teachers, even the minister. They said Ralph Brooke was a mature, respected member of the community, and I was a hysterical girl. They were right—I *was* a hysterical girl, and with good reason. No evidence of foul play, they said. Lorraine's death was ruled a suicide. I stayed hysterical, and my father sent me away to a private school in Massachusetts. It was really some kind of a hospital, but he told everyone it was a boarding school. There they half-convinced me I was crazy. Eventually I got straightened out enough to get through college, then went to New York and wrote *Oblivion Falls*. It was the only form of justice I could get for Lorraine. After that I got blocked—couldn't write about it any more. Couldn't *think* about it any more. Couldn't write about anything. When I got pregnant myself, I went off the deep end—and, in order to survive, I just had to put everything away and start again." She paused, then looked down at her hands. "Including the baby."

I hesitated before I asked it. "Was Ralph Brooke the father of your child?"

She glowered at me as if I'd made an obscene suggestion. "Are you out of your mind? Of course not. I was wild in those days— wild, boozed up, and a little crazy. But not *that* crazy. Brooke was around, of course, part of the Village scene. I ran into him once in a while—small world, the Manhattan literati—but mostly I kept my distance." Milly rose from the table and fetched a coffee pot. When she had refilled our cups, she replaced the percolator on the back of the stove, sat down again and sighed. "I don't know for certain *who* the father of the baby was. Could have been almost anyone. But there was *one* man. He was a writer as well as a teacher." She gazed out at the far-off hills. "I understand the boy became a writer?"

"Yes," I replied. "And a damn good one. *Damn* good."

She made no response.

"One thing I'm wondering about, Mrs. Finch," the lieutenant asked, "how'd you come to have Brooke's typewriter?"

"Ha!" Mildred Deakin Finch replied, "I stole it. I used to go up to Lillian's in Westchester, and one weekend Dash dragged Brooke along. On Sunday, when I left for the train to the city, that nice typewriter was sitting there by the back door, and I snatched it up. It'd serve him right, I thought, if I used his own typewriter to write a novel showing him up for the nasty killer he was. But, of course, I was blocked—couldn't write. I took that typewriter with me wherever I went, but I never even opened the damn thing."

The ensuing silence stretched out beyond comfort. Finally the lieutenant spoke. "Was nothing further ever done about the death of Lorraine Lapierre?"

Milly shrugged. "I've been incommunicado since 1959. As far as I know, until just last month when the professor here shot him, that murderous son-of-a-bitch Brooke went scot-free."

Syverson sat ramrod straight in her ladder-back chair. Her pale eyes swept the foothill slopes as if she were reconnoitering for enemy troops. "We've got Brooke on two counts of first-degree homicide, of course, Mrs. Finch," the lieutenant said, "and he'll be put away for the rest of his life. So . . . So I don't know if you even want to think about this—but the statute of limitations never runs out on murder."

. . .

have two cardinal rules," Lolita Lapierre said, "I don't sleep with cops, and I don't talk to them."

Sophia slid her eyes over at me. I tightened my lips, but I didn't think it was a personal jibe. How would Lolita in Stallmouth, New Hampshire, know about my relationship with Piotrowski? As a matter of fact, how did Sophia know about it? I thought we'd been pretty circumspect.

Sophia and I had driven up to Stallmouth to take Lolita out for meatball subs and beer. My treat. After having pointed the police in her direction, I owed Lolita something other than a simple rote apology, and I told her so. I'd suggested a trendy little bistro I'd spotted in the center of town, but Lolita had opted for the Italian Delight. She never could develop a taste for cassoulet, she said, and the Eye Dee had the best meatballs in New England. That was fine with me.

The restaurant was doing a good business this Friday evening. Townspeople, students, college workers, and faculty jammed the long, narrow room, lured by the seductive aroma of tomato and garlic that wafted from the kitchen behind the shiny chrome pizza ovens. A long counter stretched beneath a hanging menu offering pizzas, subs, salads, and pasta dishes. Lighted beer signs in bright reds, yellows, and greens clashed with a flamingo-and-aqua full-wall mural of Neapolitan boatmen. A dark-haired, ponytailed waitress had just delivered our meal.

"When the New York State detectives came around asking questions about Milly Deakin and that reporter that got killed, I clammed up," she told us. "Just on principle—in my family we were never too fond of the police. Then that skinny, bleached-out cop started harping on Jake Fenton's murder, and I lost it. I knew Jake, you see, knew him pretty damn well." She paused, then bit into the steaming sub.

"He taught here last year, didn't he?" I sprinkled hot pepper flakes on top of the Parmesan that oozed over my meatballs. Yum.

She nodded. "And he taught *me* a few things, too, if you know what I mean. I'd just broken up with my regular guy—over something really stupid, it turns out. We've worked it out now, and we're back together. But I was on my own then, and in the spring Jake and I had some good weeks together. Even planned a trip. Then that damn reporter comes nosing around, asking Jake questions about his birth."

"Oh," I said, carefully returning the dripping sub to my plate. "When was that?"

Lolita cast me a quizzical glance. "Sometime in June. Why?"

I shrugged. June. That must have been why Jake was so interested in the *Times* article about Mildred Deakin.

Lolita went on. "So, that reporter—Katz—told Jake there was a possibility Milly Deakin was his mother. Got him so upset, he brooded all summer. Like after forty years he should give a shit about someone who never gave a shit about him! So I tell him about my connection to Milly, and he asks me tons of questions about her—her disappearance. Everything. Then he reads *Oblivion Falls* and starts going on and on about my cousin Lorraine. Then we go to Greece. What a bummer. He just wants to be back in Stallmouth, and I keep thinking about Richard. So we come home, and Jake starts hanging around the old folks, picking up gossip. Tells me one night he thinks he knows just exactly what happened to Lorraine. Me, I thought she'd killed herself. That's what people always said. The shame, you know. These narrowminded little towns can be hell. But Jake said some codger who taught at Enfield got rid of her—well, he wouldn't have been a codger in the fifties, of course. Seems Lorraine was threatening to tell the whole town he'd knocked her up, Jake said. Jake said it would serve the bastard right if he blew his cover. But . . . he was so plastered that night, I didn't pay much attention to him." She shrugged. "I should of. That's what got him killed."

"You can't second-guess these things," I said, more to myself than to her. I drank beer. The restaurant's clientele had gotten noisy as more students joined their friends. A waitress passed with a huge pizza on a pedestal tray. It was loaded with pepperoni and sausage. A tableful of guys greeted it with cheers.

"Sorry I'm late, Lolly," said a male voice from behind us. Richard Graves pulled out the chair next to Lolita, bent down and kissed her on the cheek. He wore Day-Glo-orange-and-black spandex bicycling gear, and his gray hair was secured in its usual ponytail. "We've met, of course, Karen," he said, placing a manila file folder on the table and slipping into his seat. I gaped at him. He turned to Sophia. "And you, you must be Sophia. Haven't I met you, too?" He squinted at her, puzzled, as I recalled her innocent-student act the night we'd attempted to scope out the Stallmouth English Department offices. Then he shrugged, extracted glasses from a pack at his waist, and checked out the menu board over the counter. "I'm starved. How are the subs?"

I glanced over at Lolita. "This is Richard," she said. "My boyfriend."

"Oh." Richard. Her boyfriend. Lolly's regular guy. Now the quarrel between Monsieur Ponytail and Jake the night of the book signing made sense.

After he'd placed his order, the Stallmouth College English Department Chairman turned to me. "When Lolita said you were taking her to dinner, Karen," he said, "I wanted to come along. I have something to show you. You remember the day you dropped by the office asking questions about the Department's faculty back in the fifties?"

I nodded.

"You got me curious about Ralph Brooke's association with Stallmouth. Then when, well. . . ." He checked Lolita out with a sideways glance. "When Brooke was accused of murder, I had a student assistant go through the Department records from the 1950s. Hell of a job, but she turned up a number of . . . er . . . intriguing artifacts. Here, take a look at this." He opened the file folder and handed me a mimeographed sheet, purple lettering on cheap white paper.

English Department Notes
Stallmouth College
April 1953

"Whan that April with his showres soote
The droughte of March hath perced to the roote. . . ."

Like all Aprils from time immemorial, this is a
month of beginnings and endings. For the Stallmouth
English Department and its denizens, here are a few
events of note.

Promising young novelist, Mr. J. D. Salinger,
will read from his work on the twenty-fourth of this
month. Following the reading, the author will be
honored by the Department with a cocktail party at
the home of Professor D. Whitely Manley. As the immortal Emerson wrote to the young Walt Whitman,
we "greet you at the beginning of a great career." We
anticipate a long writing life and many distinguished
works from Mr. Salinger.

Professor Austin Deakin's long-awaited mono-
graph, *The Great Poem and its Organic Principles,*
has just been released by Harvard University Press.
The study has been more than a decade in the making, but our esteemed chairman's dedication to the
men of the department, both colleagues and students,
has been preeminent among his concerns. " 'Tis education forms the common mind: / Just as the twig is
bent, the tree's inclined."

Our young colleague Professor Ralph Brooke
has heard the call of the wider world and has chosen
to leave the groves of academe and go on the road
for a year or so with a few literary pals. Our loss will
prove the gain of the literary enclaves of San Fran-
cisco where he has determined to head at the end of
this academic year. *Carpe Diem,* young friend. "Had
we but world enough and time. . . ."